LET'S START OVER

RIVER LAURENT

AUTHOR'S NOTE

Ahh... it's the end of one journey and the beginning of another. For this will be my last book as River Laurent. From hereon I will be writing as Iona Rose.

Why, you ask.

Because I will be using the River Laurent name for my new streetwear brand. Yup, for those of you who are not on my newsletter, now you know. :)

Thank you so, so, so much for your readership and support. It has given and will continue to give me great joy and sense of belonging.

As always I send you all my love and best wishes for the new year. May it be wonderful, awesome, and amazing for you and me.

xoxoxo

BLURB

Ivy

Cooper Page was my first love. God, I was so crazy about him, I handed him my heart on a platter, but he went away to college, and left me and my broken heart behind.

What did I do? I ran away to the Big Apple to make a new life, a life without him. But I could never forget him, not those beautiful green gems. They followed me right into my dreams.

Then something terrible happened to me, and I had no choice, but to head back home while I licked my wounds and healed again.

I thought one hundred percent Cooper would have moved on. A man like him would never stay in a small town, like Springston, Texas.

But I was wrong Cooper *was* in town.

And he was even more gorgeous than he'd been back in high school.

He was also the owner of the bar I'd walked into looking for a job.

Cooper

You could have blown me down with a feather when Ivy Johanson walked into my joint. No one could be that lucky.

I knew then we were meant to be together. She was always my greatest regret, and all I wanted to do was start over, give ourselves a second chance, but it was going to take way more than just a wish. She had Do Not Touch signs put up all over her luscious curves. Who could blame her. Everything she knew about me was tainted by the past.

I never was one to give up. She was the one woman I'd never been able to forget.

Yup, I planned to win her back come hell or high water.

Sooner or later I was going to taste those delicious lips again...and this time I was NEVER letting go.

ACKNOWLEDGMENTS

Thank You

Leanore Elliott
Brittany Urbaniak
Kristin Moran

The subway was stuffed full that evening. So packed it was almost suffocating. A woman's leg brushed against my knee, and I pulled myself into an even smaller bundle, shifting in my seat to leave some space between me and the guy that smelled like a brewery.

Alcohol bothered me now.

I'd started to hate the stink of it, the way it could turn a perfectly normal man into a monster. I found the transformation terrifying. One moment everything was fine as he was talking and laughing, then the switch. For no good reason, dark rage took over.

The subway rattled along the tracks and I tried to keep my eyelids from closing. God, I was so damn exhausted. The couch was uncomfortable so I didn't sleep well last night. All I wanted to do was get home and relax, but I knew Brian would be waiting at home for me. I wondered what kind of mood he'd be in, what kind of night I was in for.

Sometimes when I got home, he was in great spirits ready to

chat and ask me how my day was. He'd sit beside me and treat me like I was a human being. IT would be the way he was during our first dates, when it was all honey and roses. Back then, I'd looked at him like he was the moon and stars. I was blinded by all the flash in him. You couldn't properly understand the phrase, charm the birds off the trees, until you met Brian. Heck, the charming bastard sure charmed me off my tree.

Who could blame me? He was kind and gentle with me, even in bed. None of the 'take that, you slut', or 'suck my cock, bitch', talk. He seemed to really care for me, and I loved being around him. He was amazing...for the first six months.

Then, without warning, the first sign came that all was not well in my paradise. Okay, it wasn't the first sign. When I thought about it, he always had a mean streak in him. He liked calling me thunder-thighs or fattie, but calling me fat wasn't exactly abuse. I did need to lose a few pounds. Some men called me curvy or voluptuous, but Brian thought I needed to lose at least thirty pounds.

Anyway, that day I came home from work and found him almost incoherent with rage because I had put his favorite hoodie in the dryer. What did he expect, that I'd wrap it up in a towel and dry it flat, like it was a delicate cashmere sweater? At first, the sight of his red face spitting with fury as he yelled at me was so astonishing, I was too stunned to react, but when he started advancing towards me, I ran out of our apartment.

I wandered the streets for an hour in shock. I had no best friend in the city I could go to or call and tell what had happened. As the cold seeped into my bones, I decided I would tell him to leave. After all, it was my apartment. He moved in with me because he said he couldn't bear waking up without me next to him, but he still had his own apartment. Actually, a better one than mine.

When I came back, he was sorry. He was so sorry tears ran down his cheeks. He even kissed the soles of my feet to show me how much he loved me, how sorry he was. For a week and a half it was paradise again. Then it happened once more. This time, he'd been drinking. He was so full of rage, for a reason so insignificant I can't even really remember why anymore, he balled his hands into fists.

I stared at him in horror as he swore at me and called me ugly names. When he advanced, I ran out again. This time, I was utterly determined to boot him out, but I came back to the Brian I had fallen for. The one that could charm the birds off the trees.

But I wasn't a damn bird.

The things he called me were unforgivable. I told him I wanted him out. He told me he'd lost his apartment. Practically sobbing, he confessed he was basically homeless. He told me he was upset and frustrated because he lost his job two weeks ago and he was running down his savings. He'd wanted to tell me but he didn't know how to.

I couldn't believe my ears. This was the guy who called me a worthless, fat slut less than an hour ago.

He confessed that not having a job or a home made him feel so impotent, he was taking it out on the only person he loved in the whole wide world. Then it was meltdown time, while he spewed out about how much he needed me, how much he loved me, how he couldn't live without me. He begged for one last chance. He promised he'd surprise me with how different he was going to be.

I wasn't a bird, but I wasn't a heartless monster either.

I told him I would support him through this hard time, but if he ever tried what he did today, he was out. And I'd call the police to evict him if I had to.

He wept with relief. That would never happen, he swore. Then he ran a bath for me and washed my back. That evening he cooked for me. The steak was a bit burnt, but the candle-light made it look okay. When I left for work in the morning, he was already up and scouring the net for work. But he never found anything, never even got so far as going for an interview.

Slowly things started to slip again. When I came back home, he was often drunk, or on the way there.

My clothes were too tight, too revealing, too much. It made me look like a whore. Once he spent thirty minutes grilling me about who I was fucking since I wasn't fucking him. The answer, of course, was no one. I'd lost all interest in sex. Espe-cially, his type of rough, ugly sex. I couldn't even stand the thought of it.

Then two weeks ago, it happened again. He punched the wall and made a hole in it. I looked at the hole in the drywall and realized I didn't love him. Maybe I'd never loved him. I was just a hapless bird that had been dazzled by his enormous charm.

I watched the drama unfold with desensitized eyes. I watched him rage, then start crawling back, but there was no coming back from this. Not for me. I told him we were finished. He didn't cry this time. He stalked into the kitchen and grabbed a knife. He'd held it against his wrist and said that if I left him he would do it. He would kill himself and write my name in his blood.

This shook me to my core. Even when I thought about it later, it still sickened me. My blood ran cold at the idea that an action I took could result in someone's death. It would hang over my head forever. I would never be able to forgive myself. No, the trick would be to leave with a polite note.

I'm so sorry, but I just can't do this anymore.

*H*e would be mad, but killing himself would be pointless if there was no one to watch.

I couldn't kick him out. My conscience wouldn't let me, but I knew I needed to get out. I needed a change. My whole life sucked. I had no real friends. I was living with a man I didn't love, and as much as I hated to admit it, I was stuck in a dead-end job. It was always my great dream to work for a newspaper, and I was ecstatic when I got this job, but it seemed as if my big dream and opportunity had petered out pretty quickly. It was clear my career was going absolutely nowhere. I couldn't remember the last time I received a raise, a promotion, or even a simple, 'job well done, Ivy' comment.

Not to mention the fact that my boss was a complete pig. The man couldn't even be bothered to address me by my name. It was never Ivy. Instead, it was sweetheart, honey, baby, and darlin.' Who wanted that? A boss that treated you as if you were some sort of fluffy bunny.

I needed to change everything.

And I would do it too, but I needed security. I didn't want to jump from the frying pan into the fire. So I started making plans.

Someone at work had an apartment that would be available for rent in about a month and a half, so I talked to my landlord about leaving. He was cool with it, as he only needed a month's notice, anyway. I'd found a home.

Bit by bit I started bringing in my most prized possessions into work and storing them in the broom cupboard. Maria, the cleaner knew what I was doing and even though it was only sentimental stuff like photo albums and diaries, she started locking the cupboard every night when she left.

As the subway rattled along, I closed my eyes and told myself everything would be okay. I would turn things around for me. Start a new life. Find new friends and another job.

Tonight I would go home, shower, have my meal, and go to bed early. Hopefully, Brian would probably be passed out on the couch. If he wasn't...I would just avoid antagonizing him.

I didn't know why, but today my stomach felt as if it was tied into knots. As if my body was anticipating something. Maybe the possibility of having to deal with Brian drunk, but not drunk enough to pass out. The closer my station loomed in the distance, the more I wanted to hop off of this Subway and just bolt.

Get the hell away from him.

1 4th Street came up out of nowhere, and a chime echoed through the car. The doors opened and people poured out into the station. My body was stiff with tension, as I followed them out. I stood at the top of the steps and glanced around at the restless city.

I missed home.

Yes, New York had been kind to me when I first moved here. Like everyone else who came to the big apple I too, was taken in by the glitz and glamour. A hungry young journalist ready for anything the world could throw at her.

But now, the longer I stayed, the more I felt like I was trapped. The New York dream hadn't happened for me and I just wanted to get out of here. To escape.

I gripped my bag close to my body and started walking home. Our apartment wasn't far from the station. The closer I drew to my place the more my heart started to beat in my chest. My body knew something my brain didn't. My mouth went dry, my hands were clammy. I quickly wiped them down my black pencil skirt.

I sucked in a deep breath at the entrance of the building where I lived.

"You're strong. You're not a little coward," I told myself sternly. "Anything happens, you'll just call the police." I touched my cellphone and it was there, my security blanket.

Even so, I took the stairs just to avoid getting to the apartment any sooner. TVs echoed through the doors I passed, a stereo on the top floor, blasted out rap music, the smell of cooking filled the air. With great determination, I trudged past a world of lives that were probably more satisfying than mine, and finally stood in front of apartment 410.

Squaring my shoulders, I slipped my key into the lock and steeled myself before I opened the door. In a nice, loving relationship, I might have been greeted by the smell of food and a warm meal after putting in such a hard day at work. But I wasn't.

My heels clicked on the floor as I closed the door behind me. I slipped off my shoes and padded into the living room. Brian was in his favorite chair, the TV turned to football. A nearly empty bottle of vodka stood on the table and an empty one lay on its side on the floor.

I shuddered. One bottle was not enough.

Not tonight. Please, not tonight.

Brian liked to push me around verbally and tell me what to do, but he'd never laid his hands on me. That's what I told myself over and over even though my gut was telling me something was different tonight. Brian was spoiling for a fight.

"There you are, Princess." Brian slurred as he turned his head and gave me a lopsided grin.

I hated it when he called me Princess, because I knew what he wanted when he called me that.

"I've been waiting for you. What took so long?"

"Had to hand in a story." I dropped my bag into the couch. Are you hungry? I can make us something to eat if you are."

"I'm starving, chubby cheeks," he said with a wicked grin on his lips. "But...come here first."

I tensed up. Obviously, this was not going to be a smooth night. "Let me make us something to eat first, huh?" I said as lightly as I could. I made my way around the couch of our tiny apartment. I guess I already knew what would happen. When I was in range, Brian lunged forward suddenly and grabbed my arm. His thick fingers held me a little too tightly and I squirmed in his grasp.

"Come on, Brian. I need to make us some food, then I think we should both turn in for an early night."

"An early night," he groaned and pulled me closer until I stood between his legs. Trapped. "We always have an early night nowadays. I thought we could stay up and have some fun. Like we used to. I haven't seen my cock disappear into your pretty face for so fucking long, I bet you've forgotten what it tastes like to have a mouth full of my cum."

"I'm exhausted and I need a bath," I said as I tried to wriggle away. "My boss was a real dick today and the subway was more crowded than usual. All I really want is a shower and some sleep for the night."

"You always say that," he grumbled petulantly. "When is it my turn to get a little attention around here?"

He tried to push his hand underneath my skirt, but my hand stopped him in his tracks. I shook my head. "I mean it, Brian. If you had the kind of day that I've had you'd just want to relax right now too."

"Is that your way of saying that I don't have a job? That I don't have a reason to be tired because I'm unemployed and useless?"

I shook my head. "No, that's not what it is at all. I was just saying that I had a hard day and I'm not in the mood."

"And I'm telling you that I haven't had anything from you for weeks. That's bullshit," he growled as his hand ran up and down my thigh. "You need to stop pushing me away or I'll get suspicious." His eyes narrowed. "Are you letting your boss fuck you?"

"Don't be so stupid. I can't stand him."

"Let's go in the bedroom."

I actually shuddered. The last thing I wanted to do was touch, or be touched by him when he smelled like a bar at closing time. "Maybe tomorrow," I said as I pulled hard out of his grasp. "I'm starving right now."

"Ivy," he called.

Lucky for me I managed to maneuver away from him and disappear into the kitchen. As soon as I was safe from his grasp, I sucked in a deep breath and gripped the counter. I told my body to relax. I shook my head at myself.

Running away in my own home. Horrible. My body desperately wanted to flee.

"Why'd you run away from me?"

Brian's hot breath wafted against the back of my neck and set my teeth on edge. The smell of booze entered my space and choked me. I held my breath and tried to block out the aroma as he kissed the back of my neck. "I told you I want to eat and then get to bed, Brian."

"We haven't fucked in ages."

"Not today."

"When then?"

"Maybe tomorrow." I was exhausted by him, work and the conversation. Even if I couldn't eat for the night, I wanted to curl up and get some sleep. Either way, I wanted Brian to stop touching me. I turned around. "I'm going to go to bed. Work wiped me out."

Brian pressed me against the counter with his body. "No. I'm bored of waiting."

I grimaced as he pressed his lips against mine. That acrid taste invaded my mouth and it took everything to keep from gagging. Brian's body pressed against mine. I squeezed my eyes shut and tried to endure it. If he got his kisses maybe I could put him off for another night because I sure as hell wasn't in the mood tonight. "Brian I——"

"Shhh." Brian's fingers yanked at my button-up blouse. The top two buttons flew off and pinged against the floor. His other hand reached up my skirt.

I jolted. It was one thing when he was pushy, but he was going too far. My hands grabbed him and shoved his hands away roughly. This was it. I couldn't take another minute of him trying to touch me. I slapped my hands on his chest and shoved him away from me. "Brian, I said stop. God, I don't want to have sex right now. I shouldn't have to keep saying it."

"What do I have to do, clunk you over the head and fuck a lump of lard?"

"Fuck you," I snarled. This time, he'd gone too far.

"What's your problem, bitch?"

"Don't call me that," I growled. "I'm so sick and tired of you doing this shit."

"You should be happy I even want your lumpy ass. No one else would want to fuck you even if you paid them."

I glared at Brian. It was bad enough he tried to break me down, but this was beyond hurtful. It poked a sensitive nerve. What if I left him and no one wanted me? He wasn't the first man to reject me. Hell, it went all the way back to my first love. An image of Cooper flashed into my mind. I shut it out instantly. At every turn, he tried to beat it into my head that he was the only person who would ever want me and I hated it.

"I'm going to bed," I muttered. "I've had enough."

"Fine, at least fucking give me a blow, then. You know how much you like your meat raw."

I shook my head in amazement. It was like talking to a brick wall. A horny brick wall.

He pushed his sweatpants down and pulled his naked dick out. It was hard and aroused by the thought of forced sex. "Come on, get over here, and put that dirty mouth to use."

While he had his jerking meat in his hand, I tried to streak past him, but with surprising speed for a drunk man, he grabbed me with his other hand. I tried to twist out of his grasp, but he held me tightly. His other hand left his cock and yanked at my shirt. Then his lips came for me again. Anger bubbled up inside of me and for the first time, I didn't want to shrink away and hide.

It was everything. The rudeness, the lack of care, the smell of his breath, his rough-dry hands, the unwashed, smelly dick pressed against me. I didn't want him anywhere near me. And he knew that. But he just didn't care. He just wanted what he wanted. I'd had enough of men pushing me around for one day.

"I said stop," I yelled.

He completely ignored me and let his tongue trail on my skin.

I whipped my hand as far back as I could and swung it forward until it connected with the side of his head. Full force. The sting reverberated up my hand and traveled up the length of my arm.

Brian's head jerked back, then stayed in the position I'd slapped it into. His hands had fallen away from me, but I couldn't move. I stared at him in shock. As much as he pushed me, I'd never lost my temper with him before or retaliated. In fact, this was the first time in my life I'd ever hit anybody.

Slowly, he turned his burning eyes to me. "You think you can hit me and get away with it?" His voice was very quiet, full of menace. His eyes were that of a stranger. I had lived with this man and never seen this side of him. Far, by far, worse than the man who had clenched his fists and called me names.

I backed away from him. "Stay away from me..." My voice trembled, as I tried to get some distance between us. "Just stay back."

"Bitch!" Brian lunged for me.

I couldn't run fast enough. My head slammed against the wall so hard I saw stars. The impact took my breath away and I couldn't even scream.

Hands wrapped around my throat and squeezed. My eyes widened. Brian's face was black with uncontrollable rage. It was terrifying. He gritted his teeth and pressed his body against mine as his hands tightened. I tried to scratch at him with my nails, but it was like scratching an elephant. He never even felt it. He just continued to strangle me. I could see the expression in his eyes changing to one of curiosity and strange excitement. He knew he was killing me and it was arousing him. I could feel my mouth gaping like a goldfish. I was begging him to let go, but only strange choking, gasping, rattling sounds came out of my throat.

My vision wavered and grew dark. Bit by bit, the room began to disappear around the edges and I knew that was it.

I'm going to die.

I'm going to die.

I'm going to DIE.

Panic rose in my chest as I tried frantically to breathe, but no air was pulled into my burning lungs. And Brian, he smiled as he strangled me. Was this sick, unholy look the last thing I would see before I left this earth? Would his ugly face haunt me for all eternity? I stared back at him in disbelief. Was this it? Was this all I was going to have in this life? My lungs felt as if they were going to burst. My whole body was pulsating. The edges grew and grew. Soon it would be all black...

Then, he made a mistake. He moved back slightly, so he could jerk himself off as he strangled me.

It was the only chance I had—my knee yanked upward and crashed into his balls. Brian let out a scream of agony. His hand left my throat as both his hands were needed to clutch helplessly at his crotch. Leaning my head against the wall, I sucked in great, big rasping breaths. My lungs wheezed as they tried to regulate themselves again. Dizziness made me stumble.

"That...is it," I wheezed. "I'm done with you. I'm done with this city. I'm leaving. I never want to see you again." I coughed against my fist and the skin on my throat burned and throbbed. I knew I'd have a nasty looking bruise by the morning, but I had survived. Now, to escape, while I still could. Quickly, I turned on my heels while he writhed in agony on the ground. I darted for my bag, shoved my feet into my shoes and made a dash for the front door.

"Do you really think I'll let you go? You belong to me. You're mine! Do you hear me, you bitch? You're mine."

I turned to look at him.

He was staring at me with an expression I will never forget. It was evil personified. "I'll hunt you down and drag your ass back, you'll see," he promised. "You'll never get away from me, Ivy Johansan."

My blood turned cold. I knew he was dead serious. I would never be free of him as long as I remained in New York. I would always be looking over my shoulder. I had to get away from him.

That look in his eyes as he strangled me shot shivers through my spine as I ran down the stairs. He'd come so close to ending my life while he just smiled.

Chapter Four

IVY

I stood at the bus station and stared at the little man behind the screen. He looked bored, like he'd seen too many customers and didn't give a fuck about any of them. I knew I was no different.

All I had on me was my bag which I clutched to me as if it held diamonds and precious pearls. In reality, it was just upsetting that I had left everything behind. I had nothing. None of my clothes, my laptop. Thank God, my pictures and my little knick-knacks were in the broom cupboard, but I wouldn't be able to access them at this time of the night.

At least I had my ID and social security card, but that was it.

I pulled my collar around my neck. I didn't know what was next. I had dreamed about moving on and having a new life, but not like this. I had nowhere to go.

"Ma'am, are you going to buy a ticket or are you going to stare all day?"

I blinked at the ruddy-faced man behind the glass. I wished I had the answer. All I knew for sure was that I had to get out of New York. Where was I going to go? I had only been in two places my whole life. Springston, Texas, and New York.

Could I really go back to Springston?

It seemed bizarre to go back to the one place I said I'd never return to. Except I had no idea what to do if I didn't get on that train to Texas. And the thought of going home was almost comforting.

"Yeah. I'm going to Springston, Texas. A one-way bus ticket to Springston, please."

He nodded and I couldn't believe I was actually going back home. Dallas was an hour away from Springston, but it was the closest major city to the tiny town. Springston was one of those places where everyone knew everyone. Everyone went to the same church, and everyone knew who your parents were, and what you had done throughout your life.

There were no secrets in Springston.

Was I really ready to go back to that? I left because of all the pressure, all the memories that still haunted me. Now I was about to hop on a train and go right back to it, the gossiping women, the parochial men, the lazy, nothing to do lifestyle. But it wasn't that I had run away from. No, I could have lived there all my life if not for what happened with Cooper.

I didn't know what choice I had in the matter.

It was either go back to Texas, stay in New York, or go somewhere else where I had no support or job. At least back home, I would have my old apartment. Having a place to live would at least take some of the burden off of my shoulders.

At least, I wouldn't have to worry about where I would lay my head at night. And that was a major concern.

And anyway, Cooper was probably long gone from Springston.

"All right," the man behind the glass said as he typed into his computer.

Just a few seconds later, I held a ticket and clutched it in my palm as I walked over to a seat and settled on it. I looked around me without seeing anything. My mind was filled with Springston. It was a place that held a thousand memories. Some of them amazing, some horrible.

The worst of the memories were about the fact that my parents were both dead and how they'd died. In a car accident when I was just graduating college. And now, I was twenty-seven and I had never gone back home once. Springston, without them to light it up, would be like a different world.

My mother was the upbeat, peppy type. She always donned an apron while cooking up a feast for what seemed like kings and queens, when the people around her dinner table were really just my father and I.

My father was the calm, quiet, stoic type. He liked to spend his time fishing, hunting, and napping in his favorite chair in the living room. I could still remember the scent of his cologne, Old Spice, and his deep rumbly laughter.

Now none of that no longer existed. The apartment they left me had sat empty for the last five years. It was the apartment they lived in when they were first married. After years of scrounging, they managed to save enough to move our little family to a pretty, little single-story house.

After their death, I rented the house to a lovely couple with two small children. It's what they would have wanted. That house was meant for love, laughter, life. In fact, it was the reason I could afford to have my own apartment in New York.

I didn't want to rent out a storage unit so I used the apartment to store some of the belongings I hadn't been able to part with when I emptied out the house.

Well, at least I will have somewhere to live. I knew that I could regroup there and get my shit together. I would look for a new job since I wouldn't survive long on my meager savings, and I would start anew. Somewhere else.

The bus pulled into the depot and I climbed aboard with the other passengers. I couldn't help but think how we all looked like lonely, lost spirits in the night. I shuffled to the back and found a place where I could sit comfortably. I realized I hadn't even had time to grab my cell phone charger.

The journey from New York to Texas wouldn't be short and I was sure when the bus made its next rest stop I could find an emergency charger. For now, I wanted to relax and forget the world existed. There would be plenty of problems to face when I was back home. I leaned my head against the seat and closed my eyes.

Wow!

Chapter Five

IVY

The bus bumped and shook along from New York all the way down to Texas. Sometimes, I glanced out of the window and watched the country go by. Other times, I passed out and cherished those moments of peaceful, blissful, uninterrupted sleep.

God knows Brian never allowed me a moment of peace. There had been more than one occasion when he'd deliberately woken me up out of a dead sleep, so he could pump into me.

Don't think about him. Don't think about New York. Don't think about the job you've abandoned without any notice. Don't think about any of it.

I decided to forget any of it even existed. This was a chance to start over. Clean slate, nothing to lose, the chance at a happy life.

When we finally arrived on the outskirts of Texas, we stopped for a break. I had to find a charger for my phone. As I waited my turn at the register, I stared at the diminishing battery. When I lifted my head, a man was hovering near me. I glared at him, but he came closer, anyway.

"You've got that look on your face. It's like you're running from something. Are you?"

I looked him up and down with hostile eyes. I'd had it with men interfering in my business. "What's it to you?"

"I just wanted to tell you that if you're using the same phone whatever you're running from can probably track you. I don't mean to sound paranoid or anything, but I know for a fact that people trace other people that way. You look scared, so I thought I would let you know.

I blinked up at the man. He was completely right, of course. I'd watched enough spy movies to know I needed a new phone. For some reason, my head had been so jumbled with stress, paranoia, anxiety that I hadn't realized there was an easy target on my back. I dropped the phone as if it was on fire and my heel crash down on the screen.

"Thank you," I said in a shaky voice. "I guess I hadn't properly realized that."

"No problem. I've seen my fair share of people in bad situations. I know that look you have in your eyes. I didn't want to alarm you, but I'm glad that I was able to warn you. We should head back. The bus is about ready to go."

Shuddering, I followed the man back to the bus and boarded it. The thought that Brian might have some way to track me back to my hometown was terrifying. We had never really discussed where I was from before.

Great, now I have to get a new phone.

The cost of a new phone was nothing compared to the fact that I was still alive. My hand reached up to my throat and I touched the burning, throbbing bruise that must, by now, be etched into my skin.

Any feeling of sleepiness was gone and I ended up staring out of the window the entire time and thinking about the fact that I had left everything behind and would have to start from scratch. It was still kind of daunting to think about.

"Springston," the driver called.

I quickly jumped out of my seat ready to be finally off the bus for good.

Exiting the terminal, I flagged down a taxi and told the driver to take me to the apartment. It was too late to stop anywhere as the sun had disappeared ages ago. The taxi stopped outside my apartment and I stared up at it with a strange sense of loss. It looked dark and empty. It was strange knowing that I was all alone.

I paid the driver and trudged up to the top floor where Rosa lived. She kept a spare key for me. I prayed she was in. She wasn't, but her surly husband gave me the key. I went back down to my floor and let myself into my apartment.

Light flooded the space and I sighed as I looked around the dusty space. It wasn't huge. Two bedrooms that were modest in size, a darling little kitchen trimmed in light blue and white and a living room with a small TV. There was no internet at the moment, but I would worry about getting it set up once I found a job.

Then I wandered through the apartment and was surprised by how put together it still was. There were some cobwebs and the fridge was empty, but other than that, it was perfect. And peaceful. I never realized how much I'd missed the quietness.

The main bedroom was the biggest, so I decided I would take it. I dusted off some sheets and a blanket from the closet and made up the bed before I tumbled into it. Sleep claimed me as soon as my head hit the pillow. I was grateful for that.

Chapter Six

IVY

As soon as I woke up, my first stop was a shower. I stood underneath the water until it went from searing hot to freezing cold. Once I stepped out, pruney, and surprisingly satisfied, I stared at the clothes I'd worn from New York.

"I definitely need some new clothes."

There were none in the apartment besides a few old pieces. My mother's wedding dress that I couldn't stand to part with, and a few clothes that I'd left behind years ago. Everything else had been shipped to New York or donated.

I shimmied into the blouse, the pencil skirt, and the heels I had arrived in. It would have to do.

When I walked outside, I was hit with my first problem. How was I going to get where I needed to go with no cell phone and no way to call a taxi? I was used to taking the Subway, or simply stepping toward a curb and lifting my hand for a taxi. I no longer had that luxury.

I decided to find someone with a cell phone. If I remembered correctly, there was a diner a couple of blocks away. Fingers crossed they would remember me and let me use their phone. I should call work too and let them know I wouldn't be coming back. Then I have to call Maria and arrange how to get my stuff back here.

Linda was not in, but a waitress let me use her phone to call a taxi.

My first stop was a clothing store where I purchased the staples that I would need. I opted for button-ups, skirts, flat shoes, sneakers and some laze around clothes, basically, jeans and shorts. I dressed in one lot of clothing and asked the woman that owned the store if it would be alright if I came back for the rest of my haul later that day.

My very next stop was to an electronic store. I decided against going to my usual carrier and getting a phone from them. I wanted no ties with anything from my old life. I opted for a prepaid phone that I could top up monthly. Once I had a phone in my hand, I felt a little more positive about my day.

It was time to get a job.

I held my head up and went to my first destination. The local TV news station. It was exciting to be in the building. As I looked around, I visualized myself working there. I could do this.

"Hi," I said cheerfully, as I stood at the receptionist's desk. "Could I speak with whoever is in charge?"

The blonde behind the desk looked at me curiously. "What is this regarding?"

"I was hoping to talk to someone about a job. I'm a journalist."

I must have passed whatever test she performed in her head because she picked up the phone on her desk and dialed someone. I glanced around the lobby while she quickly and almost under her breath, relayed what I'd told her. After a few more whispered interactions, she hung up the phone.

"Unfortunately, we don't have any open positions for new journalists. We're fully staffed."

I frowned. "There's not even anything I could apply for. Like in a back-up position? In case there's an emergency. I would seriously take any position you have. I've worked as a journalist for nearly five years in New York."

"Unfortunately no, hon. My boss just said she doesn't need anyone and even if she did, she doesn't hire anyone with less than ten years of experience. Maybe try the Springston Sun? They might be hiring."

My heart sank. I guess I shouldn't be surprised. I was never good enough in New York, so I guess this isn't any different.

I shook myself out of that way of thinking. If I kept this up, I would get sad and depressed and that wasn't what I needed. Instead, I thanked the blonde and focused on heading to the newspaper office. There was still hope. I wasn't beat yet.

The newspaper wasn't too far away and I walked it. I figured the less money I used the better. When I stepped into the Springston Sun's offices, I was filled with renewed energy. This would work. I had five years of newspaper experience in New York under my belt. They would have to say yes.

"Could I speak with someone in charge of employment?"

"That would be Terrance Colt. Let me get him," the woman behind the desk said. "You can sit there in the meantime."

I settled into the chair she indicated. At least I would get to actually meet the employment guy from the Springston Sun. As I waited, I went over what to say in my head. My foot bounced up and down until I heard a deep voice.

"Can I help you?"

I hopped up and shoved out my hand to the man in front of me. "I'm Ivy Johanson."

"Terrance Colt."

The man was short and his reddened face reminded me of Brian. That wasn't a great thought to have right as I was trying to impress the man who would hopefully be my new employer.

He pumped my hand and released it.

"I'm looking for a job. I was a journalist in New York for five years and I have more than enough experience and the proper degree. I primarily did—"

"Not to interrupt you," he said as he did exactly that. "I don't need any more journalists at the moment. I don't have a need for any new staff, really. This is a small town paper. Turnover is low. Maybe try some of the bigger cities."

"Oh," I said in a small voice. "Thanks for meeting with me, anyway."

"No problem. Sorry I couldn't help."

"It's okay. Thanks." I walked outside and the sun hit my skin. It was still as sunny as before, but my hope had died. My stomach growled and I wrapped an arm around it. I should probably put some food inside of me. The last thing I'd had to eat was a bag of chips at a rest stop. At least I could stop by the grocery store and do some light shopping before I went back to the apartment.

What was I going to do? If I got a job in a bigger city, it would defeat the purpose of leaving New York. Not to mention it would be harder to get to and even then, I might not get hired.

I sighed as I walked along. The stress that I had pushed off before came back full force. If I couldn't find a place to work then I would be shit out of luck.

The grocery store wasn't far away, but I was distracted by a bar tucked away to the side. Red Royal. A sign in its window caught my eye.

Waitress needed.

*I*t wasn't what I wanted to do, but a job was a job. At least I could keep the lights on and food in my belly until I found something else. I ran my fingers through my hair.

I pushed the door open and once inside, glanced around the darkened interior. My eyes adjusted to the dimness of the space and I could see it wasn't half bad. It was pretty spacious with red upholstery, a few pool tables, a karaoke machine and a few dart boards in the back. It looked exactly how a small town bar should look.

"Hey there. Can I help you?"

I glanced up and froze as my eyes landed on the bartender. He was tall, definitely over six feet. His golden blond hair was slightly longer than I remembered. Wisps of fine gold graced his neck. His strong jaw was clean shaven. And those eyes. They were exactly how I remembered them. The blue-green orbs stared back at me.

Cooper Page.

I hadn't seen him since I left this town. My breath stuck in my throat.

Even back then, he'd been a sweleringly hot guy with a strong build and taut muscles, but he'd grown even more devastating, even more dazzling with the years.

My first love.

And the first man to break my heart.

Chapter Seven

IVY

I stared at Cooper.

He stared right back at me. Then his eyes widened in shock of disbelief. When he regained his power of speech, he shoved his hands into his pockets, as if he didn't know what to do with them. "Ivy Johanson," he breathed. "I thought your face looked familiar. How the hell are you?"

"I'm good. I'm great. I'm just... Wow. Sorry, I really didn't think I'd be bumping into you today."

Cooper grinned suddenly and one mind-blowingly sexy dimple flashed at me. I had pretended to forget just how absolutely intoxicating he was. Those deliciously broad shoulders, the manly jaw, thickly muscled arms, and the mischievous eyes. To be honest, I hadn't laid eyes on anything so fine in a long time.

"What are you doing back in Springston?" he asked as he finally pulled his hands out of his pockets and reached for a towel, which he slung over his shoulder.

"I thought a change of pace might be nice," I said as I tried to stop staring at his body, only to find my eyes glued instead to the curve of his sensuous lips.

"Didn't think I'd ever see you back in these parts again."

"Well, I didn't think I'd see you here either."

The last time I saw Cooper Page was when he was taking my virginity in senior year. My face grew hot at the memory of his body gleaming in the moonlight as he pounded into me. I'd thought we had something special. That was why I gave myself to him, but I was wrong. Dead wrong. Cooper had left me high and dry and went off to college without a word.

It had shattered me. He was the other big reason I didn't want to be in or around Springston. So much heartbreak had occurred in my life in this quiet, quaint little town, and I didn't need or want to be reminded of any of it.

Remembering what he did to me, made me sober up and stop staring at him. Besides, what was the point? I couldn't be with him. There was no way in hell. Not after what I'd just gone through. I needed to cool it on the men.

"I've been back for a while," Cooper said as he grabbed a bottle of whiskey and poured some into a glass. Then he downed it in one swallow, before he turned back to me. "After college, I ended up moving back here so I could help my parents out."

"How are your parents?"

"My dad passed two years ago, but my mom's still going tough. Wrangling kids, working, singing. She's never changed."

I frowned. "I'm sorry to hear about your dad."

"Thank you. That's the way life goes," he said, but his jaw hardened as he glanced down at the bar.

The saddened look on his face broke my heart all over again. He had always been the type to hide who he really was. What he really felt. Even back in high school, I had been one of the few that saw beneath the bad boy exterior. I couldn't stop myself as I laid my hand on top of his and gave it a squeeze.

Cooper glanced up and the far-away look in his eyes faded, replaced with something I couldn't quite put my finger on.

I pulled my hand away as if I'd been burnt.

"Right, now that you're here, what can I get you?" His voice sounded strange.

"Oh, I don't want a drink. I saw the sign out front that you're looking for a waitress. I wanted to apply."

Cooper cocked a brow. "You want to be a waitress? I thought you went to school for journalism."

"How do you know that?"

"Small town." He chuckled. "You do know everybody talks about everybody around here, don't ya?"

"Yeah, don't I know it."

"You sure you want to waitress, Jo? It won't be fancy like the job you had in the big apple."

It was strange hearing Jo again. He was the only one who ever called me by my shortened last name and made it sound special and sexy. I shrugged. "I need a job. That's all that matters."

He waited as if to give me a chance to explain myself, but I didn't want to get into a whole discussion about my life. The things that I left in New York needed to stay there. If I brought it up it would only be more painful and I couldn't handle that. Not yet.

Cooper looked me up and down as if he wanted to push the subject.

I didn't care how much he wanted to know, I was too stubborn to give in and tell him a damn thing.

He must have seen the fire in my eyes and knew when to give it up. "Alright," he said with a nod. "Do you have any experience?"

"How hard could it be to carry food and write down orders?"

His eyebrows rose. "When it's busy? Really hard. Why do you want the job if you think it's beneath you?"

I rubbed my arm. "Sorry, I didn't mean it to sound like that. I do really want the job. It's close to my apartment and I'm great with people."

He hesitated.

"Look, I know I'm probably not the best option with having no experience and all, but I can pick up on things fast and I don't have any other commitments so you know I'll always be here when you need me."

"Is that right?" Cooper drawled as his eyes lingering.

My cheeks burned. I cleared my throat. "That's right," I said firmly.

"Whenever I need you, huh?" he mocked.

I groaned. "Don't get any ideas."

"I'm a red-blooded man not a piece of stone, Jo, but I don't touch my staff."

He stated this, but the look in his eyes said otherwise. That hungry look made every inch of my skin break out in goose-bumps. There was no way he wasn't mentally undressing me and bending me over the bar.

"So, can I have the job?"

Cooper considered it. "I guess, I can show you the ropes and give you some training. I need someone soon though."

"I can start whenever you need me."

He rubbed his sturdy jaw. "Now. Do you think you could do that?"

I nodded eagerly. There was nothing I wanted to do less than sit alone in my apartment. "Of course.

No matter how he'd abandoned me in high school, I found it impossible to look away. He really had matured into a drop-dead sexy, totally irresistible man. His lips pulled into a grin, which only made the situation worse. God, I wanted to kiss that mouth and work my way down all that hard muscle...all the way down to.... Jesus, what the hell was I thinking? Working for Cooper has to be the dumbest idea that I've ever had. It wouldn't end well.

But it wasn't as if I had a choice though. A job was the one thing I needed to keep living on my own. There was no one to fall back on if I messed up and couldn't pay for myself. I'd be on my own and I'd starve. I needed the job. I was on the run. There was no telling if or when Brian would pop up. Falling for someone else was strictly off limits.

Stop staring at his biceps like an idiot and shake his hand.

"Thank you," I said as I offered my hand toward him.

"Don't thank me yet."

"Even so, I truly appreciate the opportunity," I insisted.

"So formal," he teased, but he smiled as he reached out for my hand. Cooper's big hand engulfed mine.

His calloused palm slipped against mine and I wondered how those hands would fit on other parts of my body. How they would feel as they dragged across my flesh and caressed me.

I really need to stop doing that.

I definitely couldn't afford to sleep with him again. I forced myself to think about how hurt I'd been when he broke my heart the first time. Going down that path again wasn't an option. I pulled my hand away and quickly fidgeted with the hem of my shirt.

Cooper waved a hand at me. "Come through to the back. I'm sure I have some spare aprons back there. I'll show you the ropes."

"Thank you," I muttered as I walked after him. My eyes traveled down his body and landed on his ass. It looked good enough to grab and squeeze underneath the snugly fitted jeans he wore. I shook my head.

Keep it together, Ivy!

Chapter Eight

COOPER

What the hell was life doing sending her into my bar?

W I hadn't seen Ivy since the night I sped off on my bike. I still remember her face, soft in the early morning light. I was gone that afternoon. Off to college. At the back of my mind, I knew I was leaving behind something precious, but I was too young. I didn't understand how rare it was to have a real connection with another human being.

I know better now. I've never found the same connection I felt with her with another other woman. Oh, they tried, how they tried, but none of them were her.

When her parents died, I was still at college and I'd tried to reach out, but she never answered. Then, just like that, she was gone, off to start a shiny new life in New York City.

I'd never stopped thinking about her. The curvy, doe-eyed girl who I'd never forgotten. When I came back to Springston, I put my feelers out for information about her. Springston was known for its twitching curtains. There wasn't much that the folks around here didn't see. Hell, I wouldn't be surprised if they knew what was in my garbage. The women were the worst, but the men didn't do too badly either. Everybody was curious about everybody.

I learned little snippets of news about her. She had rented out her parents' home. She had an apartment full of her stuff. They speculated that she planned on returning. Otherwise, why would anyone pay rent to keep their old stuff. I agreed. I changed my plans. I bought this bar and decided to wait for her. One day, one day soon, she was going to come back to Springston.

And I would be here waiting for her.

That day was today. You could have knocked me down with a feather when she turned up in my bar. I couldn't fucking believe my eyes. It felt as if all the blood in my body had rushed down to my feet. She was even more beautiful than I had remembered.

I opened my office and walked in. She followed behind. I turned around to face her. God, my eyes wouldn't stop staring at her.

She was looking around. "It's a mess in here," she said as she straightened up a stack of papers that threatened to topple over.

"I don't get much time to clean. The bar is always full and when it isn't, I don't want to waste my time with cleaning."

"Still," she muttered as she wiped errant dust onto her skirt.

I folded my arms. "You just got hired. Do I have to fire you already?"

Ivy grinned and my world tilted on its axis. She looked good enough to eat when she smiled like that. I quickly refocused on my task of locating an apron for her before I got myself in all kinds of trouble. "Here you go," I said as I opened a box and found the aprons. I passed one to her. "And here's an order book and a pen. That should be enough to get you started off."

Ivy took the apron and tied it around her waist. Maroon looked good on her. Once it sat right, she took the booklet and pushed it into a pocket and the pen into another. She glanced up, tucked her hair behind her ear and smiled. "What do you think?"

"I think it suits you," I said as I fought back the strong thrust of arousal. My dick twitched eagerly. Ivy Johanson did things to me, wonderful, strange, amazing things. She always had. "Why don't you go out front and wait for me? I'll be right back."

Ivy nodded and walked back out into the bar. I leaned my head against the office door and forced myself to calm down. I wanted her with an intensity that was making my head pound. I'd been too young to love her the way she needed when we were younger, but damn I wanted to try again.

I'd only been around her for a few minutes and I was already rock hard. I rubbed a hand over the bulge in my jeans, and my body responded by pulsating.

"What the hell was I thinking?" The last thing I needed was to let my own lust cloud up my brain and spoil things. I had a plan and I wasn't blowing it all from lack of control. I had managed to stay focused for so long. That couldn't change now.

I squeezed my eyes shut and forced myself to calm down. Once the erection disappeared, I sucked in a breath and headed out to meet her.

She was sitting at the bar easily chatting to one of my delivery guys. The fool looked besotted.

I felt jealousy rip through me. I wanted to tear his head off.

This whole thing would not be easy.

Chapter Nine

IVY

I t already felt like a big mistake.

There was no way I would be able to work with Cooper without losing my mind. So far, we'd only spent a little time together in his bar and I was already climbing up the walls. How was I gonna work here all the time when I felt overwhelmed in less than an hour?

Cooper leaned over the sink to show me how to use the dishwasher. We were in the kitchen in the back of the bar. Here, the usual staples were produced. Onion rings, greasy burgers, French fries, hot wings. "We have a cook that comes in every day, but sometimes he needs a little help with the dishes when things get too busy."

At least that's what I thought he said. It became so hard to focus when every word out of his mouth was deep and sexy as hell. The water from the sink had splashed onto his shirt and it gripped his muscles tightly.

Suddenly, I suspected that the universe was doing this to me on purpose. Cooper was being dangled in front of me like bait on a hook. He might look delicious, but I would end up with a bruised soul and a broken heart.

But it wasn't like I had a choice. As long as I worked here, I could afford to eat and live like a normal human being. If I turned this job down there was no telling where I'd find another job in a small town like Springston. Most people got a job, worked at it, and died at that job. So I knew there weren't going to be a ton of open positions just waiting for me to be picky.

I would just have to wait and look for something better once I felt more secure. After all, I intended to be here for a very long time. My dreams of city life had shattered into a thousand pieces. I knew now it wasn't what it was cracked up to be I had no plans to leave anytime soon. Right now, I felt as if I needed my small, safe hometown, where I could lick my wounds in peace.

"Since it's Friday, it's going to be busy," Cooper said as he straightened and dried the front of his shirt with a towel." So you'll probably have a long shift."

"It's a good thing I suppose. I can jump in feet first." I chewed my lower lip. "I hope I don't make too many mistakes."

"You'll do great. Don't worry about it. If you really get stuck in the weeds, I'll help you out."

I smiled gratefully at him.

Then his expression changed. "Right. Follow me."

Cooper led me back out to the front where his day bartender worked behind the bar. Melanie was a stunning woman, tall, leggy and big breasted. She welcomed me right away. I liked the way she smiled at the customers and her laugh was loud and crazy. She was a character, that was for sure.

"How you gettin' on, shug?" she asked as she cleaned down the bar. "Is Cooper helping, or is he just talking your ear off about nonsense?"

Cooper laughed. "Don't undermine me in front of the new hire. Why don't you get back to work?"

"I'm always working, hon. That's why your pockets are so full of money."

I smiled at the two of them, but a little knot tied in my belly. They had such an easy way about them that I wondered if more might be going on. Was he dating her? You couldn't blame him if he was. She was gorgeous, confident, and outrageously fun.

This troubling thought stayed with me even as we walked from behind the bar to the tables that filled up the rest of the space. The Red Royal was a lot bigger than I'd first thought. Different from when you just glanced around the room. It all seemed to change when you were actually memorizing where the tables were and the numbers associated with them.

"Ok, so you'll just come up and take their orders and bring them to the bar, or to the kitchen in the back. Easy, right?"

"Kind of," I muttered as I tried to remember which table was which. "Why can't there be actual numbers on the tables?"

Cooper laughed. "It's not that hard. Look." One of his hands wandered down to my lower back and perched there. He pointed to the tables as he directed me around the room.

Abrupt like, my brain just completely powered down. My

heart raced at the pressure of his hand on my body and I swore I'd melt if he didn't remove it soon.

How could he still get to me like this? We hadn't seen each other in so long, but the moment I laid eyes on him, it was like I got sucked into it all over again. Like no time had passed. It was more surreal than those Salvador Dali paintings with the melted clocks. I shivered.

"You're not even paying attention to what I'm saying, are you?" Cooper asked, his hand dropping off.

I glanced up at him.

His eyes bored into mine, so sexy and alluring, something else lurked there too. Lust.

The way he looked at me made me wonder if he was having the same issue, I had. A strange expression crossed his face, and I sucked in a breath. He was definitely feeling it too.

"Sorry," I said quickly as I stepped away from the immediate vicinity of his magnetic, mind altering presence. "I guess I'm just still a little...overwhelmed." I cleared my throat. "One more time and I'll pay close attention."

Cooper's eyes lingered on me and my body heated as those gorgeous blue-green eyes swept along my body from head to toe and back up again.

This was terrible. Already my mind had drifted off to thinking about Cooper and me in very compromising situations. "I should go over the menu and familiarize myself with the dishes." I snatched the menu from one of the tables and covered my face with it. I needed to break up the intensity before I ended up doing something really stupid. The one saving grace was that soon, the Royal would be flooded with patrons and I could focus on work, instead of on Cooper.

Yes, this was what I thought, but it didn't happen. Instead, even as I took orders, made change, and tried to remember who ordered what and where, Cooper's eyes lingered on me. Whenever I turned around, our eyes locked before he'd return to working behind the bar.

I had to admit, I was just as guilty. Every time he was obviously busy attending to a customer, my attention surreptitiously returned to him. That grin tugging at the corners of his mouth, those strong biceps flexing underneath the sleeves of his shirt, the laugh that echoed from his lips as he chatted easily. All of it was so perfect.

Oh God, he was perfect.

Why did he have to be so damn perfect?

Cooper was strictly, strictly, *strictly* off limits.

"Sweetheart, can I get that beer or not?" a customer drawled at me as his friends chuckled.

I shook my head. "Sorry about that. Yes, I'll grab your beers right away." I pushed through the crowd and made my way to the bar.

Cooper strolled toward me and smiled. "What can I get for you?"

"Three beers," I said and leaned against the bar.

"Everything all right?"

"Everything is fine, except for my feet, which I think might be dead. I've never walked so much in my life."

Cooper laughed. "It'll get easier. Customers treating you okay?"

"Yeah, actually. They've been pretty patient with me, so that's nice."

"Our crowd is pretty laid back. You shouldn't have any trouble from anyone." Cooper pulled out three bottles and pressed them against the bar. One by one, he popped the tops with the heel of his hand.

"Impressive." I nodded. "Where did you pick that up?"

"I hung out with some very interesting people in high school."

"By that, you mean the other bad boys of the school who obviously taught you some more bad manners."

"Don't judge me."

I chuckled. "No judgment here. We all had our secrets in high school."

"Yeah? Didn't think you had any. I thought you were as pure as the driven snow."

I grinned. "That's my cover story. Right, I need to deliver these to my customers."

"Hang on, you're not going to finish this conversation?"

"Sorry." I shook my head as I carefully maneuvered the tables while carrying the beers on my tray. It took a bit of practice not to spill them all to the floor, so I had to take my time. Once the table was in range, I smiled victoriously at the fact that I hadn't dropped anything.

And then I dropped everything.

Chapter Ten

T he tray crashed to the floor, glasses shattered, and beer splashed everywhere. Especially on me. I shrieked and jumped, before I glanced up slowly.

Every set of eyes in the bar were on me. The room had gone quiet.

My stomach dropped and the urge to flee bubbled up until a hand wrapped around my arm.

"Are you okay?" Cooper asked, his face full of concern.

"Uh yeah. I think so."

"You're bleeding," he said as he examined my leg. "Let's get you cleaned up. Mel?"

"Already on it, shug," she said as she moved to clean up the mess.

"I'm sorry. I can clean it up. I did it."

She waved a hand. "It's your first day. None of us are immune to a bit of clumsiness. Go get cleaned up and then get back out here asap, so I'm not left alone with these wolves." She turned towards my table of customers and called out to them cheerfully, "I'll get you guys your beers in just a minute."

"Take your time," the man at the table replied, then he grinned at me. "Congrats on the new job."

Cooper chuckled.

I wallowed with embarrassment.

He led me through the bar and into his small office. "Sit," he instructed.

I perched on a chair.

He dug around and rustled up a first aid kit. "Let me see your leg."

I stuck my leg out and saw the streak of blood that had slid down my skin.

Cooper picked up my leg carefully and peered at it. "Hmmm...don't look too bad," he commented as he settled down in the other chair and laid my leg on top of his. Then he started to clean up the cut. "It's really not too bad," he said again and he smiled up at me. "Could have been much worse."

I groaned. "It already was worse. I can't believe I dropped that tray in front of everyone. I'm so embarrassed, I thought I was going to literally die."

"Don't be a drama queen," he mocked. "Everyone does it at one point or another. That's the nature of the job. Just be glad you didn't drop an entire tray of hot wings in anyone's lap."

My eyes widened. "You did that?"

"Yup. Hectic night, low on waitresses, only me and Mel to work the bar. Someone had to deliver the food, and if you send her out to the tables, she never comes back. She just talks everyone's ears off."

I chuckled. "Was the guy pissed?"

Cooper groaned. "I wasn't that lucky. It was a woman and yeah, she was pissed. To make it worse, she was the mother of one of my exes. To this day, she swears I did it on purpose, and won't look at me without trying to burn a hole through my skin."

I cracked up. "Okay, so maybe I wasn't so bad, after all." I couldn't think of anything worse than drenching someone's lap with hot wing sauce.

"See? You can already laugh about it now. I can kinda laugh about it. It'll be better after more than a month has passed."

"Oh, god..." I tried to breathe. "This was recent."

"Real recent." He grimaced. "Real, real recent."

"Oh, my god." I wiped at my eyes. "You poor thing. I bet your face was red."

"Nah, I took it in stride after I hid in the back office for a few minutes and I laughed. I didn't do it on purpose, but her expression... Just perfect. That and the fact that she never liked me, so maybe it was a bit of revenge from the universe."

"I'm starting to think you did it on purpose."

He winked at me. "You'll never know, will you?" He dug around and pulled out a Band-aid.

As he opened it and slid the tabs over my skin, I became acutely aware of his hand on my body. Shivers ran up my spine. When I glanced up his eyes locked on mine. I swallowed thickly. "I should get back out there. I don't want to leave Melanie all by herself. That wouldn't be fair."

"Let me get you something to dry off with. You're covered in beer." Cooper shifted and placed my leg onto his empty chair.

My eyes followed as he reached up and dug into another box. His shirt hiked up slightly and showed off a sliver of his back, the skin golden. Higher up, I knew there were tats. I wondered what it would be like to trail my fingers over his skin until he shuddered against me? Like I did that night so many years ago.

"Here we go," he said as he carried the towel over and handed it to me. "You can dry off with this. I'd use a bit of soap from the bathroom too, or you'll feel sticky."

"Yeah, I don't think I want to be sticky for an entire shift."

Cooper grinned. "Go ahead and get cleaned up. I'll meet you out front."

"Okay."

Cooper disappeared and I watched until he was gone. Once I was alone, I sighed. Some shady part of me thought he was going to dry me off with the towel and I'd held my breath just ready for him to do it. I knew how insane it was. Way too intimate—tempting fate.

I pushed myself up and walked to the bathroom. My leg stung a bit, but it wasn't too bad. I could still move and if I could move then I would work. I needed the money and as packed as the bar was, I knew Cooper and Melanie needed the help.

I wet the cloth with soap and water then wiped down my clothes the best I could. I'd have to wash them when I got home since I didn't have anything else suitable for working in a bar. I should look into getting some more appropriate clothes too. I'd bought things thinking I'd be working as a journalist, but that wasn't going to happen. At least, not anytime soon.

When the aroma of yeast didn't clog my nose I dropped the towel into the laundry basket and fixed my hair in the mirror. I sucked in a deep breath, pushed through the door and walked back out into the bar. No one paid attention to me, except to ask for drinks or food. I smiled and relaxed. All I had to do was focus and eventually, I'd be done.

I worked hard for the rest of the session. By the time I was done, I was slightly sweating and very tired. I sat on a stool at the bar and laid my head on the coolness of the wood once Melanie wiped it down. "It feels like I'm dead."

She laughed. "I'm sure it feels like it, but you're as alive as you're ever gonna be, hon."

"This place is always this busy?"

"Usually. Weekends are the heaviest, but we do a pretty good business." She swung a towel over her shoulder. "How were your tips?"

I popped up. "I forgot to count them."

"Oh shug, you're gonna want to do that. Trust me."

I gathered up the money I had tucked away and started to

count. When I was done I did it all over again and gasped. "Two hundred dollars!"

Mel grinned. "I told you. And that's just starting. This place is great when it comes to people loving a good drink and a sweet smile. Stop frowning at your ticket book so hard and you'll make even more."

I grinned happily. "I'll have to remember that."

"Congrats," Cooper said as he poured me a drink and sat it in front of me. "I think you're going to fit right in here."

I picked up the glass. "Thanks."

He clinked his against mine and I took a sip. Jack and coke. It was a classic and I drank it down too quickly. It hit me fast, warmth spreading throughout my body as the oaky whiskey laced my lips. It was the perfect way to end an oddly satisfying night.

"I just need to count up the till and lock everything up for the night." Cooper nodded.

"Mind if I get out of here?" Mel asked. "My boyfriend's waiting in the car."

"No problem. Tell Jeff I said hi. Goodnight."

"Night you two," she called as she wiggled her fingers at us.

I waved back and locked the door after her like Cooper asked me to do.

When I wandered back, he had the register open and was counting up the bills. "Can you count the change? Just mark down what it adds up to on here, and I'll set up the till for tomorrow."

"Yes, sir." I saluted. "If I can have one more drink."

"You're supposed to listen to your boss because he employs you."

"I will, as soon as he pours me that drink."

Cooper clicked his tongue.

I grinned at him.

He fixed me up another round.

I started on counting up the funds.

Once everything was done, he locked it up in the safe in his office and came back out. "I don't know about you, but I'm starving."

"Starving," I said. "I'd kill for some cheese fries, but everything's closed. And I forgot to buy groceries."

"You could always come by my place and grab something to eat," Cooper said as we stepped out of the bar and he locked up.

"I don't think that's a great idea, but I know there's a diner not far from here. Let's go grab something and then you can drop me off at home."

Cooper's brow shot up. "You're very demanding once you've had a few drinks in you."

I smiled. "That's a compliment."

He shook his head. "Fine. Let's go get you those fries and then into a bed."

"My own bed," I said as I pointed at him. "Without you in it."

"What do you think I'm going to do? Seduce you or something?"

"I remember how you used to be. You used to be able to talk your way into any girls' panties. Even mine."

"That was a long time ago," he said as he opened the passenger door to his truck for me. "I've changed."

"Does a leopard change its spots?" I asked as I climbed inside.

"I like to think so." He grinned as he closed the truck door and leaned against it. "Maybe you should get to know the new leopard. Maybe count its new spots."

I sucked in a breath. He was flirting with me. "Maybe I will."

Cooper's smile warmed me in all the right ways. His eyes lingered before he pushed off of the door. "You've changed, Jo."

"Is that a bad thing?" I asked, slightly worried.

"From what I can see? Nah, I'm just getting to know you all over again."

"Right."

"Let's Start Over?"

I smiled slowly. "Okay."

"But first we go get you that meal."

My smile became a big grin. "That would be amazing."

Chapter Eleven

Brian hovered over me, his face red. His hands tightened around my throat. The air in my lungs became like fire. I struggled, but no matter how hard I tried, I couldn't suck in a breath. My hands flailed and slapped uselessly against his body.

He only smiled and tightened his hands. I was going to die. And there wasn't a damn thing I could do about it. Brian's body weighed me down, held me in place. I fought against him. I couldn't scream no matter how hard I tried.

"Die," he growled. "Die, you bitch!"

Spit hit my cheek as he pressed harder and harder.

"You'll never get away from me, do you hear me? If I can't have you. Nobody can. I'll find you...bitch." His eyes narrowed and his hate drilled into me.

I couldn't speak. I couldn't protest. My hands slapped against him, but it did nothing. Finally, I couldn't suck in another breath and the world started to turn black around me. My vision faded, my head throbbed. Everything became black. He was laughing.

I died.

I jerked upright, my body covered in sweat. Sobbing, my hands flew to my throat and I scratched and tugged at nothing. My breathing refused to calm down as my head jerked back and forth around the room.

Nothing.

Moonlight streamed through the window. My entire body felt cold and I realized I was shaking. I pushed trembling fingers through my hair and sucked in a shuddering breath.

I'm all right. I'm all right. I'm all right.

The nightmare had been so real. I felt too afraid to close my eyes. I never wanted to see him again. I forced myself out of bed and went to the bathroom.

Stopping in front of the mirror, I glanced at my reflection. My eyes were puffy and red from crying. I lifted my head and around my throat was a bruise from his hands. I'd worn a high collar that concealed it yesterday, but in my PJs, it was so ugly and prominent. He did that to me. I detested him.

I grabbed the sink tightly and steadied myself before I turned on the cold water. Quickly, I splashed it onto my face to wash away the bad dream. It wasn't the first nightmare I'd had about Brian. Once even before he showed his true colors, I dreamed that he was a dangerous animal who has hunting me through a dark wood. It was terrifying. He found me. It was a creature, but I knew it was really him. He got on top of me and began to hurt me. When I woke up, he held me close and told me it was my subconscious mind processing something that must have happened at work. The dream was never about the person, only what was happening in your head.

I'd believed him because I'd wanted to believe him.

I shivered in the cool air as I stripped off my clothes. I needed a shower. I needed to feel clean. In a few hours, I had to head to work. It was Saturday and Melanie said that it was busy on the weekends. I had to get there and help them out.

I turned on the shower and stared at the water as it heated up and steam rose from it. My mind drifted back to New York. The look in Brian's eyes as he strangled me. Never, in my wildest dreams had I imagined anything like that would happen to me. It was wild. The rage he showed as he choked me. What had I ever done to him to deserve that kind of hatred? If I hadn't gotten away, I knew I would be dead.

I wrung my hands. It was a horrifying thing to contemplate. Just knowing that I had been living with a psychopath shook me. I'd been with him for so long and put up with so much. What if I'd stayed?

Don't think about that.

I closed my eyes and prayed that Brian wouldn't find me here. I prayed that I hadn't revealed my hometown to him in some unguarded moment. I'm pretty sure I didn't. Only because I never talked about Springston. Too painful. Anyway, most of the time he paid no attention to my chatter.

I wanted to forget about him. About the cramped New York apartment along with all of the problems and indignities I'd suffered inside it. One day, Brian would be a distant memory.

Pushing Brian aside, I stepped into the shower. It was hotter than I was used to and my skin turned pink, but it was welcomed to stave off the chill that had settled into my muscles.

Maybe this outfit would be nice. *I wonder what Cooper will...*

I jolted. Was I actually wondering what Cooper would think about my outfit? I forced myself to think about what he had done to me. Frowning, I pushed through my clothes. I had allowed myself to get a bit tipsy and hung out with him the night before. I groaned as I thought about it. I shook my head.

"I cannot do that again."

I needed to be firmer than that. Just because he'd given me a job, it didn't change the way he'd treated me in the past. The way he'd taken my virginity and stabbed me in the back? That wasn't okay. That would never be okay.

It was a pattern really. Cooper broke my heart and ignored me. Brian abused and pushed me around. No man was ever going to do that to me again.

I finally settled on a pair of jeans and a comfortable maroon t-shirt. I pulled my hair into a neat ponytail and I snagged the apron that I had washed and dried the night before. Then I headed out and walked to the Royal as my heart thudded in my chest. No matter how much I scolded myself... I couldn't take my mind off Cooper.

~

"*T*here you are. I was about to call you and see if you weren't planning on showing up," Cooper called as I walked into the bar.

"Of course, I was. I just overslept a little. Bad dreams. Sorry."

He tilted his head and stared at me.

Suddenly, I felt like he could see right through me.

"Alright, well get your things put away and come back out here and help. We're already getting flooded."

I glanced around. He was right. Already, the bar was filling up with patrons. People chatted and laughed as the smell of beer and alcohol filled the space.

I walked to the back and stored my purse away in Cooper's office. Then I quickly tied my apron around my waist. When I turned around, I jumped. "God, Cooper. Why are you sneaking up on me?"

"I wasn't sneaking. I walked right up to you and you didn't hear me. Is something wrong?"

I shook my head. "Nothing's wrong. I'm just ready to get started working."

"Are you sure?"

"Yeah," I said as I picked up my order book and brushed past him. "I'm fine."

I felt his eyes on me as I fled the office and took up my position in the bar. I would not drop anything tonight, I was going to focus. I wasn't going to worry about Cooper. He was my boss. We didn't need to be more than that.

"Four beers," I said as I walked up to him and Mel.

"I'll get it," Cooper said.

"Oh, and three old-fashioneds."

"Okay," Cooper said as he grabbed everything. "Hold your horses."

I leaned against the bar. At least leaning against the bar gave me a bit of relief. I lifted one foot after the other and rolled my ankle. The relief on my feet felt amazing and I was glad to have a short moment to myself.

"Coop, can I get another Manhattan," a woman purred beside me. "And your phone number?"

I glanced at the woman out of the corner of my eye. She had big, red curls that spilled over her shoulders and a mischievous grin. She looked at Cooper like a predator assessing her prey.

"One second," he called back.

"Me too, Coop," another woman smiled as she pushed her tits forward. "Although I'll have a real drink. Whiskey, neat, double."

I watched the two women exchange glares and I shook my

head. They're falling all over him. It was ridiculous. But what truly surprised me was how Cooper seemed immune to it.

"One Manhattan and one whiskey, neat, double," he confirmed back and got right into making their drinks.

I couldn't help the smile that curved my lips. No matter how much they threw themselves at him, Cooper seemed only to be focused on his job. He slung drinks, mopped up spills and smiled at everyone.

He wasn't flirting with any of them!

Why do you care?

True, Cooper was obviously single and he didn't need to ignore other women for me, but I still felt better that he paid them no attention.

"Here's your drinks," he said as he handed my order to me. "Hey, some of the other staff are coming in tonight, so we'll be able to get a break in a while. Want to take it with me?"

I chewed my lip. "Why?"

"I just figured we could catch up some more. I tried last night, but you had your mind on one thing and that was fries."

"I guess I was pretty out of it. Yeah, why not?" I picked up my tray. "Just let me know when."

I supposed I at least owed him that much. He had given me a job and a good one at that. I was making more than I thought I would make and it wasn't a bad gig. I could catch up with him for a bit and still be professional. Right?

I put my head down and kept working. Melanie was right

about one thing, the more I smiled and joked with the customers, the bigger the tips were. And it was nice to talk to people who weren't as preoccupied and jaded as folks back in New York. Some part of me enjoyed coming back home and settling into a peaceful life.

By the time my break rolled around, I was ready for it. My feet ached and I needed about a gallon of water to rehydrate. Mel gave me a bottle from behind the bar and I walked outside.

The smell of blue bonnets clung to the air and I inhaled deeply. I closed my eyes and my body relaxed. Smelling those flowers reminded me of being young again. Exploring the woods with my friends. And it reminded me of my first time with Cooper. The way he'd held me in his arms and made me feel so important before he'd ripped it all away.

"Are you okay?"

I jumped out of my memories. *Why am I so jumpy?* It bothered me that I seemed on edge around everyone lately. Mostly, men. I thought about Brian and the way he'd jumped on me and I wrapped my arms around my body. "Yeah, I'm all right. I was just thinking."

Cooper's eyes examined me and I couldn't shake the feeling that he knew something was up. It was uncanny how much he seemed to be able to see.

"Want to sit in my truck and get off your feet?"

I nodded. "Actually, that would be amazing."

"After you," he said as he nodded toward his truck.

Chapter Thirteen

COOPER

There was something troubling Ivy. I could see it from the way she shielded herself. She seemed withdrawn and quieter than she'd been the night before. What was going on with her? She looked like a woman haunted by something.

"Man, that's better." She sighed as she sank into the seat and leaned it back a bit.

I slipped my key into the ignition and turned on the radio. Dolly Parton's voice drifted over the waves. What else would it be but *Jolene*? "Are you going to tell me why you decided to quit your prestigious job and come back home?" I asked.

Ivy laughed. "Prestigious. That's a laugh. It was just a job like any other place."

"Do you miss it?"

She shrugged. "Honestly?"

"Of course."

"No. Not even one bit. I thought I would miss at least some of it, but the job was nothing like what I thought it would be. It was a glorified secretarial position."

"I'm sorry, Ivy. Did you never get to report on anything important?"

"No. I was thrown scraps. Small, local things no one cared about that they could stuff into the back of papers, and on webpages no one read."

I watched her carefully. Her voice was flat and empty and she wouldn't look at me either, but I knew instinctively that something else was bothering her. What? "Are you sure you're okay?"

"Yeah." She sank deeper into the seat and propped her feet up on the dashboard. "I guess I didn't sleep well. What about you? Is this what you always wanted to do in life?"

I shrugged. "Not really, but I like what I do now."

Ivy nodded. "Tough hours to have a girlfriend though."

I glanced at her and saw the way she eyed me. What was she looking for? My eyes automatically zeroed in on her juicy bottom lip and I had to fight the urge to reach out and run my thumb over it. God, I wanted to kiss her. I turned away from her and stared straight ahead.

"The bar does take up a lot of time, but I'm not exactly ready to date anyone right now. Most of the women that come in here get too drunk and want to round the night off with me, but I'd rather get to know someone."

"Like you got to know me?"

I raised a brow. "Are you talking about high school?"

"Yeah," she mumbled. "I guess I am."

"Are you still pissed about that?" I asked softly.

"Hmm, let's see. You told me how great I was, hung out with me all the time, then you took my virginity and disappeared, so yeah I'm pretty pissed about it."

"Look, Ivy, I'm real sorry about how I was back then. I was a conceited, egotistical asshole, and what I did to you was fucked up. I don't have an excuse for my behavior. All I know is I was young, dumb, and reckless. I thought the world was my oyster and I could just reach and take anything I wanted. No consequences, no regrets."

"Cooper—"

"No, I mean it. I've always regretted leaving you like that. You were special. It was only after I went to college and real-ized the world didn't owe me nothing was when it hit me that I'd left an important person behind."

Her shoulders stiffened. "You don't have to say all this."

She didn't believe me, but it was true. Leaving her was the thing I regretted the most. Ivy back in high school was the smart one, but she was funny too and kind when it came to helping others. I'd thought she was hot back then, but when I left I realized it was more than that. I loved being around her. She made me feel like I could do anything, and I had taken all of that for granted. "Do you think you can ever forgive me?" I asked as I searched her face.

Ivy seemed to think it over. Her face scrunched up before she slowly shook her head. "No," she said quietly. "I appreciate you giving me this job and everything, but what you did was awful. It messed me up for a long time, and I can't just forgive you like that. Sorry." Then she hopped out of the passenger seat and the door closed quietly behind her.

I would have preferred it if she had slammed the door.

She stalked off to the bar, yanked the door open and disappeared inside.

I sighed and ran a hand down my face. "Shit."

It would be a lot harder than I thought it would to make up for the past. And for her to let go of it. On top of that, I had other problems. Like the fact that whenever she was around I lost my marbles, wanted to throw her against a wall and pound the hell out of her. Life had pushed us back together for a reason, and I wanted to listen to it the second time around.

After a few more minutes alone, I slid out of my truck and locked it up. When I walked back into the bar Ivy was smiling at a group of guys and laughing as if she was having the time of her life. I wanted to throw those leering bastards out of my joint. I hated them, but there was not a damn thing I could do about them. Or any man who made eyes at her. Not yet, anyway. But soon...

My jaw tightened as I walked by her. I felt her eyes as they stared at my back. It wasn't like I could blame her. I was the one who screwed her over all those years ago. Now it was just payback time.

By the time I glanced up, she was back to work. Every time she came up to the bar, she gathered her drinks and disappeared with her lips pressed together. I wanted to make it better. No, I *had* to make it better. Ivy had walked through my door and I felt shit I hadn't felt in ages. I wanted her and I don't give up on what I want.

"See you, guys!" Mel called as she raced for the door after we'd closed up and counted all the cash.

"Bye Mel," I called as I grabbed my keys.

Ivy waved, then she became as quiet as she'd been with me all night. We walked out together and her eyes traced up and down the street before her shoulders dropped and she looked a little less tense. Was that a little piece of precaution she learned from the big city?

The key clicked in the lock and she jumped.

"Hey, do you want me to walk you home?" I asked. "It's almost one and I'd feel better if I knew you made it home safely."

"No, thank you. I'll be able to get home fine."

"Really, I don't want you walking out here at night. There aren't nearly enough lights in this part of town."

"Cooper, no offense, but I'd rather make it on my own. Thanks for the offer, but I'm just not ready to be your friend yet. Goodnight."

I watched as she walked off and frowned. There was nothing I could do if she didn't want me to look out for her, but it still worried me. I had to figure out a way to fix things and quickly.

I let Ivy go once. There was no way in hell I would do it again. I sat in the truck and watched her go down the road, when she was about to turn the corner I started the truck and drove to the corner. I waited until she was about to get out of my sight and followed her again. In this way, I kept her in my sight until she walked through the entrance of her apartment building.

I was so subtle, she never knew I was there with her the whole time.

I t kept happening. I crawled into bed and jumped out of it after a horrific nightmare with tears running down my cheeks. After that, I slept badly and woke up tired. I stood in front of the mirror in the bathroom and poked at the bags that had developed under my eyes.

Sighing, I opened the medicine cabinet and took out a compact of concealer. I went to work on the dark circles that made me look exhausted and tried to hide them as best I could. The last thing I needed was anyone commenting on my appearance. I didn't want anyone to know my nightmares had gotten so bad.

It had been a week since I'd started working at Red Royal. The tips got better the more the regulars got to know me and I was making enough to sustain myself. The only problem was that I couldn't get Brian and that murderous expression on his face out of my head. I kept expecting him to show up and finish the job he started.

All I could see in my head was how much of a high it had given him to watch the life start to go out of my eyes.

Even though I was dead exhausted when I got home, I still struggled to sleep. I would lay there for hours, staring at the ceiling, afraid of every little noise. Even though I told myself a thousand times there was no way he could track me down, my body was sure he was coming back to get me, and I hated that feeling.

My alarm went off on my phone and I scrambled out of the bathroom. Snagging my jacket and I headed for the bar. As I walked, I thought about Cooper.

The last private conversation we'd had played over and over in my head. Had he really changed? Cooper insisted that he had, but I wasn't completely sure. I did see some changes, like how responsibly he managed the bar and how dedicated he was to his work. Also, he didn't flirt with any of the woman who'd tried to get his attention the way he used to do when we were still in school. And some of the women offering themselves to him were really good looking too.

"Hey Jo, we're a little slow right now," Cooper said as I came out dressed in my apron with my hair pulled up and out of the way. "But that's not going to last long."

"Fridays," I mumbled as I tucked my book into a pocket. "I'm looking forward to it really." At least working would take my mind off of things. The less I thought about Brian, the night-mares, or the way Cooper glanced at me when he thought I wasn't looking, the better. I needed to focus.

"Are you feeling all right? If you're sick, you don't have to stick around," Cooper frowned. "You look exhausted."

Leave it to him to notice how tired I am even after I tried to cover it up. Cooper seemed to be one of the few people in my life who could read me like a book. He'd always been that way.

"I'm fine," I said as I tightened my apron strings and nodded. "I just didn't sleep too well last night, but it'll be okay."

"Are you sure?"

"Yes." I sighed. "You don't have to worry. I won't drop a tray of chicken wings in anyone's lap."

"I'm not worried about that, Jo," he said gently. "I'm just making sure you'll be all right. You know how crazy it can get."

"I know. I really don't think it will be that big of a deal. I can handle it."

"Ok. Suit yourself."

Even though he said it, I got the feeling that he would keep a close eye on me all night. He really did act as if he'd changed. The old Cooper was only worried about himself, but the new one seemed to care about everyone. His customers, his employees... me.

If he was anyone else and if I hadn't been so hurt by him already, I would have adored him. My eyes kept getting drawn to him as he worked and laughed behind the bar. The way his eyes lit up made my stomach flutter. Everyone around him was enthralled and I'd never realized how much they clung to his every word.

Especially, women.

God, the way they drooled over Cooper! As if he was a delicious meal and they'd been starving hyenas. It was almost entertaining the way they tripped all over each other just to grab his attention for a fraction of a second. Because that was all he gave them. A smile, a drink, a polite word, then he was back to work and chatting with all of them, not singling any one person out.

My gaze couldn't be torn away from him. When I was busy, I threw myself into work, but as soon as it quieted down a bit, and people went back to singing to the karaoke machine and sipping their drinks, my eyes went back to him.

Why couldn't I look away?

Cooper's arms looked irresistible contained inside the blood red tee he wore. He pushed his hair back with careless fingers every time it fell into his face and I watched every woman's eyes follow that small movement. They were as enamored as I was, but there was one difference.

He looked back at me.

Every so often, our eyes met and he seemed to see right into my soul. Or his lips would lift in that sensuous way and my body heated up all over again.

I was worried about letting him in again, even as a friend. I'd be damned if I allowed myself to repeat the same mistake all over again.

"Jo, can I get a drink or what?"

I rolled my eyes before I turned to the man at the table.

He'd sat with his friends and as far as I could tell, he was a regular. He was okay to start with, but once he had a few drinks in him, he'd become a pain in the ass. "I'm Ivy," I said as I pulled the pen out I kept tucked behind my ear. "What can I get for you?"

"Cooper calls you Jo all the time."

I blinked at him. "What?"

"Cooper. He always calls you Jo. I've heard him yell it through the bar like a hundred times tonight."

I tried my best not to narrow my eyes at him. "And he's the only one that calls me that. What can I get for you to drink?"

"The usual, baby," he drawled.

I turned to walk away and his hand grabbed my ass. My body froze. This was exactly how Brian used to grab me. My mind went blank. I couldn't move. No matter how much I told my feet to go I felt trapped, suffocated.

Cooper's eyes suddenly locked onto mine and he was over to the table in a few long, purposeful strides. "Get the fuck outta here, Randall," Cooper snapped as he slammed his hand on the table.

"What the hell for?" he demanded, looking perplexed.

Cooper's face was dark with fury. "What did you say to her?"

"I ain't said shit to her."

"Jo?" Cooper asked as he touched my arm. "What did he say?"

"He grabbed my ass," I whispered. Suddenly, I felt stupid. It was a stupid thing that I should have been able to handle on my own. Instead, I had exaggerated it out of all proportion and now everyone stared at us.

"Get the fuck out. I'm not going to tell you again. If you and your friends don't get up and leave, you're going to have a fist in your face, and then I'll call the cops. Out! Now!"

Randall clicked his tongue. "Fucking, trouble-making, city bitch," he muttered.

Cooper cocked his fist, but I grabbed his arm. I didn't want him to get in trouble over me. I should have been stronger. Something that stupid shouldn't have messed with my head at all. If not for the memory of Brian, I would have handled it in a completely different way.

Randall took off with his friends while Cooper wrapped an arm around my shoulders. He tugged me against his body and we stayed that way until they were completely gone. Cooper led me into the back and turned me to face him. "You're shaking. Sit down," he said, pointing to a chair.

I sank into it and didn't fight him on it.

Chapter Fifteen

IVY

Cooper walked away and came back with a cold glass of water in his hand. He handed it over to me.

I sucked it down until there was nothing left. I shuddered. As if not getting enough sleep wasn't bad already.

"Better?" Cooper asked as he took the empty glass.

"Yeah. Thanks." I bit my lip. "I'm sorry I caused a scene and you lost a customer because of me."

"Hey, it's not your fault. I should be saying sorry about that asshole. I've never had any issues out of him."

"Until I came along," I finished bitterly. "It seems like I attract bastards wherever I go. That's my superpower."

"That's not true."

"You have no idea, but that's the truth. I've accepted it." I shrugged as I wiped my palms off on my apron to get rid of the water. "Anyway, I should get back to work. I'm sure it's getting packed out there."

"If you need to take a minute, then take it."

"I'm fine."

"You keep saying that, but it's bullshit. Now, sit down, take a minute, and collect yourself. Stop pretending everything is okay and let yourself calm down before you go back out there."

I blinked at him. Did he just snap at me? But it apparently worked because it jerked me out of trance like state. I nodded and Cooper's shoulders relaxed. He smiled and I saw the relief in his expression.

"Stay here until you're ready to come back out and get back to work. I'll cover you for now."

"Thanks." I smiled softly. "It actually means a lot that you're doing this."

Cooper waved a hand. "No problem."

I watched as he disappeared back out into the bar. The noise from it flooded the back for a minute before the door closed and I was cut off from the world once more. I felt positive that he saw me as more than his employee, but the fact that he respected my boundaries. It made me want to forgive him a little bit more.

My body relaxed bit by bit while I sat on the chair. Thoughts of Brian were forced out. I hated how my body responded by freezing up when I got scared. It shook me to my core. What if someone really wanted to hurt me and I froze up like that?

Once I was closer to normal again, I adjusted my hair and clothes, then took a deep breath before my palm pushed against the cool wood. I went back out into the bar with my head held high. A few eyes followed me, and I was surprised when people began to comment about how glad they were that Cooper kicked him out.

After that, I threw myself into my shift. Cooper watched me the whole time, but I almost didn't mind. I knew he was looking out for me and wanted to make sure I had no more problems. Thankfully, the people at Red Royal were sweet and they treated me well.

In an hour, the place picked up once more. The exhaustion from constant lack of sleep took hold and I started to forget orders and mix up tables. No matter how hard I tried, I couldn't keep anything straight.

I growled as I stared at the pad. "What the fuck did I even write?" My frustration grew with each new order, but I knew I had to keep it together.

"Ivy, can you collect the glasses from table twelve? I think everywhere else is full and people are waiting." Mel nodded toward the people standing at the entrance.

"Yeah, I've got it." I hoofed it over to table twelve and wiped it down before I loaded up my tray. Once I balanced the empty glasses, I turned toward the bar and tripped over my own feet. The glasses crashed to the floor and I groaned.

Again? Fucking seriously!

I called myself every name in the book in my head as I moved to my knees and quickly collected the shards. They stacked onto the tray one after the other. I reached for another and yelped. I yanked my hand back against my chest and stared at it. "Shit," I breathed. "That's just great."

"Jo?" Cooper yanked my hand out and frowned. "Shit, that's pretty bad. Come here." He pulled me to my feet.

I didn't fight him. My palm throbbed from where the glass had cut through my skin. Blood dripped and trailed us as we shuffled into the back and he stuffed me into his office. I glanced at the clock. It was almost closing time. Another hour and we'd be shutting down, but I couldn't even make it that far. I felt like such a fool. Any other boss would have fired me by now. I was nothing but trouble.

"Damn woman," he growled as he wiped down my palm with antiseptic wipes. "I'm gonna have to start charging you for all the broken glass."

"I'm sorry," I whispered. I don't know what came over me, but my bottom lip trembled. Then the tears started. They rolled down my cheeks as I sniffled and sucked in shaky breaths until my body hurt.

"Hey, I didn't mean it. I'm really just worried about you."

"I'm okay," I sobbed. "I'm fine. I'm just—I'm so tired."

"I know," he soothed. "I know you are. I can see that."

Cooper's fingers brushed over my cheek. I leaned into his palm, calloused with hard, honest work. A far cry from Brian's soft white hands. He wiped my tears away and then his hand was gone as he dug into the first aid kit. A pressure wrap was applied before he wrapped it with vet tape and made sure it was secure. "How's that? I know it's a bit tight, but once the bleeding slows, you can take it off and we can replace it with something else."

"It's okay," I said as I wiped my eyes. "Thank you."

"You know you can tell me if something's going on, Jo. You don't have to carry everything all by yourself. It'll eat you alive."

"I don't want to keep you. There's a full bar of people waiting out there for you," I croaked.

"Fuck them," he growled.

I sank against him and buried my face in his chest, then. It was such a relief to hear the strong steady beat of his heart against my cheek again. Cooper's arm wrapped around my back and he rubbed it gently while I cried. I wasn't quite ready to tell him about my life, about Brian. I did love the way he held me however, the way he comforted me as I wept until I'd cried myself completely out.

"Feel better?" he asked as he snatched up a couple of tissues and gave them to me.

I sniffed. "Yeah. I guess I do. I haven't cried in a long time like that."

"Maybe that's what you needed then?" Cooper brushed fallen locks off my cheeks and tucked them behind my ears.

The warmth of his fingers against my skin soothed me. I sighed softly before he leaned forward.

"Whatever has you so worried, you can stop right now. I'm here for you, okay? I'll protect you," he said quietly. "I'd do anything for you."

My heart melted at his words. And then his lips captured mine. I didn't freeze. I didn't hesitate like I did with other men. It was like coming home. I moaned against his mouth and pressed forward more as my body sought his out. I ran my fingers over his cheeks and he cradled the back of my head in his strong hand. His mouth plundered mine as if he had been waiting for this moment for years and he just could not get enough.

Our bodies pressed against each other and my lips grew numb from kissing him so hard. We came up for air and sanity returned to me once more. I blinked, the haze leaving my mind as I quickly jumped to my feet and stepped away from him.

What the hell was I thinking? Kissing him, letting him off the hook for what he'd done to me all those years ago? I couldn't fall for it all over again. "I have to go."

"Wait, Jo."

"I'll see you for my next shift," I called over my shoulder as I dashed from the office.

I couldn't believe I'd kissed him like that. What the fuck was I thinking? I ran out of the bar. I needed to get home and figure out what the hell was happening to me.

Chapter Sixteen

COOPER

The bar felt empty and lifeless without her. Maybe it was just because I missed her face. She was always smiling when she was dealing with customers, or I would pick out her laugh from all the other laughs in the room. Hers was that special.

"Quit staring at the tables. She ain't gonna magically pop up and smile at you," Mel said as she leaned against the bar and smoked a cigarette.

"Didn't I tell you not to smoke in here?"

Mel shrugged. "Why not? It's not like it's banned here yet. Might as well enjoy it while I can."

I rolled my eyes. "Whatever."

"Stop being so fed up and go get your girl," she said as she pointed at me. "I know that's what you're thinking about."

"What are you saying?" I growled.

"Ivy. You know, the one that lets you and no one else call her Jo?"

"What about her?"

"You miss her, you big dumb ass." She laughed. "Why don't you go by her place and check on her?"

I snorted. "Yes, because your boss that you still pretty much hate, showing up at your door is a total turn on. I mean—"

"Too late now, cowboy," she drawled. "You said what you said. I'll let it go, though, because I'm not stupid and neither are you. You can always say you came to check on her. She did cut herself after all."

"I guess that's true," I muttered as I wiped the same spot for the hundredth time. "She'll probably throw me out though. She's always had a temper on her."

"And I bet you love it." She grinned.

I frowned. "You know what? I don't pay you to flap your mouth."

"You pay me because I am an enigmatic and amazing human being who can call out your bullshit from a mile away. Now..." She sucked in smoke and exhaled in my direction. "Get the fuck outta here and go get your woman. We aren't creatures that should be allowed to stew on our own, you know. She'll come up with every reason why she should leave you alone if you let her."

I waved a hand in front of my face and scowled. "I'm supposed to be working."

"On what? You're going to wipe a hole in the counter if you do it one more time. Anyway, we're closing in an-hour. You go talk to her and I'll hold down the fort. If things magically get too crazy, I can always call you and tell you to haul your ass back here. Besides..." She frowned. "There's something up with her and I really am worried. She seems so nice, but I've seen that look before. Something's going on with her. Make sure she's really okay."

I leaned forward. "She won't tell me what's going on."

"She will, if you keep being there for her and giving her time. I mean kissing her may not have helped..."

"How the fuck do you know about that?" I growled.

"I came back to check on you guys and saw it through the crack in the office door." She chuckled. "I will never follow you two back there again."

I wiped a hand down my face. "You're gonna be the death of me."

She laughed heartlessly. "Live with it. Now, go check on Ivy and makes sure that she's okay."

I glanced around the bar. It was practically a ghost town anyway. The only people left were a couple of out of towners, two truck drivers on layover and a table of regulars who showed up every day no matter the time. It was only a handful of folks and they all looked content just sitting at the bar smoking and drinking.

"I do want to go see her," I muttered.

It was more than that though. Much more. I wanted Jo with the kind of passion most people wouldn't understand. She was the perfect person for me and as far as I was concerned, we needed each other. Or maybe I just really wanted her to want me too.

I had every intention of convincing her that she was meant for me.

I'd stood back when I found out she had found her dream job and was trying to make it in the city, but now that she was back. I had no intention of losing her for a second time. I couldn't. I'd walked away from her once, but I couldn't do that again. Jo was special and she was going to be mine.

"That's more like it," Mel cheered.

"What?"

"That look of grim determination."

I stared at her. "You can see that in my face?"

"Hell yes! Go get your girl, Tiger. You both deserve to be happy. I've watched you run this place for too long and you haven't been with anyone. You need to go back to enjoying life and having fun."

"I guess you're right about that. I haven't gone out and enjoyed myself in a long time. It's always bar, home, sleep, repeat."

"Well now, you have a reason to shake that up. Get out of here. I'm telling you, I can handle the bar. I've done it for you in the past, haven't I?"

"You always come through, Mel. Don't forget to lock up if I'm not back by tonight. Well, you know what to do. I don't need to explain it to you."

"Thank you very much," she called as I jogged around the bar.

"I'm calling my boyfriend to come hang out with me though."

"Tell him I said hi. Don't let him drink the whole bar."

Melanie chuckled. "Yes, boss. Good luck!"

I headed for my truck with a spring to my step. Everything was quiet, calm and I liked the change of pace. I climbed into my truck and drove to her place. I still remembered the times I used to sneak into her bedroom back at her parents' home late at night. More than once, I'd climbed into her bedroom window and spent the night there. That was before we'd ever fooled around but I'd gone from sleeping on her floor to holding her in her bed. I wanted to get back to that.

When I arrived at her door, I double-checked to make sure I was still presentable. The button up shirt was still passable, but the jeans had a streak of blood, her blood around the knee. It wasn't my finest attire, but she'd seen me in worse back in school.

Was I trying to impress her?

Hell, yeah.

It was so deeply buried in my subconscious I didn't fully realize it. I shook my head at how infatuated I was. But who could help themselves? Jo's curvy body, silky hair and warm eyes would make any man lose his head.

And there was nothing wrong with that.

I knocked on her door and waited. My hands felt restless. I should have grabbed some flowers from someone's garden or something, but I didn't want to overwhelm her.

I wondered if she would even answer the door after the second knock. Maybe she was already in bed.

Then the door creaked open and she peered out of the crack. She was wrapped up in a pink robe. She clutched the edged tightly to her body and frowned. "Cooper? What are you doing here?"

"I wanted to see how you were doing."

"Oh," she said before she opened the door fully. "You can come in."

I followed her into her apartment. It was the same as it had been that one time I came up here with her to pick up a rent check for her father. The same faint blue and white wallpaper on the walls. The same tidy little dining room and quaint kitchen painted sunny yellow and trimmed in white. I doubted it had changed since the times I'd sat at the kitchen counter with her and studied. Well, she studied as I teased and prodded at her until she giggled and shoved me away.

"This place brings back memories," I said looking around. There were still photos everywhere of Ivy with her parents. One with her father in front of the Thunderbird that they'd died in later. Another, with her mother when she was just a little girl. I knew how painful it had to be for her to lose everything. She had no family and that must have been a difficult thing to deal with, especially when she was still so young.

"Yes, it does," she said quietly.

I turned back to her. "I'm sorry about your parents."

"So am I." For a second there was a heavy silence, then she forced a smile. "Coffee?"

"That would be nice."

I watched as she strolled into the kitchen, her robe fluttering around her curvy legs.

Ivy poured a mug for me and one for her before she brought them over and set them on the counter. She placed cream and sugar beside the mugs. Then she looked up at me with a small grin tugging at her lips. "Remember when my dad caught you touching me and yelled at you for a solid twenty minutes?"

I groaned. "Oh, god. There are things I do want you to remember, but that isn't one of them. I almost pissed my pants! No one scared me, but that man. He was terrifying. I don't blame him. If I had a daughter that looked like you, I'd be walking around with a shotgun all the time."

She laughed, but a little sadly. "My dad was a sweetheart. He just wanted the best for me. I'm pretty sure that one day, I'll be the same way with my kids."

"You know? Me too." I laughed. "I can't imagine anyone getting away with the things that we got away with, but my child is not going to be so lucky."

Ivy grinned. "And yet, we always complained when our parents were the same way."

We smiled at each other for a minute, quiet as we sipped our coffee together. In the soft yellow light from the lamp, she looked like an angel. The dark shadows under her eyes were still visible, but she still looked... entirely fuckable. Like a stunning woman who deserved all the love in the world with her hair loose down her shoulders, her eyes misty with memories.

"Let me see your hand."

She held it out toward me.

I took off the compression binding I'd put on and looked at the wound. It had already closed nicely and I was glad. "Tomorrow, I'll re-bandage it in something less restrictive." I laid her hand down on the table top carefully. "I wanted to apologize for... the kiss. You were distraught and shocked. It wasn't appropriate and I shouldn't have done it."

Ivy peered at me before she slowly nodded. "I don't think either of us was thinking straight." She put her mug down and toyed with her fingers. "Let's just forget about it, okay?"

I nodded. "Well, in honor of forgetting it, could I take you out to dinner Monday night? The bar is closed and we could kill our day off together."

"Oh, I don't know," she whispered. "I don't think we should go out together."

"It's not going out," I said quickly. "It's just the two of us grabbing a bite to eat and mending all the shit that happened in the past. Think about it, there's so many good memories that we shared. They shouldn't all go up in smoke because of one dumb thing I did when I was a kid. I want to fix it."

Jo glanced at me and fidgeted with the hem of her robe.

I knew she was on the fence. I just had to give her one thing that would push her over the edge into saying yes and giving me a chance. "Maybe I don't deserve forgiveness," I said as I took her hand. "But I'd like to try and earn it if that's alright with you. What do you say?"

She sighed and her shoulders relaxed. "Fine," she finally said with a smile. "But this doesn't mean anything."

"Nothing," I said with a big, happy grin. "Just us going out for a nice meal."

"Ok." Suddenly, she looked worried. "Uh, where are you taking me? I have nothing here to wear."

"Nothing fancy," I assured her quickly. "Just a good meal. You can wear whatever is comfortable for you."

Ivy smiled.

I wanted to reach out and pull her body to mine, but I took a step back. "Right then, I'll see you tomorrow."

When the door closed behind me, I felt a smile that lit up my face. And it was a big fucking grin too.

Chapter Seventeen

COOPER

I sucked in a breath.

Jesus.

Nothing to wear!

She wore a little black dress that hugged her curvy figure and showed off her cleavage. Strappy black shoes completed her outfit. She'd done her long hair in big, loose curls that spilled all over her shoulders and made her look like a Botticelli painting.

"Wow," I breathed.

"What?" She laughed. "It's nothing special, but I figured no matter where we go, you can't go wrong with a little black dress."

"You're right about that," I muttered as I told my boner to calm the fuck down.

Ivy grinned. "Stop staring at me like that! You're making me feel shy."

"Why? I think you look awesome, that's all." I laughed and reached out for her arm. "Let's go get dinner."

"I should warn you. This is not going to be a cheap date. I'm starving."

I laughed but my head was spinning. *Date!* She said date. I also loved that she let me touch her. She slipped her hand into the crook of my arm as we walked down to my truck. I opened the door for her and helped her inside before I closed the door and jogged to my own.

"Where are we going?" she asked when I slid in and the truck roared to life.

"A little steak house not far from here. The food is good and they have soft music and candlelight. Women like that sort of thing, don't they?"

Ivy smiled softly. "I don't know about other women, but it sounds divine. I can't wait to check it out."

Something had changed in her. It felt like the confusion from our encounter in my office had slid away. I turned on the radio. Bruce Springsteen was singing *Born in the USA*. We both looked at each other and laughed. It used to be our favorite song. As if on cue, we both started singing along. Suddenly, it felt as if I was with my best friend, as if the long painful years of yearning for her hadn't passed.

Soon, we pulled up to the restaurant.

"Jordan's!" she cried out happily. "Oh, my God! I haven't thought about this place in so long. Not since you brought me here."

I smiled. "We snuck in a bottle of wine and I kept pouring

you glasses of it, and the waiter couldn't tell if we were old enough to be drinking or not. And when he asked for your ID, you deserted me and ran like a lunatic."

"What was I supposed to do?" She laughed. "I was so scared we were going to get into trouble!"

"So you left me high and dry," I scoffed.

Ivy's shoulders bounced up and down as she slapped a hand over her mouth and laughed heartily.

Damn. I'd never seen anything as beautiful as her laughing.

When she collected herself, she swiped her finger underneath her eyes and shook her head. "My father was right, you were such a bad influence on me."

I laughed. "You're so full of shit, Jo! You got me into trouble more than once and then laughed when I got caught. I might have been a bad boy, but you were the enabler."

"Maybe I was a bit wild back then," she replied as she smiled at me. "But you were the catalyst. I was as good as gold until you showed up."

"Oh, yeah?"

"You calling me a liar, Cooper Page?"

We stared at each other for a while and the urge to grab her and kiss her was so fucking strong I had to throw myself out of the truck. If I stayed that close to her, with her beautiful eyes on me, and the sexy scent of her soft perfume all around me, I would lose it.

I opened her door and extended a hand. She slipped her hand into mine, but pulled it away as we reached the doors.

We slipped inside and were seated somewhere in the back. I felt glad for that. It was quiet, warm, with a perfect view of the setting sun outside. "What do you want to eat," I asked as I picked up the menu and stared at it to keep from staring at her.

"I don't know about you, but I'd kill for a good steak and a side of potatoes. I haven't had that in so long."

I frowned. "How? I'm sure plenty of places in New York have that."

For a second, a strange look crossed her face.

I just got a feeling I had touched a raw nerve. Then it was gone.

"Well, they do, but...everyone's so caught up in being healthy. I was sucked into it too. For the past few years, I've eaten mostly salads and kale."

I wondered why there was a pause before she said *everyone*. Was it some man that had shamed her into living on rabbit food? I pushed down jealousy. Well, whoever he was, he was gone now. It was me sitting in front of her. And this time, I wasn't letting go. "Did you just say kale?" I asked as I scrunched up my face.

Ivy burst out laughing. "Don't judge! I wanted to fit in with everyone else, so I gave up the good food and settled for the healthy. Stop making that face at me. Stop it."

"I can't help it. I'm really bothered you haven't had a *real* meal." I reached over, snatched up her menu and put it with mine.

"What are you doing?" she asked with a laugh.

"We're getting ribs. Potatoes. Mac and cheese. And not a vegetable in sight."

Ivy grinned. "That's disgusting. Come on. We're going to get sauce everywhere."

"That's the way you're supposed look after you've eaten ribs. Anyway, they hand out bibs here."

"Forget it. I'm not wearing a bib."

"Suit yourself," I said as I flagged down the waiter and ordered just that.

By the time it arrived and was placed in front of us, Jo looked like she was ready to be self-conscious. So I picked up a big bone and bit into it like a wolf.

There was nothing left for her to do but pick up one of her own and dig in too. I grinned as she buried her face in it and I stifled a chuckle. She would think I was laughing at her and that would be the last thing I wanted to do. I thought she looked gorgeous just being herself. The girl I'd known all those years ago.

You have to fucking stop staring at her like this.

But I couldn't tear my eyes away from her. I literally devoured her with my eyes.

Ivy finished up her food and glanced up at me as if she suddenly realized that I even existed. She licked her fingers, then picked up her napkin, and dabbed at her mouth daintily.

After the way she had eaten, the effect was deliciously funny.

"What are you grinning about?" she asked.

"I don't think I've ever seen anyone put away food that quickly."

Jo groaned. "Shut up. I know I must have looked like a pig, but I haven't had food this good in a long time. It was amazing." She sighed as she held up a hand.

"What are you doing now? Ordering more?"

She glared at me. "No. I want a beer."

I chuckled. "I love seeing this side of you. I know you think I'm being a smart ass, but I'm not. I really do like seeing that you're enjoying yourself."

"I have to admit, it feels good to indulge a little. I was so wound up in New York."

"I'm sure you were. I'm glad that you came back."

Jo smiled at me.

Damn, I swore my heart just stopped for a minute. Thankfully, the waiter walked over before I blurted out what my mouth was dying to say. How could I blame myself? How could I not want to be with her? Everything about Ivy was exactly what I'd been missing from my life.

"Could I get a beer, please?" Ivy asked the waiter. "And one for him too."

I raised a brow. "Are you ordering for me now?"

"You ordered for me," she countered as the corner of her mouth quirked upward.

"Fair enough." I nodded at the waiter. "I'll take one too."

When he returned with them, Ivy took a sip and sighed deeply. She smiled when she put the bottle away.

It took everything to keep the imminent erection down and under control at that sight of her drinking beer straight from a bottle. I still remember the last time she wrapped that delectable mouth around my cock, even though it had been years. "I'm guessing you really missed beer too."

"I did." She nodded. "I was never really allowed to have it back home."

"Allowed?"

Ivy blinked and the smile faltered on her lips.

What I saw there made me want to ask her what was going on.

Before I could even open my mouth however, she waved it off. "Anyway, it's nice to have a night out and grab a beer. Thanks for bringing me. I guess this is an acceptable apology."

"You guess?" I said. "What else can I do to have you completely forgive me?"

Ivy tapped her chin. "Dessert wouldn't hurt."

"You're enjoying this, aren't you?" I laughed. "Getting to boss me around for once in our lives."

"Well, since you're my boss now, it makes it even funnier to mess with you. I suppose I shouldn't be too hard on you though. I don't want to go into work tomorrow and have you get your revenge."

I grinned at her. "I wouldn't do that to my friend."

Jo narrowed her eyes. "Are we friends?"

"Do you think I have some kind of secret agenda?"

"Yes."

My eyebrows rose. "Really?"

She shook her head. "Okay, maybe you don't. I don't know. I just want to make sure that you know that we're friends and nothing more. I'm not ready to be with anyone... just yet." Again, that strange expression showed up on her face.

Finally, it made me wonder why she appeared so suddenly in town without a plan or job. I nodded slowly. "I'm not going to push on you. I want to be here for you. I like your company, Jo. I always have."

Jo smiled softly. "I like your company too. Thanks for bringing me out to dinner. I'm feeling a lot better."

"See? I knew it was just the thing you needed."

"Yeah, yeah, you're very wise." She laughed. "We should get going."

"After you," I said as I waved a hand.

Jo stood up and I tossed a few bills onto the table for the tip. She walked past me and my eyes greedily roamed over every inch of her curvy frame. Mel was right. I wanted her in the worst possible ways.

Hell, this woman was setting my teeth on edge with desire.

Chapter Eighteen

Maybe I was crazy. But forgiving Cooper was almost an impulse and one I didn't want to fight. I was back home, away from a bustling, uncaring world where I was almost murdered, and I could use a friend. Especially, someone like Cooper who looked out for me. In fact, I needed someone in my corner.

"Are you sure you want to go right back home?" Cooper asked as he peered at me curiously.

I thought it over. Did I want to go back to the quiet, dark apartment that sometimes made me uneasy? Not particularly. Brian popped into my head too much when I was alone. Every noise, every creak made me freeze with fear. And the nightmares—

"How about a walk around the park?"

"This time of night?" I asked as I raised my brow.

"Did you forget this isn't New York? Our parks are nice at

night and I could use a walk after all of that food I stuffed into my face."

I laughed. "Actually, I could use that too. Those ribs were far heavier than I remembered."

"Good. That just means you had a good meal."

I rolled my eyes. "If it was up to you, I would weigh a thousand pounds."

"Nothing wrong with that," Cooper purred. "I like a bit of weight on a woman."

I slapped his hand. "Don't be a pervert, or I'll go home."

Cooper threw up his hands to protest his innocence. "I was just giving you a compliment, that's all! Not being perverted here at all."

"Uh- huh. I'm keeping my eye on you. I remember how you used to be back in the day."

"I was young and hormones are a bitch. You know I'm not just trying to get into your pants. Honestly, that's not who I am—"

"Anymore, you mean?"

"Alright, anymore," Cooper agreed with a long suffering sigh as we arrived at the truck. He held open the door for me and waited until I climbed inside. "I've calmed down a lot over the years."

That was true. I'd watched him at the bar. The quiet way he worked with determination and skill showed how true that was and his lack of flirting with even stunningly gorgeous women reinforced his assertion that he had in fact, changed.

Which was surprising since most people seemed incapable of change, but not him. He had really done a 180.

Cooper climbed into the truck and started it up. As it roared to life, I realized there was a smile on my lips that I hadn't even realized was there. Hanging out with Cooper was the most fun I'd had in ages. I'd hardly ever laughed with Brian. Not even at the beginning.

We pulled up to the park and Cooper switched off the engine. Then he jumped out of the truck and came around to my side before I could even get find the door handle. I hopped out and we strolled away from the truck.

What a strange feeling it was not to have to lock the truck.

The paths were well lit by the soft glow of lamps. There was a pond nearby and the sound of toads croaking filled the air. The sun had disappeared and the coolness of the night was perfect.

"Do you miss New York?" Cooper asked, his face turned towards me.

I didn't look at him. I chewed my lip. Do I miss it? That was a hard question. I missed the great food, the hustle, the bustle, the way the city seemed to be alive and have a constant pulse. I missed the variety. But that was all a façade. No one in New York seemed to be truly happy. They were all chasing dreams that were just around the corner. It just seemed so easy to get pushed aside and thrown away in a big city. Whether it was a job or a relationship, you could be dismissed in the next five minutes and replaced almost imme-diately. Which then made everybody selfish, rude, discon-nected, vaguely depressed, and cold. Yeah, that pretty much summed up the attitude of everyone in the city.

And then there were people like Brian.

I frowned when he popped into my head. He was the past. I wasn't giving him headspace while I was with Cooper.

"Maybe for a minute or two, but it died very quickly. Nothing compared to how much I missed Springston when I left it. Everything's slower here and people appreciate life. They're not just rushing through it until it's gone. Maybe there isn't as much to do here, but it's a good place." I nodded. "Maybe this is the place I need to be more than any other."

"I was the same," Cooper said as he wrapped an arm around mine. "And I appreciate it for the same reasons. There's not a ton of pressure on me. I don't feel like I'm going to lose my shit from stress and I still have time to take off and be myself, you know? I realized when I moved back here, I really like it here."

"Do you think you'll ever leave?" I asked as we stopped and settled onto a bench.

"Leave Springston? Why would I ever want to do that? Everything I've built is here. A bar that's doing well, a house that I've had constructed just the way I want and a quiet life that's full of peace and friends. I don't think there's much more I want. Sometimes, I think people chase rocks when they have diamonds in their backyards." Cooper's fingers caressed my skin and brushed a dark lock off of my cheek. "Why do you ask me that? Are you planning on leaving again?"

I shook my head. "That's not on my agenda as far as I know. I'm still getting settled in here."

"Will you tell me if you plan to take off anytime soon?"

I smiled up at him. "You'll be the first to know."

Cooper held up his hand and extended his pinky. "Promise?"

I laughed, but his eyes were like a puppy's. The pout on his face was both comical and heartwarming. I wrapped my pinky around his and kissed my thumb as he kissed his. "I promise I won't just up and leave." I smiled. "As long as you do the same."

"Where the hell am I going?" he asked as our fingers pulled apart and he leaned against the back of the bench. "Everything I want is here. I'm here for the long haul, babe."

My heart fluttered in my chest and I blinked in surprise. Just those words were enough to do that to me? Here for the long haul. It was what I had wanted from him when I was younger, but I never dreamed he would actually tell me that. "I'm glad you were here when I got back," I confessed. "I had no idea what I was going to do for a job. Let's be honest, most people wouldn't have given me the time of day, considering I have zero experience in anything except journalism for which there is no need in this town."

"A real shame because you're a fast learner. I mean, sure you tend to drop things every once in a while—"

I groaned. "Oh please, don't bring that up. I'm pretending that it never happened since I've almost died of embarrassment twice now."

Cooper laughed. "At least, your injuries were minor. And my point is that even though you've dropped a few things and taken a few wrong orders, you're good at what you do. You're upbeat and warm, which the customers love and the best part is when you get it wrong, you own up and fix it right away. I don't have a single complaint about you. You're amazing."

I waved a hand even as I felt my cheeks grow warm at his extravagant compliment. Being praised felt so foreign to me. My parents and teachers were the last people that told me I was good at anything. Ever since I moved to New York, it had been a constant barrage of insults and tear downs until I started to feel like I was nothing.

I shivered and rubbed my hand up and down my arm. Just thinking about the way Brian and my boss used to bully made me feel small again.

Cooper wrapped an arm around me and pulled me tighter against his side. His hand rubbed up and down trying to warm me up.

The thing was he had no idea I wasn't cold on the outside, my heart was just frozen inside. I felt as though he was melting it as he tried to give me comfort that I had been denied for so many years.

"Are you okay?" he asked quietly.

I stirred and blinked. "Yeah, I'm fine. Sorry, I guess I started daydreaming all of a sudden. I'm fine."

Cooper looked like he didn't totally believe me, but he didn't push it either.

I felt glad he was holding back instead of interrogating me. When or if I was ready to tell him about my life back in New York, that's when it would happen and not a moment before. I was barely over what happened. As I thought about it, my hand fluttered up to my throat as if I could still feel Brian's hands tightly wrapped around it.

Cooper frowned. "You say you're fine, but then you get that look on your face."

"What look?"

"It's like a mix between panic and sadness. You look like you're ready to crawl out of your own damn skin."

"I guess that's a good way to put it," I mumbled.

And it was true. Sometimes, I did feel like I wanted to crawl out of my own skin. Especially when I thought about Brian and the hell he put me through. I felt angry with myself. I should never have let him humiliate me. Calling me horrible names while we were having sex was pure abuse.

Keep him out of your mind.

I want to do that. I desperately want to stop thinking about Brian, but I was still worried that he would come after me. Today was the first day that fear had started to slip away. Maybe he didn't want anything to do with me and I could finally be free. Maybe I could start a new life. I deserved it.

"I'll tell you about it someday," I said as I took his hand and gave it a squeeze. "I promise. For now, I want to finish enjoying my night out with you. I've been having such a good time and I don't want it to end. Let's walk around a bit more before I have to go back."

"Whatever you want," Cooper said softly.

We wandered through the park hardly speaking, but there was no need to speak. Everything was simply perfect. Besides wildlife, the place was so calm and peaceful. I'd had to cut through the park back in New York and the feeling that I was going to be mugged had lingered the entire time. I didn't feel that way here, or maybe it was because of Cooper.

Once my legs started to ache, we climbed back into the truck and he drove me to my place. Cooper hopped out and helped me down before we made our way to my front door.

By the time we reached it, I fidgeted with my fingers. "Thanks again for taking me out tonight," I said, smiling softly. "I guess I really needed to get out more than I realized."

"I'm just glad you let me. I needed to have a little fun myself. I'll see you at work tomorrow?"

"On time and ready to work." I grinned. "I might drop a few things, but no one can say I'm not punctual."

Cooper chuckled. "That is not the kind of thing you should be telling your boss." He brushed my hair off of my cheek. "It is good to have you as a friend again."

"You too," I breathed. "I sure could use one here."

Cooper smiled and leaned down.

I sucked in a sharp breath as his soft, sexy lips hovered above mine. It felt as if time had completely slowed down and I couldn't think straight. I licked my lips, sure that I was going to taste him when he moved and brushed his lips against my cheek. Cooper kissed my skin and I tingled all over.

I want him. I want more of him so badly it hurts.

I ran my hand down his arm and gave it a squeeze. The muscles underneath the palm of my hand only riled me up more. I wanted to feel him on top of me, hot, hard and eager. All of the desires that had died in me when I was with Brian had come back furiously. I needed Cooper. I could already feel his hands all over my body and I wanted it to be true.

"I should get going," Cooper whispered as he pulled away slowly.

I blinked. "Oh? Are you sure? If you wanted a cup of coffee or something I could make some for us."

"I better not," he said as he straightened up and adjusted his clothes. "I'll see you at work tomorrow."

"Drive safely."

Cooper smiled and ran a hand down my arm before he turned and walked away.

My heart sank watching him jog down the stairs and head back for his truck. I bit my lip so hard it hurt.

Maybe it was for the best. As much as I wanted him, it was still a horrendous idea to give into those urges that coursed through my body. We were friends, nothing more. I had to be okay with that. Falling into bed with him could only lead to complications. Why risk making life complicated when it was finally going right?

I fished my keys out and unlocked the door when I realized I could hear Cooper's truck outside. He was in his truck, waiting for me to go inside before he left. I let myself in and switched on the light. As soon as I did, I heard his truck move away. I glanced around the empty apartment. It felt so lonely being here all on my own.

I still kind of wished he would have come in for a while. Even if things didn't progress beyond chatting and watching bad TV together, it would have been nice. I was tired of being without someone I could truly connect with. For too long it had seemed my only options were men like Brian or being on my own forever.

I quickly locked the door and shook off the gloom that threatened to settle in. I knew that wasn't true. There was something between hell with a partner and being lonely. Cooper popped into my head and my heart squeezed in my chest.

"What is wrong with me?"

I was the one that said we could only be friends and nothing more. Clear boundaries were set, and we weren't going to go over them. No matter how tempting it was. I peeled off my clothes as I headed for the bedroom. I would now have to do something I hadn't done in a long time.

Just one good orgasm and then maybe I would be able to sleep.

Chapter Nineteen

IVY

Excitement sent my tummy into a spin as soon as I walked up to the bar. My heart was already thumping excitedly and I knew it was going to be a crazy weekend. Music poured out of the doors as soon as I opened them, laughter filled the air, but my eyes were only drawn to him.

Cooper stood behind the bar in what I started to recognize as his signature shirt. The black material stretched over his wide chest, showing off intimidating biceps. It left very little to the imagination, but I still found myself wondering what it would feel like to run my fingers down his stomach and slip lower into the confines of his pants...

Snap out of it Ivy!

My thoughts were getting worse by the day, but I couldn't seem to stop them. Every time I saw Cooper, the most inappropriate thoughts filled my head. Cooper had been on his best behavior since our dinner date. He treated me like a friend, not like a piece of ass he could throw away, the way he'd done so long ago.

"Jo!" His voice bellowed through the bar and cut through the noise. "We're drowning. Come help us out."

"I'm coming," I called as I came back to life and waded through the sea of people. "Let me put my purse away and grab my things."

"We'll hold down the fort until then," he shouted dramatically.

I rolled my eyes, but I loved it. It wasn't what I went to school for, but I had to admit, I loved being in a job where I was needed and appreciated. "I'll be back in two secs!" I dashed into the back, stored my purse and grabbed my apron. As I tied it I looked in the mirror. My honey locks had been pulled into a messy bun that sat on top of my head. I'd worn a nice pair of shorts and a tank top. The combination was comfy and cool since the bar could get a little hot at times. I looked okay.

I grabbed my pad and pen, tucked them into my apron, and went back out front.

"There you are," Mel piped up and handed me a few drinks. "Table twelve. You're saving my poor old legs, hon." She smiled as she started making another drink. "Get some orders and we'll get to whipping them up."

"I'm on it," I sang as I twirled away expertly with a tray loaded with glasses. Working with Cooper had started out by necessity and I was lousy at the job to start with, but I'd gotten good very quickly and I was really enjoying it now. There was a constant rush when I was serving customers. Grabbing orders, delivering drinks, chatting, laughing, collecting money. All of it was a whirlwind of activity and it kept my mind off of the sour spots in my life. Maybe this was what it was like to be happy.

"Coop! There you are. Make me something good, darling."

I glanced up at the loud, confident voice. There was something proprietorial about it. A woman swung her hips as she brushed past me and headed directly for the bar. Her red dress was skintight, micro short, and showed off humongous cleavage. She tossed her thick blonde hair over her shoulder. When she reached the bar, a man gallantly moved, so she could sit down. Two women trailed her and they paled in comparison to the magnetic bombshell that had just breezed in.

I already hated her.

She wiggled her perfectly manicured fingers and smiled seductively at Cooper while he was still a little away from her.

Everyone in the bar stared, but I stared even harder. She looked vaguely familiar and my dislike of her brewed in my belly.

"Victoria," Cooper said as he swung a towel over his shoulder. "What are you doing here? I thought you were out of town."

It hit me like a ton of bricks then. Oh, God. This was what Victoria Blake had become. Obviously, she'd had some improvements done and she happily flaunted them in her teeny dress. Those breasts were at least three times the size they used to be, and her hair was neither thick nor blonde. And that nose. There were changes there too.

We went to high school together and she'd been jealous of me for ages. Mostly, because back then, I was Cooper's best friend and he was the only guy she wanted. We'd been friends before that, but afterward Victoria made my life hell as much as possible and that didn't stop after high school ended.

Did she recognize me?

Neither of us looked the way we did ages ago. I used to be a tiny little thing, but I filled out over the years. I wasn't as quiet as I'd been years ago either, although I still preferred to be solitary.

"I came by to see you," she purred.

I put the tray of drinks on table twelve and marched back to the bar. I grabbed another drink order and edged my way toward them.

Victoria pouted.

Yes, those lips had seen changes too. Big changes.

"Vegas was amazing, but I missed home."

"Really? I thought Vegas would have been right up your street," Cooper replied.

She reached out a hand and slowly stroked his arm. "What can I say? It's just a stretch of sand and a bunch of colored lights when you're not with your man."

Cooper removed himself from her grasp and took a step back. The way her face fell, and the way he distanced himself was pure gold.

I grinned to myself as I handed in my orders to Mel and had her make my drinks as Cooper was obviously busy.

"I'm here, guys," Cindy jogged up to the bar and grinned cheerfully at everyone.

She was the total opposite of Mel and she was another wait-ress Cooper had hired for the busy night. She was always upbeat and sunny. Her megawatt smile could blind someone, and she really worked her little butt off.

Mel presented me with my drinks. "Make sure I didn't miss anything," she said as she started working on her next order. "I don't think I did, but it's possible."

"Let me check," I muttered as I compared my ticket to the drinks.

"Coop," Victoria purred. "When are you going to take me out to dinner? Drinks are great, but they would be even better if we hung out afterward."

"Sorry, I have a full shift and we're slammed."

"That's why you have staff," she scoffed as her eyes ran me up and down. "I'm sure even they could handle something like this. You and I haven't done anything in a long time," she grumbled as she dragged a red nail polished-tipped finger on the bar surface.

I wanted to smack her upside the head. *Nice desperation you're showing there Victoria.* It was annoying, but I got a strange sense of satisfaction from their exchange. The more she piled on the compliments and flirting, the more Cooper resisted.

He looked completely uninterested as he slid her a drink. "That'll be thirteen dollars," Cooper said with a smile.

"Really? I don't even get a drink anymore?" She pouted again. "You've changed, Coop. What has you acting so different?"

Cooper's eyes flickered and I swore for a minute that they landed on me. Before I could fully register the motion, he focused on Victoria again. I was dying to hear what he had to say when Mel snapped her fingers in front of my face.

"Are you going to give the customers their drinks, or should I do it for you?"

"Oh, sorry," I mumbled as my cheeks burned like they were on fire. "I was just—"

"I know exactly what you were doing." Mel leaned forward and lowered her voice. "Trust me, he doesn't want that hussy. If he did, he would be with her." Mel straightened up. "Now, go deliver drinks before you get us all backed up."

"Right, I'm off," I said pushing away smartly, but I was smiling as I carried the tray away.

If Mel said he wasn't interested in her, she must have seen even more than I had from their little exchange just now. I trusted Mel. She looked as if she couldn't care less about what was happening between Cooper and me, but I felt as if she was quietly cheering for us in the background.

I carried my drinks over to the table and instead of plopping the tray on the table and rushing back to the bar, I handed them out with a cheerful smile. I was definitely getting better at my job. Not dropping a single glass was an accomplishment. The smile never leaving my face as I took another table's order, but my eyes kept going back to Victoria and Cooper every free chance I had.

No matter how much he politely nodded and got on with his tasks, Victoria wouldn't pull her claws out of him.

"When is she going to give up?" I muttered under my breath as I went into the kitchen to drop off a tray of dirty plates.

"Who?"

I jumped and pressed a hand to my chest when Cindy smiled at me. Whether she had been standing there all along, or walked up on me, I had no idea. I was way too involved in my own thoughts. "Oh, it's nothing," I said as I waved a hand. "How are you doing out there?"

"Great! This place is way better than my last job. Everyone must be in a great mood tonight because they're tipping like crazy. Except Victoria. Then again, that's how she always is."

"Wait, you just started, right?"

Cindy nodded. "Yeah, but I hung out here a lot before Cooper hired me. Victoria was always here all over him. I think she likes to show him off."

"What's that about?" I scoffed. "What is he, a damn trophy?"

"I think he was for a while. You know, once you left town, he dated her for a while."

My mouth dropped open. Cindy had been in the same grade as Victoria and I when we were in high school so it wasn't surprising that she was up to date on all the drama and gossip. Most people were like that in Springston. "They dated?" I gasped as I came out of my stupor.

"Well, I say date, but it was more like a fling. You know how Cooper was back in those days. He 'dated' for all of five minutes before he was on to the next. When he first came back to town, he took up with Victoria for a while and she's never gotten over it."

"Who broke up with who?"

"Oh, Cooper dumped her for sure. It was ugly. She used to come here all the time angry as hell that he was done with her. After a while, she calmed down and switched to flirting. She's totally delusional. I'm sure she thinks she's going to get him back...one day."

"Wow," I whispered. "I've missed so much."

"You have no idea. I better get back to work before Cooper starts looking for me."

I nodded, but my mind was a million miles away. Had Cooper really changed after all? What was that saying: you can't teach an old dog new tricks? Apparently, Cooper took that statement and ran with it. What if I went out with him now, and he dropped me the way he'd dropped Victoria?

What if Cooper was still the same guy he was back in high school? The way he used women, then tossed them aside made me clench my fists.

It was more than that though. Cooper had started seeing Victoria right after he came back. That was enough evidence for me to see things as they really were. Cooper hadn't cared about me at all. He never made any effort to look for me. He just took up with the first skirt he saw. The only thing he ever wanted from me was what I'd given him, my virginity nice and easy. I'd handed it over on a silver platter.

Suddenly, I was angry. I couldn't believe I let him kiss me! The fury boiled in my belly and to my horror, tears ran down my cheeks. It shouldn't still hurt. That happened with us years ago when we were young, dumb kids.

Saying it shouldn't matter was easy, but the reality was that it bothered me big time. You never forgot your first and Cooper was unforgettable for all right and wrong reasons. I dashed my tears away and scolded myself. I was expecting too much and I needed to grow up.

How could I even fall for his bullshit again? Had he told Victoria that he wanted to be friends? Was that the reason she continued to hang around him?

There were so many unanswered questions, but I had no way of getting answers to them. No one knew what was going on inside of Cooper's head but Cooper, and I doubted he would give me the honest answers I craved.

I quickly closed my eyes and forced myself to get it together. I was at work. None of that drama mattered.

"Jo, what's wrong? Why are you crying?"

Chapter Twenty

IVY

I stiffened and slowly opened my eyes.

Cooper peered at me curiously with his eyebrows knitted and a frown etched into his forehead.

I didn't want to talk to him. I wanted to get back to work and pretend I never learned about him and Victoria. "Nothing," I said as I rubbed my face with my arm. "I should get back to work." I breezed past him.

Cooper pulled me back by my arm. "Wait a minute. If something's bothering you, would you tell me?"

I tried to yank myself free, but Cooper easily had a height and weight advantage.

Instead of using any force, he simply stood his ground and held my squirming body with one hand.

"It doesn't matter. Will you let go of me, please? Seriously, you're acting like I'm a three year old that needs a time out. Come on, I need to get back to work."

"I'm the boss, remember? I'll tell you when it's mandatory that you get back to work. Now, tell me; what is going on?"

I sighed. Every inch of my body dreaded the idea of telling him. It felt small and petty. Part of me recognized that we were just friends and it shouldn't matter so much, but the other part of me was envious as hell. "It's just seeing Victoria draped all over you. I hate it. I don't like her, I don't like the way she tries to bring attention to herself all the time. And then I found out you two were together, so I guess I just..." I trailed off as I tugged my arm away.

He stared at me. "We're not together."

"You used to be," I countered quickly.

Cooper raised an eyebrow. "Is this really bothering you? She's just someone from my past, and it's been over for ages."

"Yeah, but it started right after you came back right? I mean did you ever bother to look for me?"

"Jo—"

I held up a hand. "It doesn't matter. Like I said, it's stupid and we're not together. I need to get back to work."

"Hey," he said as he caught me again. "I'm serious. We had a brief thing and I broke it off because I was drunk and lonely one night and she came on to me. It was nothing like what we had—"

I laughed bitterly. "Just admit that we had nothing. It was a fling and it was over, then you moved on. And now, I don't ever want to talk about this anymore." I brushed past Cooper and stalked out into the bar. His words could sound as sweet as honey, but I knew him. The way he'd pursued me and then dumped me right after he took my virginity was all I needed to know. I fell for Brian's sweet words, but I was not falling for Cooper's too.

Enough was enough.

I couldn't believe I was dumb enough to consider going out with him. Of course, a man like him would be inundated with offers from women. I had to stop falling for the good parts of him and remember he had broken my heart once and he would do it again, if I let him.

I pushed all the pain and the negative thoughts down and went back to work. I'd had a lot of practice pretending everything was okay, so I was good at it. The smile never faltered from my lips as I started taking orders again. As I worked, the feeling of eyes tracking me never stopped. I knew it had to be Cooper, but I refused to acknowledge him. When I had to pick up my drinks, I purposely went to Mel instead.

"I don't know why that Victoria keeps trying," a woman said with a laugh. "It's embarrassing. She is never going to get anywhere with him."

"Seriously," her friend said. "Cooper hasn't dated anyone in ages, so I don't know why she keeps trying so hard. He's been caught up on his ex for years."

"Where did you hear that?"

The woman waved a hand. "Who knows? One of my friends might have told me last time we were here. Something about his high school girlfriend and him still being in love with her. Victoria's not the only one that's tried to snag him."

"Too bad," the first woman sighed. "He is hot."

I couldn't stop replaying what they'd said. Cooper was still in love with his high school girlfriend? I couldn't think of a single person that he'd dated besides me in high school. He was known to hook up, but I was the only one that he spent that much time with. I needed to know if it was true.

Would knowing that Cooper loved me change anything? I wasn't sure, but I had to know if that's really what he thought for my own peace of mind. It was hard to focus on work for the rest of the night, but I tried not to think about anything else besides delivering food and drinks and keeping my customers happy.

"I'm taking off," Cindy called.

"I'm going with her," Mel said as she walked from behind the bar. "You two have this, right?"

"Yeah," Cooper said.

Mel smiled at me.

I had a feeling that she didn't need to leave as quickly as she was. I narrowed my eyes at her, but her grin only grew. I swear, she was always up to something sneaky. She wiggled her fingers at me and escorted Cindy out. I locked the door and walked back towards the bar.

Cooper stayed behind the bar as he cashed up the money.

I leaned against the counter.

After a few quiet moments, his eyes flickered up to me before he resumed what he was doing.

"Can I have a drink, please?"

"What? Are you talking to me again?"

I raised a brow. "Not if you're going to be cranky." Right away, I watched the tension go out of his shoulders.

He finished stacking up the money before he stopped and glanced at me.

I chewed my lip. "I wanted to ask you something first."

"Not Victoria," he groaned. "I don't want to talk about Victoria for one more second. I had to listen to her all fucking night. I'm begging you, Jo—"

"It's not about Victoria," I assured him quickly.

"Okay," he said slowly as he put the money and credit card slips into an envelope then started heading to his office. "Then ask me anything."

I leaned on the doorframe.

He put the envelope on the table and looked at me expectantly.

It should have been easy to ask, but my mind switched between wanting to know and the feelings I would experience if it weren't true.

Cooper glanced up at me. "Well?"

"Do you—uh—well..."

"Go on."

"Still love me?" I blurted the words out quickly or I knew I wouldn't say them at all. "I overheard someone tonight saying you were still in love with your high school girlfriend, and unless you were seeing someone else then that would be me, right? Were you seeing someone else? I mean you can tell me. It's all water under the bridge now. It won't change anything between us. We'll still be like friends and everything." I stopped to take a much needed breath.

He rubbed the back of his neck. "No, you were the only one I dated in high school."

"Really?" I asked, a fountain of joy surging inside my heart. "So, it's true."

"Yeah," he said quietly before he gazed up at me. "Yeah, it's true. I still love you. I thought I would get over you one day, but it just never happened."

I swallowed thickly, but the lump wouldn't leave my throat. *He loved me. What was I going to do with that?* I never expected him to actually say those words, to know that he cared about me that way. My hand clutched my shirt so tightly my fingers throbbed before I nodded a little. "Oh, well that's... good to know."

Cooper sighed. "Yep, I definitely just made things awkward and weird, didn't I?"

"No," I said quickly not wanting him to feel strange about things. "It's just a lot to process right now."

Cooper nodded as he opened a drawer. "Alright. Look, let me drop you off at home, then I'll get back here and close up on my own."

I shook my head and sat down beside him. "I'm not leaving you alone. I'll help you close up."

"You sure?" he asked, tilting his head adorably at me.

I picked up the book where he recorded all the totals. "I'm sure." I smiled softly. "We'll leave together."

A corner of his mouth lifted into a grin before he nodded.

When he started counting the money, I stared at his profile.

He still loved me.

Chapter Twenty-One

IVY

As soon as he knocked, I knew it was Cooper. We both had the day off and I was ready to go out with him. I had no idea what he had planned, but he promised it would be a nice, relaxing day between friends.

Yeah, the friend who was in love with me.

Thinking about that night in his office made my heart hammer. Neither of us had brought it up again and Cooper had been true to his word when he said he would respect my request for us to be friends. He hadn't made a move, he hadn't said anything remotely romantic, but it was odd. I still felt as if he was waiting, wanting, and part of me was on edge too. Because I'd also been waiting and wanting.

The door opened.

I stopped and stared in amazement.

I'd seen Cooper every day for the past few weeks, but I've never gotten over how breathtaking he really was.

His blond hair had grown out a bit, but it looked good with

those sparkling blue-green eyes. He was dressed casually once again in dark jeans and a t-shirt that showed off his muscles.

I instantly wanted to run my fingers over his body but stopped myself.

"I brought donuts and coffee," he announced as he dazzled me with his smile. "Raspberry filled for you."

I raised my eyebrows.

"Yes, I remembered."

"My guilty pleasure." I smiled as I took the bag. "Let's go in. I'm about to get dressed." I was still wrapped up in my robe and wore a twisted a towel on my head.

Once we made it to the kitchen, I pulled the towel off and my still damp locks, slightly curly now, fell down my back. I opened the bag and reached inside for a donut when I realized Cooper was staring at me. I raised a brow at him. "What?"

"Nothing," he said, and quickly handed me a cup. "Coffee too."

"Mmm, thank you. I can never have enough caffeine. Where are we going today?"

"Oh, uh fishing," he said as he regained himself. "I figured you hadn't been in a long time so we can go up to the cabin, fish, and then have dinner. I thought it would be nice to get away for a little while." His lip quirked up into a grin as he added, "If you're up for it after all of that New York City lifestyle bullshit."

I rolled my eyes. "You're really trying to get under my skin with that one, huh?"

"Would it be me if I didn't mercilessly tease you?"

I shook my head at him. Cooper reminded me so much of how he used to be when we were younger. I'd loved hanging out with him because he could make me laugh no matter what the situation involved. There weren't many people who were capable of that. "I guess I better get dressed then," I sighed as I licked icing off my fingertips.

"Or you could go naked. I'm sure the fish wouldn't mind."

"Coop," I warned.

"I'm kidding! I'm kidding. Seriously though, go take your ass back there and get dressed so we can go. Hurry up, woman."

I stuck out my tongue. How did he manage to make me feel so desirable and comfortable again? I could never be carefree with Brian.

I tossed my robe onto a chair, then tugged out a pair of shorts and a crimson tank top. Pulling my hair into a ponytail, I donned a baseball cap that would hopefully protect me from the sun. If I was still in New York, I would never have left the house without a full face of makeup, but I rolled on some *chapstick* and called it a day. It was freezing.

"Ready," I called as I walked into the kitchen. "Do I need to bring anything?"

Cooper shook his head. "I told you I would take care of everything. Let's hit the road."

I followed him to his truck and settled into the passenger seat. Lately, it was starting to feel like it was my seat. It was probably a testament to how often I hung out with Cooper. I tried to rationalize and say it was better than sitting at home moping, but I genuinely loved being around him. He was upbeat, warm and ok... sexy as hell. Just seeing his face light up when he smiled was enough to make me melt.

The journey to the lake was quiet, but not uncomfortable. I remembered sitting around Brian when he was quiet and I was always tense wondering if I had somehow made him mad. Cooper's silence was comforting and laid back just like the music playing on the radio. It brought up a deluge of warm memories from my childhood, just the kind I loved to think about.

"Here we go," Cooper announced as I shook off my daydreams. "I haven't been here in a while myself."

"Wow, I forgot how small it is." I smiled. "We used to drink beers up here."

"Yep. I brought a few along with me just for old times' sake."

I grinned. "Okay, you really *do* know me."

"I keep telling you I do." He smiled as he reached over and pinched my cheek. "You just don't listen, honey bear."

That old nickname. It made me feel almost breathless with nostalgia. I quickly pretended to fight him off and rubbed my cheek.

He chuckled.

We pulled to a stop and he unloaded the supplies. I went into the cabin and looked around. Someone had definitely been here to clean it up. There was no dust, the dishes were all put away neatly, the fridge was empty, but in pristine condition, and the sheets all held that freshly laundered scent. "Are we staying the night?"

"I figured if we had a few too many beers, we could crash here. You can have the bed, and I'll take the couch. Oh, and I have spare clothes in the dresser if you end up needing them."

"You're so well prepared. When we were younger, you always used to just shrug your shoulders and tell me to sleep like nature intended."

He grinned. "Yeah, but if you slept naked, I wouldn't get much sleep. I don't really fancy ending up with blue balls."

"Blue balls. You wouldn't know what blue balls were if they slapped you with a cold fish," I huffed. "Be honest. You have never been rejected in your life."

He put food in the fridge before turning and telling me calmly, "You did."

"Only after you rejected me," I shot back.

He leaned on the counter. "You know," he said as he rubbed the back of his neck. "I didn't actually come here to fight with you."

I smiled at him. "You're right. Let's go catch us some food," I said as I stepped over and patted his shoulder.

"I packed lunch. I figured we could clean our catch and cook it for dinner."

"Sounds like a plan."

We carried what we needed outside and settled into our chairs on the edge of the lake. The water rippled as the sun sparkled on the surface. The distant call of birds and nature surrounded us. Every muscle in my body relaxed and I couldn't stop smiling at how wonderful my life had become.

"Beer?" Cooper asked.

"Oh, hell yes," I purred. "This is the best I've felt since—since..." I furrowed my brow. Years. It was the best I had felt since before leaving Springston. I couldn't believe I'd spent so many years completely miserable.

"Since when?" Cooper asked.

"Since I left," I said slowly.

Cooper lips tugged downwards. "You know, you've done that a few times now. If I talk about New York, or mention anything about the past you get that look on your face like something's really bothering you. Did something happen?"

I glanced off to the side.

Cooper's eyes burned into my skin.

I knew he wouldn't give up, not this time. And I wanted to tell him. I hadn't told a soul and it festered in my brain giving me nightmares unless I was around Cooper. "I didn't exactly have the best time out there." I stopped talking, cracked open a beer, and tilted it up. "It was horrible."

"Why?" Cooper asked softly. "I thought you'd found everything you wanted out there. I met Linda, your old friend, and she told me you were happy as a lark, dream job and everything."

I laughed. "Yeah, I was happy as a lark. I worked for an asshole that screamed at me more often than not, and humiliated me for fun. I never saw a major story because I was just the girl who made the best coffee he'd ever had. My apartment was a shoebox that consumed most of my salary. And my boyfriend?" I laughed dryly. "My boyfriend was a manipulative psychopath. He had a way of abusing me that was so borderline that I couldn't actually get angry. It's like someone giving you a banana with a needle in it. You think you've got a banana, but you bite into a needle. He was so good at it, I actually got used to his particular brand of abuse and ended up making excuses for him. Who the hell gets used to abuse you ask? I did."

I realized I was ranting. I blinked away my tears and quickly brushed my cheeks before I drank down my beer like it was water. A warm, pleasant buzz spread over my body, as I sat the empty can aside.

"You never told me that." Something tight and tense resonated in Cooper's voice.

I had never heard him sound like that before. I turned to look at him in surprise.

His jaw was clenched tight.

"I never told anyone, Cooper. Brian started out as the perfect boyfriend, and then he turned into a lazy, controlling, manipulative, aggressive bastard. At first, it was just little things; comments about my looks, or my weight, criticizing me for the way I did something, calling and texting me a million times if I was even a few minutes late, but that night I left... it escalated."

"Escalated to what?" Cooper asked, his voice barely a whisper.

I glanced over and realized his face was contorted with fury. He clenched his hand and the can dented, beer sloshed up and over the side. I realized that when Brian clenched his fist my body trembled when Cooper did it I felt no fear to myself.

"We don't have to talk about this." I said, reaching over to touch his hand.

"No." He shook his head and his hold relaxed a bit. "Tell me what happened. You shouldn't have kept something like this to yourself for so long. No wonder you've been walking around like a fucking spooked cat."

My heart warmed at how protective he was over me. That was all I'd wanted out of a relationship, someone who loved me and looked out for me. I kept my hand on his and motioned for another beer.

He handed it over and stayed quiet while I opened it and took a little drink. Once I was sure I could speak without my voice trembling, I continued, "That night, Brian had clearly been drinking and I just wanted to eat and get some sleep, but he wanted to—you know, have sex." I drank more of the bitter beer. "But I didn't want him anywhere near me. We argued and then he started choking me and wouldn't stop. I was about to pass out and I swear I saw it in his eyes. He wanted to kill me. He would have killed me if he hadn't made the mistake of thinking he could fuck me while he strangled me. I took my chance and kneed him in the balls and took off. He was screaming that if he couldn't have me no one would. That he would find me. I didn't look back. Everything I own is still in that apartment, but I'll never go back to it. I'm just happy to be free."

Cooper released a deep breath. "That fucking coward, asshole," he hissed. "How dare he put his hands on you? He's lucky he's still there because I would have fucking killed him." He blinked. "Fucking hell. That's why you used to wear all those high collars for the first week you came to town."

I stared at Cooper. Seeing him so angry surprised me. I knew he wouldn't be okay with it, but I didn't expect such a visceral reaction. I put my beer aside and stood up to wrap my arms around him.

Cooper calmed down in my arms and reached up to hold onto my wrists. "You shouldn't have to be the one comforting me. You're the one that went through it."

"Yeah, but I've accepted it, or as much of it as I can stand. I'm okay now, so don't worry about it. Okay?"

"If that bastard ever shows his face here, I'll cave it in for him. You don't deserve to be treated like that. I'll never be okay with that."

I closed my eyes and leaned against Cooper. He made me feel safe. I'd worried about Brian finding me since I'd come back home. Knowing that he would look out for me helped. "Don't beat anyone up. I don't want you going to jail because of me. I don't think he'll find me here, or at least I don't think so. I never left a trail and I never told him about this place. Even in the early days of our relationship, I must have known something was wrong, but I held back telling him about everything that was most important to me."

"Well, if he ever finds his way down here, I will make him sorry."

"Don't do that. I don't want you to get in trouble because of me. All I ask is that you look out for me if you can. I like closing the bar down with you because at least, we leave together."

"Then we'll close it down together all the time." Cooper held me tightly. "I'm not going to let anything happen to you."

The funny thing was that I believed him. It was hard for me to trust anyone, especially the men in my life, but I wanted to trust someone again. I wanted to trust Cooper. I wasn't all the way sold, but it did give me some comfort. Maybe things were going to go right for me finally. Maybe?

In the end, we didn't end up staying in the cabin. Cooper became strangely withdrawn over dinner and eventually, he blurted out that he was truly, truly sorry he had messed up my life.

I told him I was a big girl and it was my decision to end up in New York or even go out with Brian. Something had changed inside me.

Chapter Twenty-Two

IVY

I ducked into the back of the bar around noon and quickly got myself ready before I popped into the front.

"What's with the face?" Cooper asked as I walked up to the counter.

"There's no face."

He narrowed his intoxicatingly mesmerizing eyes. "There is clearly a face. Is something wrong?"

I shrugged. Nothing was wrong so much as I couldn't get things out of my head. The main thing being *him*. I had forced him to agree on us being just friends, nothing more, but I couldn't stop wanting him. Especially, after he showed how much he cared for me at the lake. I told myself it was because no one had turned me on in so long. As a matter of fact, no one had turned me on since him... but it was more than that. "I'm fine, really." I smiled and picked up my tray. "It's a good day. Relax."

Cooper nodded, but his eyes followed me throughout the bar, which only made a shiver of desire jog up my spine. *Stop looking at me or I'm going to melt.* My legs pressed together as I stopped to take an order, but I was so on edge with wanting him, I could feel myself getting wet.

Jesus, when was the last time that happened to me?

Never.

I forced myself to concentrate on my job. The more I worked, the less time I would have to stare at Cooper. Or at least that was the plan. It was much harder to execute when I came close to those strong arms or he pushed his fingers through his silky blond hair. When he smiled and it became a deep, powerful laugh... I shuddered with pent up lust.

This was going to become a problem.

Whenever I went up for drinks or carried out food, Cooper was never far from me. The scent of his cologne lingered in my nose until it drove me crazy. How was I supposed to work when he was everywhere? The man was a complete and utter distraction. How was a girl supposed to stay composed around all of that?

I felt more than thankful when it was time to close up. Mel and Cindy took off as usual which left Cooper and me alone. I took my sweet time wiping down the tables and the bar until I couldn't stall anymore. Then I trudged into the back office and took my seat where I picked up a pen ready to help record the numbers for the day.

"Look at that, you're done avoiding me for the day," Cooper commented with a grin.

"I wasn't avoiding you!"

"Then why are your cheeks so rosy?"

A hand fluttered up to my cheek and I felt the heat in my skin. Damnit. I didn't know I was showing it so obviously. My eyes locked on the sheet of paper in front of me as I pretended to be very interested in the numbers on the page. "I just had a lot on my mind," I muttered.

"Like what?" he asked. I heard the hint of a grin in there. "You can't avoid me forever. Were you thinking about me?"

I started to shut him down, but I heard the desire in his voice. He wanted me to be thinking about him. I didn't want to destroy his feelings like that, especially if it was with a lie. I chewed my lip instead until the silence spread so long that I couldn't deny his words. "Shut up," I finally muttered.

Cooper tilted his head back and burst out laughing at my childish come back.

I tried to hide my grin, but his laughter was contagious, and before I could stop myself, I cracked up too.

Cooper reached over and brushed the locks that had escaped my ponytail out of my face. "Did you get that out of your system?"

"No, there's a lot more childish nonsense where that came from, so watch out."

"I've got big shoulders, so bring it on," he drawled, his eyes twinkling.

Our chuckling died down and disappeared before I was pulled out of my chair and half-standing as our lips crashed together. Cooper's kiss was strong and possessive and I pushed my body on to the desk. I could hear papers and stuff falling to the ground as he pulled me across until I was on his side and facing him, the desk under my butt. His fingers raked into my hair and scratched my scalp. I slipped my tongue out and Cooper ran with it. His tongue swiped mine before he sucked on it. My pussy twitched.

Twitched? Yes, twitched.

I hadn't felt such a strong reaction since our first time together, but there it was again, all riled up and ready to go. "This is a bad idea," I whispered desperately. "We both know it? I thought...Oh God," I moaned as he attacked my neck with kisses. "I thought we both agreed to just be friends."

"Definitely still friends, babe," he growled as he nipped my shoulder.

"Isn't this crossing a line?" I asked as he pushed his hand underneath my shirt. That strong, calloused, hard-working hand worked its way up my sensitive belly and gripped my right breast. "I don't think friends do this."

"So we'll be friends with a little extra," he mumbled as he fondled my nipple beneath my shirt. "Nothing wrong with that."

I laughed. "I think you mean friends with benefits. Things could go very wrong."

"You worry too much. You want it, right? I saw it written on your face all day."

I had to be honest. I nodded.

"This is what you want, isn't it?" he growled as he yanked up my shirt and licked my nipple.

I gasped at the warm wetness of his mouth. God, Cooper

knew me. He wasn't so easy to throw off because he saw right through me even when I was a horny, desperate mess. I gripped the breast that he sucked on and pushed more into his mouth. "Yes," I moaned as my legs fell apart all on their own. "I—I need it."

Cooper didn't hesitate as I admitted the truth. He ran his tongue up the expanse of my throat before he kissed my lips and slipped his tongue inside. When he pulled away, he nipped my bottom lip, and sucked it hard. "God, you are so fucking fine," he muttered in that deep, husky voice of his that made my knees tremble with desire.

A gasp left my lips and I started to protest, but when my butt connected with his desk, I gave up. His hands yanked up my skirt until it was well above my waist.

He traced a finger up and down my slit, over my damp panties as he sucked in a breath. "I can feel how wet you are for me," he moaned as he glanced up at me and looked me right in the eyes. "Is this why you had so much trouble tonight?"

I swallowed hard. "Maybe…"

Cooper rubbed my clit hard and fast until I gasped and gripped the desk. "Fuck, don't do that."

"Then don't lie to me," he said as he traced my clit around the soft fabric of my cotton underwear. "And I won't have to torture you."

"Yes, yes that's why," I panted.

"That's better," he growled, but his fingers still moved in small determined circles around my clit.

I shivered. "Cooper, you're making me crazy."

"Not yet."

I was about to ask him what he meant when he gripped my panties and pulled them down my thighs. They slipped down my knees and hit the floor so fast I was sure it was some kind of record. Cooper pushed my thighs apart, exposing me in that tiny office.

Even though it was just the two of us, I shuddered nervously. "What are you doing?" I breathed.

"I'm making sure you show up to work focused next time." Cooper stroked the insides of both of my thighs. Up and down his finger slid as he caressed my skin lovingly. He leaned down and nipped my flesh before he moaned. "You have the softest skin," he hummed. "And you smell like heaven."

"When you say things like that I don't know what to do. No one has said that kind of stuff for a while now."

"Then let me make sure you realize how amazing you are, and let me remind you of it every single day."

My toes curled as he lapped at my inner thigh. Fire collected in my belly and I gripped whatever I could find to keep from losing my mind. Cooper was like a completely different man. He'd always been strong and sure, but this Cooper between my legs came with an edge of hungry dominance. I felt as if he was going to devour me. Not that I was complaining.

Cooper's name dripped from my lips over and over again as he teased my soft flesh. He licked at my slit until I froze. Pleasure tore through me and my breath stilled.

He looked up at me and grinned. "Right there, huh?"

"Everywhere," I admitted. "It's been so long..."

"I'll fix that," he purred before he lapped at me long and slow. "I'll make up for lost time."

And Cooper kept his word. His strong hands gripped my thighs as he rolled his tongue and lavished it on me. I squirmed underneath his touch, but I didn't push him away. My fingers slipped into his hair and I gripped it as he moaned against me. Just hearing him enjoy himself as he ate me out only aroused me even more.

My eyes flew open as he ran his tongue over my clit, while his fingers pushed inside me and stroked my walls before he perfectly, expertly pressed against my g-spot. It was like he still knew every inch of my body. His fingers slipped in and out, as he sped up more and more.

"Cooper," I breathed as I tried to control myself. "I'm so close."

"Then come for me," he purred. "Just let go and come for me."

I did just that.

I laid back and felt papers stick to my skin, but I didn't care. My legs shifted apart more. I gave myself up to Cooper completely, something I hadn't done with anyone since that night with him. As his fingers pushed inside of me and massaged my walls my muscles clenched around him. My back arched and I cried out as another orgasm rippled through every nerve and muscle in my body.

It felt like nothing I'd ever experienced before. My body still vibrated even after he pulled away and wiped his mouth with his arm. My head spun and I laid there, stretched out, and wired until reality started to sink into me again.

What the hell had I been thinking?

I stared at the ceiling as I realized that I'd let my pussy do the thinking, but my brain and heart still weren't prepared to start another relationship. There was so much trust that needed to be rebuilt and so many wounds that still needed to heal. I needed to be whole again. Not because I was with Cooper but because I was okay with myself again.

"You all right?" Cooper asked.

Slowly, I nodded. "I'm fine," I said as I shifted up and tugged my clothes back into position. "I'm sorry. I should get home."

"Wait, wait, wait. Hold on. You're just taking off, since when? What's the matter?"

I glanced at him.

Cooper hair was still a tousled mess, his lips were pink from exploring my body.

I wanted to reach down and kiss him. There was no doubt he was rock hard and straining in his pants, I could see the evidence, but I wasn't ready for any of that. "I'm sorry. I just —It's just too early. I'm sorry if I led you on and got you all ready to go for nothing," I muttered miserably.

"For nothing? Jo, I didn't do it because I wanted something from you." His voice was quiet, and his brows were knitted. "It's kind of bullshit that you think about me like that."

"I'm sorry. I just need time."

Cooper stood up and adjusted himself. "Don't apologize. Take all the time you need. I'm not rushing you into anything."

I stared at him in amazement. "Are you mad at me?"

"No, Ivy," he said as he collected up the cash. "I'm not mad. I'm disappointed. There's a difference. And I'm not disappointed because we didn't have sex. It's the way you think about me. Still. Why don't you head home for the night?"

"Cooper, I—"

"It's all right. I can lock up on my own. Goodnight, Ivy."

The anger I'd felt slowly dissipated. He wasn't mad because we didn't have sex he was upset because I'd assumed something about him that he felt was unfair. I fixed my hair and made sure I was paper free before I quickly exited his office.

Maybe we both needed a bit of space from each other.

W hy did I allow that to go so far? I should have left it alone. Instead, I had to give into him and screw everything up. We had finally gotten to a point where we could be friends and I had screwed it up. My brain switched from *it was my fault* to *his fault* countless times before it was time for me to gather up my belongings and head for the door.

As I started heading towards the front door, Cooper walked up behind me and I nearly jumped out of my skin. When I glanced up at him, he looked at the door and nothing else. I couldn't be upset when he looked like that. I'd never seen such a vulnerable look on his face before.

"Goodnight," I said softly before I slipped out of the door. Behind me, the lock was thrown hard and I sighed as I leaned up against the building. "Fuck."

My legs still trembled as I pushed off from the building and headed for home. A string of low light street lamps lit my path. I wasn't used to walking home. Cooper always gave me a ride home and waited until I was safely inside. Not tonight. I would have turned him down anyway, and I was pretty sure he knew that, and it was why he didn't ask.

Instead, I lifted my chin and walked on. Springston was a pretty quiet and safe town, so I wasn't worried about running into anyone dangerous. A quick and easy walk home. That was all this was.

Except, just then... every hair on the back of my neck stood up. As much as I tried to tell myself it was my imagination, the feeling of someone watching me couldn't be shaken off. I trudged onward, ready to get home and get myself a little drink before bed.

A sound echoed down a nearby alley and I jumped. My heart hammered in my chest. I shoved a hand against it. It calmed down when a cat scurried out of the dark and darted across the street and into the night.

"Jesus, Ivy. You're being stupid," I scolded myself as I picked up speed.

There was no one there. Of course, there wasn't. The eerie feeling of eyes that had followed me from the bar were my own ridiculous imagination. I knew it was probably because of the night I'd had. Going from all revved up to alone and cold was enough to screw with anyone's head.

I just had to get home. And not think about Cooper. Every time I thought about him, I wanted to go back and talk to him and tell him I didn't think he was a horrible person. It wasn't that I didn't trust him. I didn't trust anyone. I couldn't. Not yet. Not when I was waking up from dreams of dying in Brian's chokehold.

Whenever I trusted someone, it always went horribly wrong, and I didn't want a repeat of my life in New York. Not that I thought Cooper would treat me the same way Brian did, but I needed time. I didn't want to rush into anything. This time, I wanted to be sure. I wanted to be happy in my next relationship, not insecure and afraid.

I tried to shake off that strange feeling, but it never faded. No matter how fast or slow I walked, how much of my path I changed, I still felt like someone was watching me. Eyes pierced my body and I glanced around hoping to catch sight of someone. *Am I going crazy?*

By the time I reached my apartment, my heart was beating so fast I couldn't breathe. My fingers shook as I fumbled for my keys. They dropped to the ground and I cursed as I scooped them up and tried again.

"Shit, shit," I muttered under my voice.

Clink. Clink. Clink.

The key jabbed against the lock, but couldn't find the hole. I gripped my other hand and shoved the key inside hard before I sighed. Stop being so ridiculous. It's all in your head.

Click.

The key turned and I heaved an enormous sigh of relief. I stumbled inside, slammed the door, and threw the lock. My bag was dumped onto the couch while I made a beeline for the kitchen and poured myself a glass of vodka. I topped it off with soda that I had stashed away and took a few gulps before I finally calmed down.

Bit by bit, my body relaxed and a little tingle took over. It counteracted the tingles that still reverberated between my thighs and I was grateful for that. I couldn't stand one more minute thinking about Cooper and his tongue as it lapped away at me and turned me into a puddle.

God, I'm thinking about him again. It was hard not to when he'd made me feel the way he had with such minimal effort it seemed. My body had been craving pleasure, but after Cooper, I was worried that we'd crossed a line that shouldn't have been crossed.

"Oh my God, stop thinking about it!" I yelled at the ceiling. For Christ's sake. What the hell was happening to me? Only he could make me feel like I'm losing my mind.

I carried my drink into the bathroom and turned on the water. I'd ordered a few bath bombs online and I tossed one into the water. A soft, delicate rose aroma filled my bathroom.

"That's better."

A hot bath, then a mug of hot chocolate, followed by some undisturbed sleep were just the things I needed. I sat my glass down and stripped off my clothes. I hadn't even taken off my apron. Of course, I hadn't thought about it, I was more worried about getting the hell out of there and getting some space. Suddenly, I felt a little sad. I had been unfair to Cooper. Like some teenage tease, I left him high and dry. I would find a way to make it up to him.

I picked up all my clothes and carried them to the washer. I decided to grab my phone and watch TV while I was in the bath.

I padded back out to the living room and my foot touched something on the floor. I glanced down at the envelope and frowned. The mailboxes were down on the main floor. I had never gotten an envelope inside of my place.

My stomach dropped as I bent over and opened it up. It wasn't even sealed, the flap was simply tucked into the envelope itself. I fumbled with it and peeled it open. A note was folded up inside. With trembling fingers, I grasped it and I unfolded it so slowly. I think I already knew. My breath burned in my lungs from waiting for so long.

I AM WATCHING YOU.

*T*he words glared at me from the page, bold and written in red ink. I felt my head reel with fear and I almost fell. Quickly, I reached for something to lean against. My hand connected with the arm of the couch. I plopped onto it.

Brian. It had to be Brian. Of course, it was.

I couldn't think of another person who would send me something so sinister. I clutched the note in my hands and my palms ached from the pressure. Suddenly, I jumped off the couch and scrambled for the door.

There was no one at the peephole. All I could see was the stairs, cloaked in shadows and ominous with the light broken outside, but no one was there. I quickly made my way to the window and yanked the ties from the curtains. They were old school things, heavy and thick, and I was glad now I hadn't replaced them yet. Once I had drawn them shut, I made a tiny slit and peeked through them down into the parking lot, at least the bit I could see, but I had a better view of the street below. It was dark and still, a perfect Springston darkness that hinted at softness and security.

But it made me feel so terrified goosebumps cropped up on my skin and littered my arms. I took a step back. It had to be Brian. He was the only one that could ever make me feel so small and terrified. He was the nightmare in the shadows, the creature that haunted me.

Somehow, he had found me.

Silent tears rolled down my cheeks.

I would never be free. The realization sat in my chest like a stone. I had hoped and prayed that he would never find me. Things had been so calm and amazing. So I let myself get comfortable and feel safe again. If he knew where I lived, obviously he had been watching me for a long time. That meant he knew where I was, what I was doing. He was waiting, watching.

I sat on the couch frozen and shocked until I remembered the tub was still running in the bathroom. I pushed myself up and staggered to the bathroom. Shit, I swore as I quickly stepped into the water. It rippled around my bare foot. I quickly shut off the water and yanked out the drain. There was still half an inch of water all over the floor, but I couldn't freak out about it because what was waiting out there for me was a million times worse.

I tracked back out into the kitchen. My feet left wet footprints on the carpet. If my mother was still alive, she would have chastised me, but she wasn't. She was dead. So was my father. I had no one. Except for Cooper and I had managed to alienate him tonight as well.

Tears threatened to fall all over again, as I shakily poured myself another drink. I downed it faster than I should, but the pleasant warmth that filled my body was comforting. I walked over to the couch and grabbed my phone. My eyes landed on the note and a shiver ran through my body.

I should call Cooper. It was the first thought that went through my mind. I knew he didn't want to talk to me, but if I invited him over would he come? If I mentioned Brian, I was pretty sure he would shake off his irritation and come to my rescue, but then I thought about him not showing up. Him saying no.

My heart couldn't take that.

"I don't need him. I don't need anything," I muttered to myself. "I can take care of this myself."

I left the note where it was and went in search of some towels. After the bathroom was clean again, I pulled out some heavy boxes. It took a bit of struggling, but I managed to get a few heavy boxes in front of my front door. It probably wouldn't stop him from getting in, but it would definitely slow him down and maybe I would hear the noise.

Right away, I snagged a notebook and a pen and started to take note of the weak points in my apartment. The next day, I would make it my priority to buy latches for the windows, another lock for the door and maybe even some pepper spray to keep on me for my walk home.

By the time I was done, I felt slightly better.

Maybe it was crazy to be comforted by a list, but it was so much more than that to me. It was a way for me to protect myself. The list was a proactive way to keep myself safe instead of hiding away, afraid and unsure of what might happen next. When I grabbed my phone, ready for my bath now, I saw a text message. It had come in a while ago, but I hadn't been paying attention to it.

Did you make it home safe?

*C*ooper's name glared at me from the top of the message. I ran my finger over it and it took every ounce of willpower within me to keep from begging him to come over. As long as I had been home, Brian hadn't popped up. He wasn't at my door or down below, he hadn't tried to barge in. Maybe, just maybe, it wasn't him. Maybe some teenager thought the note was a good joke and a way to freak someone out.

Safe & Sound. Thank u 4 asking.

I debated about putting an x and then finally decided not to. After what happened tonight, I had to be careful that I didn't behave like a tease. Then I closed the message and walked into the bathroom. I determined that I would not be afraid of what I couldn't see.

Chapter Twenty-Four

IVY

I tried to make myself sleep, but it was harder than I realized. I was up again in an hour. I fixed myself a hot chocolate and prayed it would soothe me enough for me to sleep. All I needed was some sleep, pure, blessed release from having to think about Brian and the problems he would undoubtedly cause. I wasn't going to be afraid of him was what I told myself, but the reality was that his smiling face while he'd strangled me kept coming up like bile until I shivered with unease and fear.

When my head hit the pillow, I didn't stay asleep for long either.

Instead, I popped up alert and every nerve on fire as if Brian was staring down at me while I slept. When that didn't happen, I tried to knock myself out by drinking half a glass of vodka. I was sure I would wake up with a hangover, but it hurt more to think and dream about Brian choking me to death.

After my big drink, I curled up against my pillow and turned the TV on, but kept it on mute, just in case there were foot-steps or any noise that might alert me to an intruder. The vodka and the soundless images soothed me until I eventu-ally, relaxed and dozed off once again.

I slept until I heard something and jumped out of my sleep.

The room felt cold, freezing even. I wondered if I had left the AC on once again. More often than not, I fell asleep with the thing running and froze myself to death by morning. I kicked my legs over the side and slipped out of bed. My feet shifted against the carpet as I left my bedroom and walked out into the living room. Before I could get to the thermo-stat, a figure shifted on the couch. I froze.

He had already laid eyes on me and he narrowed them. "There you are," he growled. "Come here right now. Where the hell have you been? Who the fuck do you think you are?"

I backed away from him and ran into the wall behind me. My ability to speak had stopped working.

Brian stood up and adjusted the jacket that he wore. He lurched forward and my heart rate skyrocket. I wanted to turn and scramble back into my room, but my feet wouldn't cooperate. My chest rose and fell faster as his grin widened and stretched across his face like a grotesque mask.

I finally forced myself to move just as his hands slammed into the wall where I had been. I fell through my bedroom door and kicked it shut with my foot. Shaking, I threw the lock and screamed when he slammed against it.

"You can't get rid of me, you fat bitch!" he growled. "I'm watching you! I know where you are and who you're talking to, you slut! If I can't have you, no one can have you. Do you hear me? You're nothing without me and I'll make sure you know it you bitch!"

I wrapped my arms around my legs and buried my face between my knees. Sooner or later, he would burst through the door and I'd be dead. I tried to block out his rabid words, but they flowed into my ears anyway. The door bowed out under the force of his fists and I knew it was over. He was going to get me. It was worse than *The Shining* when Jack Nicholson went bonkers and tried to kill his family.

Then the door cracked and Brian appeared in front of me. He grinned as he lurched for me.

I screamed at the top of my lungs...

The sound of my own screaming jolted me out of my sleep. I was gasping for breath and covered in sweat. Cold tingles slid down my spine and I shuddered as my eyes flashed around the room fast. My hand reached for the lamp. I switched it on and winced as bright pain hit my eyes. Squinting, I threw my gaze into every corner until I was positive Brian wasn't in my room and it was all just a horrible nightmare.

My chest rose and fell as my heart pounded even after I knew it was only a dream. The adrenaline was taking its time to wear off and there seemed to be nothing I could do about it. I closed my eyes and focused on my breathing. Bit by bit, the fear dissipated, and I was left a shaky, sweaty mess in my bed.

I reached over to the nightstand and yanked up my phone. It was six in the morning. I'd slept only for a while, but the nightmare was apparently enough to shake me out of my deep sleep. I knew I had to work in a few hours, but I wasn't feeling it. I needed to get myself together.

My thumb scrolled over Cooper's name and stayed there for a minute. He had wished me a goodnight.

I sent him a quick text letting him know that I was not feeling very well and was going to stay home for the day. I let him know it wasn't serious and he didn't have to worry about me. I would be back tomorrow. For now, I just needed some time to myself.

I realized that Brian had got what he wanted. He had frightened me so much I just wanted to stay home. At that moment, I felt as if I never wanted to open my front door and go outside again. Why would I want to leave when I could stay safe and sound locked into my room?

Brian could be outside, waiting just around the corner to finish the job he had started in New York. Even now, I could still feel his hands squeezing my throat as life went out of me. I shuddered at the phantom sensation.

I laid the phone on the nightstand and scrunched down underneath my blanket. Fuck going outside. I didn't feel safe being exposed and out in the open.

My phone buzzed, and the noise made me jump. I gripped my pillow instinctively even though I knew it had to be just Cooper telling me to rest or letting me know he received my text. That could wait. I was too on edge to answer anyone. I would answer him when I wasn't dizzy and out of it and trembling after such a horrible nightmare.

Eventually, the buzzing ceased. I didn't want to go back to sleep, but it was better than being awake and wondering every second if Brian would burst through my door and hurt me. My eyelids grew heavy and before I knew it, my body had started to settle down as it dragged me back down for another nap.

By the time I woke up again, I still felt groggy and out of it. I reached for my phone, and saw dozens of texts and I knew I'd have to actually call, so I might as well get it over with. With a groan, I hit Cooper's name.

His phone was answered before the second ring, "Where the hell are you?" he growled.

I blinked. "I sent you a text to tell you I wasn't feeling very well. Didn't you get it?"

"Yeah," he huffed. "I got it, but it seems like bullshit. You were perfectly fine yesterday."

"I can't help that my body suddenly decided not to feel good, Cooper. Come on. I need the day off so I can heal up and then come back to work fully upbeat and ready to go. If I have to sniffle over drinks and people think I'm going to infect them, it won't be a great day anyway."

Cooper sighed. "Why do I feel like you're hiding shit from me?"

Maybe because I'm definitely hiding shit from you. Of course, I couldn't tell him that, but it was true. I didn't want him to know about Brian, or the note. All he would do was worry over me, but what if he got caught up in something that didn't even involve him? I'd never forgive myself if he got hurt or sent away because of me.

"It's not," I said as I pretended to cough. "I was fine until last night, then it hit me. I guess it's been creeping on for a few days. I'm really okay, though. I have soup and juice and if I need anything else I'll—I'll get it delivered."

"Hmm," Cooper said. "I'll be over in a little bit."

I jumped up. "Cooper, I told you I'll be okay. You have to work."

"It's a weekday, the bar will be fine. I'll see you in half an hour."

I growled. "You don't listen even a little bit, do you? I'm fine. I don't need your help. Stay at work."

"Half an hour. So get dressed."

Chapter Twenty-Five

IVY

I started to tell him to stop, but he had already killed the call. I stared at my phone in astonishment for a few seconds before I began to curse and swear. Hard-headed, dominating bastard. I should have known he wasn't going to back off.

I forced myself onto my wobbly legs and trudged into the kitchen. I clicked on the coffee pot before I went into the bathroom and cleaned myself up a bit. One shower later, my hair was no longer sticking to sweat-slicked skin. My cheeks were rosy again and my teeth were clean. It helped me feel a little more alive than when I had first jolted from my nightmare.

The coffee pot was ready to go and I poured myself a cup. I left the cream and sugar behind in favor of the strong, bitter liquid. It just might give me a boost.

Knock, knock, knock.

I jumped and almost spilled boiling liquid on me. My heart

raced. It was Cooper. What if it was Brian though? I gripped my mug so tightly, I was sure it would break in my hands.

"Jo? Open the door, it's Cooper."

The fear left me. It was just Cooper. I quickly stalked into the other room and peered through the peephole just to be sure. When I saw him, I unlocked the door, shoved the boxes out of the way, and yanked the door open.

Cooper pushed inside and slammed the door after him before he looked around. "Why are there giant boxes behind your door?"

"Oh, I was—uh, looking for something," I said as I turned away to pick up my mug and take a sip from it.

Cooper looked as if he didn't believe a word that I was saying.

I stopped while panicking internally. Just having him here was enough to soothe me, but I wanted every single precaution that I could take.

He nodded toward me. "You look like a wreck. What's going on? And don't lie about it because I can see the redness around your eyes. You've been crying."

I couldn't deny that, not when it was so visible. I shrugged my shoulders and walked over to the couch.

He followed.

When I reached the table, I picked up the note and gave it to Cooper so he could see it for himself.

He read it before he frowned. "What the hell is this?" he asked before he looked up at me. "Who fucking sent this?"

"Brian, I think," I whispered and clutched my mug needing the burning heat to keep me grounded. "I can't think of anyone else that would want to scare me. I mean unless it's some asshole kids just screwing around with me, but I don't think that's it at all. I think it's him."

"What the hell?" he muttered as he examined the note. Cooper turned it over and stared at the words before he finally shook his head. "We have to go to the police with this."

I waved a hand. "What good would that do? No one would ever believe me. Besides, I have no proof that it was Brian who did it."

"That's not the point. At least if you tell the police everything you've been through, maybe they can start to work up a restraining order, or at least you'll have a trail of evidence about what he's done and said to you. This could turn ugly really fast, Jo. I don't want to see you in danger."

I chewed my lip. Could he be right about that? I was worried they would laugh at me, but I did need to protect myself. Brian was unhinged and he had been for some time. If there was even the slightest chance that he'd found me in Springston, then I wanted to take every precaution I could find. "Maybe you're right."

"I am right. Where was this?" he asked, jerking the note in his hand. "When did you find it?"

I shrugged. "I felt weird last night when I was walking home, like someone was watching me. I thought it was just my imagination playing tricks on me since it was dark and quiet out, but the feeling stayed the whole time. And then I found this on the floor. Someone had pushed it underneath my door."

"He got into the building?"

I nodded.

"It can't be anyone but Brian, can it?" Cooper breathed.

"It could be one of your crazy, stalker, wannabe girlfriends," I pointed out. "Some people aren't exactly happy that I've moved back and most of them seem to be people you've dated."

Cooper looked at me as if I was crazy. "No one I know would go this far, Jo. You can't be in denial about this forever. If he's here and I have a bad feeling he is, we need to make sure you're going to be safe."

I frowned. "I don't want you to get wrapped up in my drama, Cooper. You have your life."

"You are my life. I'm not going to let anything happen to you. Go and get dressed so we can go to the police station."

I stared at him. "You're not going to give me a choice in the matter, are you?"

"Glad you recognize that, so we don't have to waste time arguing about it. I'll make myself a cup of coffee and wait for you out here."

I sighed, but gave up on arguing with him. Instead, I walked into my room and made sure that my curtains were pulled tightly. Once I was positive no one would be able to see me, I stripped off the robe then changed into a pair of jeans and a dark t-shirt. I tugged on my sneakers before I pulled my hair up into a bun and headed back out.

Cooper was right where he said he would be. He sat perched on one of the stools in the kitchen drinking from one of my mugs. For a minute, my heart did flip-flops in my chest. How could anyone be so effortlessly beautiful? Cooper was more than gorgeous, he was kind, protective and... more important than any of that, he cared about me.

He glanced up at me. "Ready to go?"

"Yeah," I said, shuffling from one foot to the other. "Before we go, I just wanted to say I'm sorry for the way I acted last night. You've come through for me so many times since I've been back and it was unfair of me to be so unkind. Thank you."

Cooper stood up and eclipsed me with his size. "You don't have to apologize. I know what you're going through. You can't get rid of me so easily. I'll always be here for you. Whatever you need, call and tell me. Don't ever feign sickness again, or feel you have to lie to me."

I grinned sheepishly at the look on his face. "I told you I didn't want you to get involved. Every movie or show I've ever seen shows the guy that gets in the middle gets hurt or killed. I wouldn't know what to do if I was responsible for that. I can't lose you, Cooper. I wouldn't be able to take it. You're the only one I've got left."

"I'm stronger than you think," he said softly as he reached out and gently stroked my cheek. Then he yanked me forward and I was crushed against his hard body. "And I would rather die a hundred times than let you suffer through this by yourself. Stop thinking that you need to take on the world alone. You have me now. There's not going to be any more talk of you putting up with this shit all on your own. Do you understand me?"

My voice caught in my throat and I choked on the words that were trying to come out. It was impossible to form sentences or even coherent thoughts when I felt such overwhelming emotions emanating from him and my own heart. Cooper cared about me and he reminded me of a time when other people cared as well. Maybe I hadn't had the best life in New York, but I was back home now. There were people like him, Mel, and even Cindy that cared about me and wanted me to be all right. I hadn't felt care and concern so strongly since my parents died.

I stayed pressed against the warmth of his chest, and Cooper didn't move an inch. He was like a rock I was holding on to. I felt grateful for that as I buried my face against his body and let the tears pour down my cheeks. *Am I ever going to be done crying?* It seemed like lately that was all I did, but I couldn't stop. Brian had tried to kill me. He hated me that much after all I did for him. There was so much emotion stuffed inside me that it all seeped up in a steady stream threatening to drown me and ruin Cooper's clothes.

"Do you understand me?" Cooper repeated into my hair.

"I u-understand," I hiccupped.

His big, strong hand moved down my back gently and I melted even more against him.

"Good. That's all I need to hear."

He didn't rush me to stop crying or try to hurry me along. No, Cooper just stood there with me in his arms and waited patiently. He whispered against my ear that everything would be okay, and shushed me gently until I finally calmed down.

"God, I feel like such a fucking baby," I muttered, rubbing at my cheeks. "I swear, I don't usually cry at all. I don't think my boss or Brian had ever seen me cry even once. Not even after all they put me through."

Cooper shrugged. "I don't have a problem with you crying. Cry as much as you want."

I sniffed. "I'm done... for now."

His lips quirked. "In that case, get your shoes on, and let's get this over with."

I smiled mistily at him. "Can I just go wash my face first?" I felt like a freak for sobbing so much and it was nice to hear his comforting words.

"Of course. I'll be right here waiting for you."

When I came back with my face still looking swollen but with some semblance of being presentable, Cooper took my hand in his and gave it a squeeze. I knew I had to get this done. So I held my head up, sucked in a deep breath and walked on to meet it. I couldn't let Brian turn me back into the scared, helpless person I was before.

Chapter Twenty-Six

COOPER

I'd intended to give her some space. That was what I told myself after she freaked out in the bar the night before. Clearly, there was a lot that she needed to work out and I was going to give her that space.

Until I heard the stress in her voice on the phone. And the hours of pep talk I had given myself was gone in a flash. I'd jumped up and decided to get to her right away and I was glad I did. I couldn't believe the state I found her in. Just looking at the boxes she had piled in front of her door, made me shake with fury. How dare he scare her like that? She was a complete wreck.

When she came out of the bathroom, I led her down to my truck, but only after she had checked her lock again and again to make sure it was all in place.

I kept my face calm, but I was fucking boiling inside. If he had been standing there I'd have kicked the shit out of him. Then when we got to the truck, she looked around, her head darting back and forth before she climbed in and I shut the door behind her.

"It's going to be okay," I said as the engine roared to life. "Once we get this done, we'll grab some food and we'll both calm the fuck down."

Jo nodded, but her lips stayed pressed together in a straight line.

I didn't push her. I knew it was hard taking a stand for herself, especially when she was terrified. She tried to hide it, but I could see the terror on her face and she wouldn't stop squirming.

"What's the matter?" I asked.

"It's just so... surreal. I never thought I would end up in this kind of relationship, where I had to do something like this. And what is this little piece of paper supposed to do? I mean, if he wants to get to me, he would. Does he just want to scare the shit out of me? He could have already done something last night while I was walking home."

I gripped the steering wheel hard. I let her walk home on her own last night. If anything had happened to her... My head spun with the thought. God, I would never be so careless with her again. *Never.* I took a deep breath and calmed myself down. I needed to keep my wits about me. Not lose my cool if I was going to help Jo. "We are doing this because it is a way to start a paper trail. Maybe it's not a shield, but it's a way to protect you. If he even shows his face around you, then he'll be taken away."

She nodded. "I guess that's better than nothing."

"Good. Just relax. I'm here now. He'll have to get through me to get to you."

"I don't feel well," she murmured.

"It's just stress."

"I guess you're right."

"What do you say to Chinese food and beer for dinner?" I asked.

"I say that sounds like a perfect night. I need to relax a little. I'm so wound up I can feel it in all of my stiff muscles." She rolled her arms. "Everything hurts."

"We can change that. Food and then a massage?"

Jo frowned. "I haven't had one in so long I don't think I can even remember what that feels like anymore."

"Good, then it's time for you to have the special works."

"Yes, I'd love one."

I smiled as she perked up a bit. There was still that undercurrent of fear, but at least it had lessened a bit.

It got even better once we went to the station. I knew all the guys there and they were very gentle with her. They believed her right away, and took her complaint seriously. Even though it was too cold in there and she shivered inside the enclosure of my arm, I could see it was a great relief for her to be able to tell the whole story of what had happened between her in the cowardly bully to someone who could do something about it.

When we were finished, I drove to the takeout place and ordered our food while she literally clung to me. She wouldn't let me go until we were back in my truck safe and sound.

I wasn't happy about the situation, but having Jo rely on me and cling to me meant the whole world to me. This meant she had begun to trust me again. Even if she said she still needed time, her actions told me otherwise. I wasn't going to take advantage of her vulnerability though. As I told her, I was here for the long haul. I would wait for as long as it took.

When we reached her place, she froze up in the car. Her hand was white from how hard she gripped the door handle.

I reached over and stroked her back. "I'll come up with you and check your place out first, okay?"

"No, it's okay," she breathed. "I'll be fine."

"You're not fine and you won't be until you're sure no one's up there. Just stand in the doorway and I'll check out the rest of the apartment."

"Okay," she said between gritted teeth. "Let's do it."

I searched through the apartment as she stood in the middle of the living room. Once I checked every corner of the place thoroughly, I made sure the front door was locked up and then set the food down on the coffee table. "I'm staying the night," I said as I sat down.

"I'm not sure if that's such a good idea." She hesitated then she walked over and sank onto the couch.

"I'm staying and that's the end of that," I stated firmly. This wasn't an issue that was even up for argument. "I'm not leaving you alone here tonight. I'll sleep on the couch so stop worrying. Nothing has to happen between us."

Jo's shoulders slumped. "Okay, thanks. I could keep protest-ing, but honestly, I really don't want to be by myself tonight. I'm terrified he's going to show up and that door is just a few pieces of plywood stuck together."

"If he tries that shit, I'll be right here to show him how we treat bullies in this part of the world," I promised as I opened up the bags of food and passed her a container.

She smiled. "I'm not someone who encourages or appreciates violence in any form, but I have to say you saying that makes me feel a million times better."

"That's because you're smart," I joked, nudging her. "Cooper to the rescue, hmm?"

"Cooper to the rescue." She leaned on my shoulder. "Thank you for everything today. I can't express how much it means to me that you stayed with me and made sure I was okay. I don't think I would have even left the bed today if you hadn't come over."

"I just want to make sure you were okay, that's all," I said as I reached over and stroked her hair. "I... care about you."

"Thank you for caring," she whispered, looking deep into my eyes.

Then I pulled her against my body and held her tightly. We stayed like that, pressed up against each other in the silence. I willed my own strength and power into her body.

By the time she pulled away, she seemed stronger, more confi-dent, and calmer.

I quickly dished out chopsticks and sauce, then I handed her a beer.

Jo turned on the TV and we watched some sitcom that didn't really stick in my brain. Every time I could get away with it, my eyes slid over to her. She looked more like herself than before and I felt glad I was able to help her get back some of her strength. I would never give up on trying to get her back. If anything, the day had strengthened my resolve. She could take all the time she needed, but I would always be there waiting for her and keeping her safe.

After a while, Jo yawned and stretched out. She rubbed at her eyes and I saw the tired look on her face. I picked up the remote and clicked off the television.

"What are you doing?" She mumbled sleepily. "I was watching that."

"Five more minutes and it would have been watching you. Time for bed."

She frowned. "I'm not sleepy."

"I know you're worried, but I'll be here to protect you, okay? You need to get some rest after all of the stress of the past twenty-four hours. Tell me where I can get some blankets and a pillow and I'll go get it for the couch."

She gave in. "You're right. Here, I'll get the stuff you need if you clean up the food."

"That, I can do." I gathered the leftovers and popped them in the fridge. Once all the trash was cleaned up I used the bathroom, then I walked back out into the living room to find the couch all made up for me.

She covered her mouth and yawned before she nodded at it. "I'm going to turn in. I hope that's okay for you."

"It's perfect," I assured her. "Thanks. Go ahead and get some rest."

Jo smiled and walked to her bedroom.

I kicked off my shoes and tugged my shirt over my head. When I glanced up, she was leaning against the doorframe to her bedroom staring at me. I winked and her face flushed.

"Goodnight, Cooper," she said quickly before she disappeared into her room.

"Goodnight, Jo." I grinned to myself as I stripped down to my boxers. That spark wouldn't die down. Every time we looked at each other, I felt it surge to life between us. I climbed onto the couch and tugged the blanket over my body. Jo's couch was a bit short, so I tossed and turned for a bit until finally, I was as comfortable as I was going to get and I promptly started to doze off.

Chapter Twenty-Seven

COOPER

"**G**et off of me! Stop!"

The shout ripped me from my sleep. The world was hazy and dark as I tried to get my bearings and figure out where I was. It came back in a rush... I was spending the night at Jo's place. I blinked a few times trying to figure out if the sound had been a figment from my own dreams when Jo screamed.

I was off of the couch and into her room in record time. She clutched her pillow hard as tears ran down her face. Her chest rose and fell hard and I knew she was on the verge of hyper-ventilating. I lunged into bed with her and gathered her into my arms.

She clung to me, shaking and gasping.

"It's okay. It's okay. It was just a nightmare. Nothing actually happened. I'm right here." I stroked her arms, hair and back trying to calm her down. She clutched me so hard I felt her fingernails dig into my flesh, but I didn't care. She could destroy my flesh and I would still hold her. I would die for her

I would die for her.

The thought hit me hard and suddenly, I'd always known I still loved her, but thinking about it in that moment when she was a terrified, vulnerable mess, I knew it was true. I loved her so much I would die for her.

"I saw him." Her voice trembled. "He... he was right here and ch-choking me. I can still feel his hands on my throat," she sobbed. "Why won't these fucking nightmares stop!"

"They will," I assured her. "It's just going to take some time, that's all. I know this is hard for you, but it *is* going to get better. I promise."

"What if it doesn't?" She shook her head back and forth. "What if he never gets caught and he just tortures me until he finally drives me mad? I know now that it doesn't matter where I go—h-he'll find me. He already found me here. I have to leave. I have to get out of here before he actually kills me."

I held her against my chest while she sobbed until her voice was raw and scratchy. I simply let her get all of it out. She'd been holding a lot in since she came back and what she needed was to let things out so she could face them and heal.

"Hey," I finally said as I pulled her back a bit. "You're going to be fine, okay? I'll protect you no matter what happens. No one is going to take you away or hurt you on my watch. Do you hear me?"

She looked up at me and nodded. "I hear you," she said quietly. "I'm glad you decided to stay."

"I wouldn't dream of going anywhere."

She looked up at me for a long time before she leaned up and kissed me. The moment her lips touched mine, I kissed her back.

Jo's arms wrapped around my neck and she straddled my lap. Her fingers pushed into my hair, her mouth gasping and moaning as she kissed me with every ounce of frustration, passion and lust that had slept inside of her. "I need you," she mumbled against my lips.

I pulled back for a bit and we both panted. "Are you sure about this? I know you're upset and I don't want you to do anything that you're going to regret."

Jo frowned. "Are you just saying that because you don't want me now?"

"Hell no," I said as I shook my head. "I never stopped wanting you. I couldn't believe it when you showed up in my bar. It was Christmas and my birthday all rolled up in one. But the last time we did something, you said you needed time to think and I don't want you to be rushed into this then regret it. Believe me, when I say it's hard as hell not to just throw you down right now and have all of you."

"Do it," she breathed as she stripped off her tank top and squirmed out of the panties that she'd worn to bed. "I want to forget all of this, but more than that I've wanted you for so long. Since that first night I saw you in the bar." She reached up and touched my face. "I want this."

"Look, I don't have any condoms," I said with a groan.

"I've never been with anyone else except you and Brian and I never trusted him ever. So we always used a condom."

"I've never been with a woman without a condom."

"Good. I've just had my period, so there's no chance of me getting pregnant." Even before she finished speaking her bra came off.

I was stunned by all of her naked gorgeousness. There was only one word to describe her. Beautiful. She ran a hand over her creamy, full breasts that begged to be kissed and licked. Her thighs were curvy and I loved the way they parted for me as she reached out and took my hand. She guided my palm to her breast and inhaled when I traced a finger over her nipple.

"I want you," she reiterated. "I do. So, don't hold back. I'm tired of not getting what I want."

"Whatever you want," I said, but it sounded more like a growl.

Jo shuddered in response.

I wasted no time at all getting out of the black boxers that I'd worn to bed before I climbed on top of her. My lips crashed against hers, desperate and hungry as I drowned in the taste of her. Her body pressed up against mine, her pebbled nipples shoved against my chest as her tongue teased my lips.

I let her tongue inside of my mouth and caressed it with my own. My teeth sought out her bottom lip and I tugged it out as she moaned and wrapped her legs around me.

Jo was on fire, her skin felt hot as she rubbed herself against me desperately. "More," she moaned when I released her lips. "Give me more, Cooper."

I nodded, too engrossed in her body to reply back with coherent words. My lips traveled over her chin and left a string of kisses to her throat. There, I stopped and took my time, licking and nipping until she cried out from underneath me. By the time I shifted to put my cock inside of her, I wanted her to be drenched and ready to take every inch of me.

My lips moved downward and I covered her collarbone with kisses before I moved down to her chest and buried myself within those glorious breasts. I grabbed one and groaned as I opened my mouth and sucked her pink nipple inside. She tensed, her back arched and I rewarded her by flicking my tongue back and forth over her intoxicatingly erect nipple. I wavered between slow, torturous, and fast. I raked my teeth against her nipple and she cried out my name before I did the same to the other one.

"Fuck, you taste so fucking good," I growled.

I couldn't get enough of her. My head spun as I came up for air and released her nipple. I blew a soft breath on both of them and grinned when she shuddered in response. My mouth continued its journey south, lavishing her soft belly with attention before I pushed her thighs apart and sighed at the prize.

She was already dripping wet. I ran a finger down her slit and collected her slick juices on my finger. I held it up and lapped at it moaning at how sweet she tasted.

She watched me the whole time, her teeth buried in her lip as she ran fingers over her nipples and tugged on them.

"And you look amazing," I breathed up at her. "I can't take my eyes off of how beautiful you are."

Jo groaned. "You're not supposed to say things like that."

"Why not? It's true," I said as I rubbed her clit with my finger.

"Oh God," she groaned and tossed back her head. "Cooper," she panted. "Fuck me, please."

"Not yet." I wasn't quite done with her just yet. I intended to make her forget every fear she had, every thought of the bastard that decided to hunt her down like an animal. I wanted to take her worries and fears and get rid of them, even if it was just for a little while.

My fingers opened her up and I dove between her shapely thighs. Her juices touched my tongue and I reveled in how good she tasted. I lapped at her, eager and turned on. My hand wrapped around my own cock and I tried to quiet it as I flicked my tongue over her clit and heard her suck in a sharp breath.

"Cooper," she moaned.

Yes, keep moaning my name. That was the only name I wanted on her tongue. I wanted to be the one to give her unlimited comfort, pleasure and love. That was my one and only goal with when it came to Jo. I wanted to make her happy.

I pushed her thighs apart as she tried to close them because of the overwhelming pleasure she felt. However, I couldn't let her get away so easily. I pushed two fingers inside of her and wiggled them until I found her G spot. I swear it quivered at my touch as I stroked it softly and pressed until her mouth fell open in an amazed gasp.

Jo was teetering on the very edge, but I wasn't ready to let her go just yet. Instead, I sucked in her entire clit. She screamed, the sound loud in the quiet room except for my slurping noises.

She ground down against my mouth obviously needing and wanting more of what I could give her. I released her swollen pussy and pushed three fingers inside her. Her body arched off the bed and worked them back and forth while I gently sucked at her clit. Her legs trembled and she moaned long and loud as the first orgasm washed over her. I felt the way she clamped down around my digits and watched as she came once, then again.

She stared at me in wonder as if she had never experienced a multiple orgasm before.

"Now, you're ready," I stated as I climbed between her legs. I gripped myself and slipped my thick cock along her slick entrance. Up and down. I knew I was bigger than most men, so I gathered up her wetness before I slowly pushed myself inside.

Her eyes widened with shock at the intrusion. "Jesus, you're so big," she cried.

"You will get used to it. Just relax."

As she relaxed, I pushed more and more of myself into her deliciously warm wet pussy. Inch by slow inch, I sank into her. When she had taken all of me inside her, I began to thrust gently. She groaned and her arms wrapped around me as I rocked back and forth.

She writhed and rolled her hips, her breathing shallow pants.

I had slept with so many women for the wrong reasons that I'd forgotten just how amazing it could really be.

"You're teasing me," she groaned. "I know you are. It feels so good, but I want all of you."

"Don't worry," I breathed, as I nipped her earlobe. "I'm going to give you all of me." Capturing her mouth, I rocked myself inside her slow and deep before I released her lips, pulled all the way back and then rammed myself into her.

She shuddered underneath me and her mouth opened. I grinned at her response. I lifted up and slammed back inside again. A gasp tore from her lips as I lifted my hips and dropped them once more. My skin slapped against hers, the wetness of her pussy making the sound even more exhilarating. Our breathing went from deep and eager to sporadic and wild. Jo's nails raked down my back and I knew it would be littered with scratch marks the next day, but I wouldn't have wanted it any other way.

Our bodies worked in unison.

She pushed back against me and whispered how much she needed me. It drove me onward and made me desperate to fill her up in every way imaginable. The pleasure climbed and climbed until I felt it in my gut. My cock twitched hard, ready to explode as she reached up and kissed me.

I reached between our bodies and rubbed her clit with my thumb. Jo immediately stopped kissing me, her mouth slack against mine as she made a little animal sound of her approval. I picked up speed stroking her insides and circling her clit as I grunted and tried to hold back for just a little while longer. Jo's hands gripped the sheets, the blanket, her pillow, anything she could find to ground herself.

"I'm gonna come," she cried. "Oh God, Cooper. Fuck, yes!" Her body tensed and she shook underneath me hard.

I had very little time to think about how beautiful she looked with her mouth open and in the throes of an orgasm as her muscles clamped around my cock, squeezing it, milking it for its seed.

I jerked and bucked and I knew I couldn't hold back anymore. Quickly, I pulled out of her velvet walls and jerked myself hard and rough. The last thing she needed was an unplanned pregnancy. We were going to have kids, lots of them, but only when she was ready.

I groaned as spurts of thick cum shot out and splattered on her belly. The whole time, she kept her eyes on me.

I held her gaze. "Fuck," I groaned when I couldn't milk another drop. I was already overly sensitive, so I moved my hand away and hissed a little. "Are you okay?" I asked Jo when I noticed the out-of-it expression on her face.

She nodded slowly. "Yeah, I'm excellent."

She slurred the words and I found that adorable. I got off the bed and vaulted into the bathroom. I quickly ran a towel under the hot water tap, wrung it out, and came back to clean her up. Her eyelids were heavy as she whispered, "Brian hadn't once cleaned me up after sex."

I hated the sound of his name on her lips, and I hated thinking of her with any other man. But I also knew that until she was able to put him out of her mind, she would automatically keep making comparisons for some time. And if they were favorable comparisons, then I was going to let it ride. "You deserve to get pampered every single time."

"Am I that good?" she teased.

"You're that special."

Jo's cheeks reddened adorably.

I ran my hand down one flushed curve before I kissed her softly. I straightened up, took the towel back and cleaned myself up too. I walked back to her room and leaned on the doorframe. "You look like you're about to pass out," I observed.

She smiled. "I do feel amazing. That was just what I needed."

"I'm happy to help," I said as I pushed myself off of the frame. "Try to go back to sleep."

She held out her hand to me. "Only if you sleep with me."

They were the words I had been waiting a lifetime for. I smiled and walked into the room. She scooted over and I climbed in behind her. My arms went around her.

She sighed contentedly. "That's better," she murmured. "Stay with me, always, Cooper."

"I'd never dream of leaving." I kissed her shoulder and laid down behind her. Her breathing calmed down almost instantly and I knew she'd fallen asleep. I tightened my grip on her and she sighed in her sleep. The heat of her body warmed me as we snuggled underneath the blanket.

Jo was damaged and scared. She reminded me of a timid deer in the woods and I didn't want to scare her off. After tonight though, maybe she was finally warming up to me. Maybe she would let me love her the way she deserved to be loved.

The next nightmare never came. After I fell asleep all wrapped up in Cooper's strong arms there had been nothing but peace and calm. It had been so long since the darkness dissipated and I was able to wake up the next morning alive and refreshed.

I didn't even move. Instead, I stared out of the window and smiled as I listened to Cooper's breathing against my ear. His arm was still slung around my stomach and I loved that. I was always trying to move Brian's hand away, but I didn't want to get away from Copper, I wanted to stay in this position until I absolutely couldn't put off ending the moment.

Of course, that was when my bladder decided it absolutely could not hold on for another second. I scowled and huffed. *You couldn't have just given me ten more minutes, could you?* I didn't want to move. What if I got up and when I came back everything had changed and the world was shitty again? I wanted to live in this fairytale for a while longer, the one where Cooper loved me, life was perfect, and I didn't have to be afraid anymore.

I gave up on the notion of staying in my wonderfully hazy warm state any longer. If I didn't get up soon, I would end the fairytale by peeing my bed. I tried to move without waking Cooper, but the minute I tried to get free, his arm wrapped around me tighter. I yelped as he yanked me back against his body and rubbed himself against my back.

"Where the hell do you think you are going?" he grumbled in that husky, deep, just-woke-up voice that was enough to make any girl drop her panties.

"I have to go to the bathroom. Let me up."

Cooper ignored me. He buried his nose into my hair and dragged it to the nape of my neck. His teeth bit me and his tongue traced patterns over my skin until I tingled from head to toe. I tried to roll away from his eager mouth, but he was faster, stronger and more determined. He pressed me to the bed and wrapped his hands around my wrists. "In a little bit," he breathed. "You can get up when I'm done with you."

I squirmed under his body and that intoxicating, lustful gaze. It spoke volumes about exactly what he wanted to do to me. My eyes flickered down his still naked body and saw the huge erection that was pointed right at me. I swallowed hard. "As much as I would love to enjoy that," I said with a pointed nod to his dick. "The only thing you're going to get is me peeing on you. Unless you like golden showers in the morning, I suggest you free me this minute."

Cooper tilted his head and laughed. "Alright, but you're coming straight back, right?"

I grinned. There was the faintest hint of a pout on his lips and I wanted to kiss him. How the hell did someone as rough and tumble as he could be, look so adorable at the same time?

It warmed my heart. "Yes," I whispered. "I'm coming right back to you. I didn't want to leave in the first place, but nature calls."

"Right. Off you go." He leaned down and captured my lips.

The kiss was so soft and tender, but it built and built until I felt as if I was melting. I spread my legs for him on instinct. I was craving his great big cock buried inside of me again. It seemed as if he had grown even bigger since our first time and I hadn't felt so deliciously full since then and damnit, I wanted it again.

"You have to pee, remember?" He grinned as he reached between my thighs and rubbed my clit. "You should do that first before we start things up again."

I groaned. "Worst. Timing. Ever. Oh, God," I moaned and grabbed his wrist. "Stop doing that or, I swear I'm going to pee all over you."

Cooper chuckled and pulled away. I watched as his hand wandered to his lips and he licked and sucked each wet digit clean. My eyes fixated on the scene before me. I was almost ready to shove him onto the bed and impale myself on him. Instead, I shook my head at my own weakness.

He smirked at me like a demon.

"Bathroom," I said, and threw myself from the bed. "Be right back."

"Don't take too long," he called after me. "I don't know how long I can wait."

I shivered. I'd missed this side of him. Don't get me wrong, I loved how he could be soft and sweet, but seeing the crazy, wild, domineering side made me just as happy. And it was more than that. I could trust that he wouldn't hurt me, he'd never go too far and leave me afraid and distant. That's why Cooper was different and why I wanted to ride him until I was sore and exhausted.

By the time I joined him in the bedroom, he ducked past me and went to use the bathroom himself.

He came back out with a grin on his face... like a shark about to bite its victim.

I squealed as he jumped on me, but honestly?

I wanted to be bitten.

We spent the whole morning in bed.

When we weren't having sex, we fell asleep for little power naps before we woke up and repeated it all once more. We only stopped once Cooper was drained and his mouth was sore from getting me off again and again. The man was a beast. Forget one or two rounds, he used everything in his power and every part of his body to make sure I was sated. And for once, I was not only sated, I was on cloud nine.

"Drink," he said as he nudged me with a bottle of water. "I don't know about you, but I'm dehydrated as hell."

I grabbed the bottle from him and downed it as the plastic crinkled and crushed under the force of my palm. Water slipped from my lips and dripped onto my chest. I only came up for air damn near at the bottom and realized Cooper was staring at me. I ran an arm across my lips. "What?" I asked as my face flushed.

"That was so fucking hot," he breathed. "Maybe I can go one more time."

"No." I laughed and held up my hands. "God, no! I can't take one more time. If I orgasm again, my clit will fall off and run away to safety. You stay on your side."

Cooper grinned and eased himself into bed. He opened his own bottle and drank some water down before he sighed contentedly. Reaching over, he tugged me against his side.

I chuckled as I rested my head on him.

"No regrets?" he asked softly.

I shook my head. "Surprisingly, not one. I really thought I would have some problems, but with you, it's... familiar. Like coming home, but new too. I know that doesn't make any sense..."

"It makes plenty of sense," he said as he brushed his lips against my forehead. "It's how I feel about you."

My heart hammered in my chest. How had I survived so long without Cooper by my side? I didn't feel judged, afraid, or unsure. I didn't feel insecure about my body because it was more than clear he loved me just the way I was. I just felt... happy. And in his arms, I felt utterly safe.

I reached out and took his hand. "Thank you for staying with me and making sure I'm okay. You don't know just how much it means to me."

"You're mine and I'll always protect what's mine."

I felt my heart skip a beat. I loved it when Cooper was possessive about me.

He was quiet for a minute before he ran his thumb over my hand. "You know, I've been thinking a lot since the day before."

"About?" I asked, suddenly nervous.

"Nothing bad," he said quickly and soothed the butterflies in my stomach. "I was just thinking that you should move in with me. I don't like you being here on your own and I can't stick around twenty-four-seven unfortunately, when I have to be at the bar. So, I figured you could pack a suitcase and stay at my place, at least until all of the insanity blows over." He searched my eyes anxiously. "What do you think?"

I chewed my lip. *Move in with him?* He just wanted to keep me safe from Brian. I wanted to believe that, but I knew there were deeper feelings at play. I would never forget the mistake I made of letting Brian manipulate me into allowing him to move in with me. If Cooper and I moved in together this early in the relationship, would we be setting ourselves up for disappointment?

I sat up so I could look at him. One look into his eyes and I knew he was serious. Cooper wanted me to move in with him for real. I swallowed thickly, tugged the blanket up over my naked body as if that would hide my vulnerabilities and tucked an errant hair behind my ear. "I really appreciate you offering to let me stay with you—"

"But?" Cooper asked with a wary look on his face.

"But I don't know if that's such a good idea. There's so many factors at play here and things could get messy fast."

I saw the frown on his forehead and I immediately felt bad. He was trying to do something nice for me and I was shooting him down. I almost caved and gave in, but the memory of the way my relationship with Brian had disintegrated so fast after he moved in with me was still fresh on my mind.

I didn't have a relationship with Cooper, but what we did have, the protective friendship and the amazing sex... I didn't want to see it go. I didn't want to lose the one thing going well in my life.

"I know it can," Cooper said with a nod. "Don't think I'm not taking this seriously. I've thought about it, I thought about it more last night. I think the best option for you is to stay with me, so you have someone with you all the time. I noticed you didn't have nightmares last night, and you would probably sleep better without all of the stress of looking over your shoulder."

I chewed my lip. "That would be nice. Waking up every day feeling like a zombie isn't exactly doing me any favors. I just don't want things to change between us. I don't want it to turn into another horrible situation."

Cooper picked up my hand. He kissed the back of it softly, his warm breath caressing my skin.

When he pulled back, I stared up at him a bit more relaxed, but still concerned about messing up everything that we had slowly built together.

"Things aren't going to change, Jo," Cooper said as he shook his head. "We've naturally gotten along since we were kids and I really don't think that's going to change just because we move in together. Do you?"

I chewed my bottom lip. "I don't want to think it'll change

things, but I've been wrong about things and... people in the past."

"We're different," Cooper insisted as he grabbed my chin and made me look at him. "I would never do anything to hurt you and if you wanted to stop this," he said as he gestured between the two of us, "then I'll stop whenever you're good and ready. Not that I wouldn't miss it but you get to call the shots here."

I shook my head. "How do you always know just what to say to me to calm me down? You've always done that to me."

"I don't know," he said slowly. "I never really paid attention to other people and what they wanted, but with you it's different. I want to make sure that you are happy."

My heart swelled at his words. No one had ever shown the care and concern like he did for me. Maybe it would be okay to let him in, even if it was for just a little bit. I leaned up and kissed him. "Are you sure you want to take this on? Brian's still out there and I saw something in his eyes that night that is truly scary. He hid it well, but he's evil. He really meant it when he said if he can't have me, no one will. That promise means hurting the people close to me. I didn't have any close friends back in New York, but even those few acquaintances I did have he drove away. I don't want you to get caught up in the middle of it and end up getting hurt."

Cooper climbed on top of me and pinned me to the mattress. His lips traced patterns over my cheek and down the curve of my throat. For just a moment, I forgot every worry and fear I had. When he touched me like this, it was easy to only see the good in life and ignore everything else.

"Hey," he whispered against my ear.

I reveled under the warmth of his breath. "Yeah?"

"I know you might find this hard to believe, but I can handle myself. You don't have to worry about me, okay? Just let me take care of you. Let someone else do the caring for you for a change. All you need to do is be safe and happy."

I caved at his sweet words and the weight of his strong body against mine. Maybe he was right... it was time to stop trying to do everything on my own. If he could keep me safe and I could enjoy his company then what was the point of resisting? Slowly, I smiled and shook my head. "You've always been able to talk me into the craziest things."

"Is that a yes?" Cooper grinned as he grabbed one of my breasts. "I'm going to need an actual confirmation here."

"Yes, it's a yes." I laughed. "Stop that or you're going to start things up all over again!"

"You say that..." he moaned against my nipple, "like it's a bad thing."

"You know we have to leave this bed at some point, right?"

"Five more minutes," he mumbled and flicked his tongue expertly over my nipple. "And then we'll go out and get food. Scout's honor."

F ive more minutes my ass.

I glared at the sexual but beautiful deviant as he rinsed off body wash in the shower. It was almost impossible to stay angry at him when every muscle glistened and suds graced his skin, but I had to. It was the principle of the thing.

"That was not five minutes. Are you even a Scout?"

Cooper turned around and winked at me. "Okay, I'm not a Scout, but I don't know what you're complaining about. So maybe it was an additional forty, give or take."

"Everything is sore," I groaned and dropped the glare for favor of a pout. "I swear, I can't even move."

Cooper grabbed me against his body and kissed my shoulder. "Then I'll take care of everything."

I started to protest, but damn when the man was on a mission, he was set on that mission. He used his hands to rub soap on me. Then he somehow managed to persuade me to spread my thighs while he held the shower spray inches away from my swollen clit and let the hot spray hit me there until I climaxed in a delicious, throbbing rush.

Once we were done, I yelped as he carried me to the bed and sat me down on it. He pushed me onto my back and began to dry me off. "You don't have to do all of this," I argued as my cheeks burned.

"I like doing it." Cooper grinned. "Besides, any excuse to touch you is a good one." He went off in search of his clothes.

I rolled onto my side. *He's kind of perfect.* No one had ever taken care of me the way he did. And I knew it wasn't just to get in my pants like it was with most guys. After all, he had already gotten into them multiple times and he still spoiled the hell out of me.

"Wear this one for me," Cooper said, bringing me out of my thoughts. "I think it'll look good on you."

I glanced up at the red orange dress that he held in his hand. It was a nice summer dress, a bit on the shorter side. It showed off a lot of leg and a bit of cleavage. I had loved it when I had bought it, but I hadn't worn it yet, because I was too self-conscious.

Brian had a habit of dictating what I could and could not wear, especially when we went out together. He never wanted eyes on me that weren't his. He would never say... no you can't wear this, or don't wear that. It was more like... that just makes you look like a two-dollar hooker, but go ahead and wear it if that's the look you're going for.

Cooper was completely different. He clearly wanted to show me off. He wasn't insecure like Brian.

"Okay." I smiled as I stood up and shuffled over to the dresser. "I'll wear it for you." My heart hammered in my chest at the thought of showing so much skin, but Cooper's smile made it worth it.

He placed a delicate kiss to my ear and started to get himself dressed.

I slipped into the dress and smoothed it down carefully. I took a deep breath and a leap of faith before I stood in front of my mirror and checked out the results. "Wow," I muttered. "That's a lot of skin on show."

"Wow is right, but not because of too much skin," Cooper breathed as he squeezed my arms. "But because you look so fucking beautiful. I could throw you over my shoulder, carry you to bed and eat you out all over again."

"Don't you dare," I warned. I lifted my dress and showed him how my clit was so swollen it was protruding against the material of my panties. "Look what you've done to me. My pussy is throbbing right now as it is."

"Now why would you show me that?" He took my hand and placed it on the hard bulge in his pants. "Look what you've done to me by doing that."

I grinned. "Touché."

Cooper traced his finger over the exposed skin on my chest.

I'd always been a little heavier than the average woman and I was worried about it, but not when he touched me with such reverence and called me beautiful.

I smiled at my reflection and to my surprise. I loved the person that smiled back. I raked my fingers through my hair. It had naturally curled up a bit, but I liked that too for the first time in a long time. "You know, I haven't been able to look in the mirror for a long time."

A frown touched Cooper's lips as he caressed my arm. "Why not?"

"I hated who I saw there. And then I couldn't tell who I was even looking at. I didn't recognize myself anymore. I wasn't dressing like myself. I wasn't talking like myself or even thinking like myself. I was a stranger and I let it happen to myself."

"That's not true." Cooper's grip tightened. "You lost a lot all at once and then you ran into people that decided to take and take instead of give. That's not your fault." He growled. "That's why I get so fucking pissed when I think about that coward. Anyone would be lucky to be with you, but all he wanted to do is fuck it up, and then come back to harass you. He'd better hope I never see his face."

I smiled up at him and patted his cheek. "You're so wonderful Cooper. Come on, let's go get lunch. I'm starving."

"I guess, if we're not having sex, we might as well refuel." Cooper slid his hand into mine and never let me go.

I didn't try to pull away, why would I? There was comfort in his warm, strong hand. I didn't feel like I had to look around, or feel scared and intimidated like I'd done before. If soft, cowardly Brian was going to get to me he would have to go through a hard and determined Cooper first, and I would bet money that wouldn't end well.

"Where are we going?" I asked once the truck roared to life.

"Since you're all dressed up, I was thinking that little French bistro you were talking about the other day. We'll have to leave Springston, but I have the whole day off. Mel already agreed to cover my shift. I think she just wants all of my money, and all of the bar tips."

I laughed. "You have to admit, she's a smart woman."

"One of the smartest I've ever met and that's why she scares me."

"Just a little huh? Maybe I'll tell her that you said that."

"Don't you dare," Cooper growled. "She'll never let me live it down and the last thing anyone needs, is more of Mel's shit."

I cracked up. I could already see that wicked little grin on her lips. Yeah, she would torture him for sure.

"Wipe that look off of your face," Cooper said as he poked my thigh. "If she tortures me, I'll torture you. I don't think you..." His hand shot up my dress.

At his pressing, I moaned from being overly sensitive.

"... can you handle that?" He smiled gently. "Can you?"

"No, no, you're right. I'll keep my mouth closed," I said as I pretended to zip it shut and toss the key. "I'm done!"

"Good." Cooper grinned before he held onto my thigh and gave it a squeeze. "You're lucky you're so damn cute. Mischievous, but cute."

If he complimented me anymore, I was sure my face would just permanently freeze into a grin. My cheeks were already protesting. I hadn't smiled so much for years and it felt good to be so carefree.

We pulled up to Cafe Nicolette and I let out a delighted gasp. The red brick, the twinkling lights that must look amazing at night, the garden out front and the small benches that had been placed in it, all of it was so pretty.

"I'm sure you had better back in the city," Cooper said as he took my hand.

"You know, I can't say I did. Everything was either grimy or so... so polished and modern. No one would appreciate how beautiful something so quaint and old-fashioned like this really is, and if they did they didn't show it because they would be afraid of being sneered at for not being sophisticated enough."

"I love that you do appreciate it."

Cooper led me into the restaurant and we were seated next to a large glass window with a view of a different part of the garden. Everything inside was decorated with cream and red colors. It was romantic and sweet with the soft music playing through the room.

"It's beautiful here. I seriously feel like every stressed out bone in my body is relaxed for once." Then I peered at the menu and nearly choked at the prices. "Maybe I should have looked the prices up before we came all the way out here."

Cooper pressed a finger onto my menu and pushed it down to the table. "Stop looking at the prices. I can handle it."

"Are you sure? I know I don't have enough on my bank card right now," I said as I nibbled at my thumb.

"Jo, I make a lot more than you think. Trust me, I'm comfortable and I can handle this. If I didn't think I could swing the bill, I never would have suggested this place." He smiled. "So, please relax. I might get annoyed."

I wanted to protest, but his eyes said that he was serious. A smile slowly spread across my lips. "What happens when you get annoyed?"

"I haven't thought that far ahead..." He laughed. "Don't question things I can't give you answers to."

I grinned. "That's the best time to ask them."

"Smart ass," he muttered as he flipped through the menu.

I chuckled and flipped through mine as well. If only he knew how timid I was back in New York, how much the smart ass hadn't come out in ages. My heart sped up in my chest for him and I had to shake it off before I could properly examine the menu and order my food.

"Oh, my God," I hummed. "I don't think I've had food this good in a long time. This is amazing," I said as I picked up another oyster.

"I'm surprised I actually like this stuff. I'm more of a steak and potatoes man—"

"Don't I know it," I said with a grin.

"This isn't bad though," he continued. "Maybe I need to expand my horizons a bit more. You can pick the next restaurant too."

"Really? Good, because I have an entire map planned out of all the places I want to visit around Texas and outside of it too."

Cooper grinned at me.

My cheeks went red. Yeah, I sounded like an excited little kid, but I was free for the first time in... like ever. Eventually, Brian would have to back off and I could live the life I wanted to live. I was never meant to be stuck in one place unhappy and closed off from the world.

"Jo," Cooper said softly. "I really missed the hell out of you when you were gone." He reached across and took my hand. "I hated it when I heard you left. It might not have seemed like it, but it really fucked me up for a while."

I blinked. "It did?"

He nodded. "Of course. You were my other half when you were here and I didn't appreciate it until I was in college." He sucked in a deep breath. "I want you to give me, give us, another chance. All I want to do is be with you and make you happy the way I should have done years ago."

Oh, my God. Was Cooper actually pouring his heart out to me? There was so much hope in his eyes as he gazed at me that my stomach dropped. Am I ready to be in another relationship? There was so much going on with Brian still in the picture, but I did have feelings for Cooper. A lot of feelings. Hearing him say he wanted to give it another go I was both excited and terrified all at once.

"Jo?" he prompted softly.

I glanced up at him. "Can I think about it? It's not a no, but I do need to think some things over with everything that is going on. Is that okay?"

Cooper slowly nodded. "Of course. I would never try to push you into anything. If you need time, I can wait."

I squeezed his hand. "Thank you. I appreciate you being so patient with me through all of this. I never used to be so fragile."

"You don't have to apologize," he said quickly. "I get what you're going through, at least partially and I know why you need time. I'll be okay waiting."

"Seriously..." I sighed. "Thank you." I hadn't been given time to think in my past relationship about anything. It was do or face the consequences. Now that I was with Cooper, I found it was still hard to let go of the mindset I had before to appease someone. I didn't have to do anything I wasn't comfortable with. Cooper's words just confirmed that.

"Should we order dessert?" Cooper asked.

I smiled. "Dessert sounds like heaven. Let me go to the bathroom first."

"I'll be here," he said as I stood up. "Probably ordering one of everything," he muttered.

I chuckled and shook my head. As I walked past him, I ran my hand across his shoulder. I was one seriously lucky girl. I strolled past the tables and felt eyes boring into me. As I glanced off to the left, I saw a familiar face.

Victoria. She sneered at me, her eyes narrowed as she openly stared me down.

A million thoughts went through my head, but in the end I settled for ignoring her and popped into the restroom.

As soon as I walked out of the stall, I bumped into someone. "Oh, sorry about that. I wasn't—"

"You need to back the fuck off."

I stared at Victoria in astonishment. Had she really followed me to the bathroom? Were we in middle school? I brushed past her to the sink and turned on the water. "I don't want to do this," I sighed. "Can we just... not?"

Victoria scoffed. "You have a lot of nerve asking anything from me when you're trying to steal what's not yours."

I rolled my eyes. "What are you talking about?"

"You know what I'm talking about, bitch. Cooper. We've been working on getting back together for a while now, and suddenly you pop up and try to ruin it for us. You have no idea what you're getting in the middle of, so you need to back off and crawl back to whatever rock in New York you were living under."

I'd been quiet for so long, just letting people push me around and have their way. I wasn't going to do it with her. I turned off the water, yanked down some paper towels, and dried my hands. "From what I've heard..." I tossed the paper into the trash, "... Cooper wants nothing to do with you. I know you two had a bit of a past, basically you jumped him when he was feeling lonely and very drunk, but he's sober now. Don't you think it's time *you* let it go?"

Victoria's eyes narrowed and she folded her arms across her chest. "You have no idea what you're talking about. Cooper and I have been secretly sleeping together this whole time. Why the hell would I go to his bar and hang around him like that if we weren't? I'm not some desperate groupie," she said as she flipped her hair.

I pressed my lips together. I wanted to slap her, but I also didn't want to go to jail for someone like her. Could it be true? Cooper wouldn't still be sleeping with her and then climb into bed with me, right?

There was no way. No way in hell. Cooper wouldn't do that to me. I sucked in a breath. We weren't together formally. It wasn't like he couldn't sleep with anyone else if he wanted to. I couldn't even rightfully get angry about it.

Despite the logical part of my brain, the insecurities reared their ugly head again. What if it was true? If he were sleeping with Victoria after he told me that he wasn't, I wouldn't be with him. I wouldn't even consider the possibility. We would barely even be friends if he had lied to me. "Why should I believe you?" I asked her, not letting the doubt show on my face.

Victoria's lips curved into a grin. "You know Cooper. Let's be real, he's never been the settling down type."

"So, what's your point?" I scoffed.

"My point is that if he didn't settle down for you years ago, what makes you think he's going to do it now? I mean honestly, grow up. You had your chance already and he's clearly not into you that much if he's still coming over my place once the bar closes. So, I'm going to warn you one more time. Stay the hell away from what's mine and you won't get hurt." Victoria turned on her heels and stalked out of the bathroom.

As soon as she was gone, I leaned against the sink and my shoulders sagged. The fluttering feeling that had been in my stomach all day died. I tightened my fists and felt my nails sink into my palms.

"Breathe. Breathe," I muttered to myself as I took a steady breath.

I quickly turned and splashed some water on my face. The

cold woke me and took down some of the heat in my cheeks. When I felt like I could handle it, I slipped out of the bathroom.

Victoria's eyes followed me as I walked back to my table and sat down.

"There you are. For a minute, I thought I was going to have to come find you myself. They brought dessert. What's wrong?"

I stared down at the table until I collected myself as much as possible and glanced up at Cooper.

His fork hovered mid-air, a frown on his lips as he searched my face.

I refused to let Victoria see me cry, so instead I held my head up and confronted the situation directly, "Are you fucking Victoria?"

Chapter Thirty-Two

"**W**hat?" Cooper asked as his mouth gaped open.

"You heard me. Are. You. Fucking. Victoria? Don't even think about lying to me, because I swear I can't take one more lie out of one more person's mouth. If you're not going to be truthful and open, you might as well take me home now and leave me alone. I can't stand another moment of unnecessary pain."

"What?" he repeated looking entirely lost.

"You heard me," I said quietly.

"I don't understand what you're going on about? Why would you suddenly think that I'm sleeping with someone? We've been fine since last night and all of a sudden, you spring this on me? It's more than a little bizarre and not only that, it's incredibly insulting. When have I lied to you since you've been back? Every time you ask me something, I'm upfront even when you don't want to hear it. I don't understand why you would think I was even capable of hiding something like that from you."

"I noticed that you still haven't answered my question," I said as I crossed my arms in front of my chest. "All of those pretty words mean nothing if you can't be straight with me. Are you sleeping with Victoria? Yes or no? It's a simple question."

"It's a bullshit question," Cooper muttered. "We both know, I'm not."

"I don't know that," I snapped back at him. "For all I know, you could be doing anything with anyone. It's not like I'm around after you drop me off home at night to monitor your every move."

"What do you want from me? Do you want me to prove it somehow? Here," he said as he dug into his pants. "Here's my phone. Go through all of the calls, the texts, go through my social media for all I care. You'll find a lot of messages from women, but you'll see I haven't responded to anyone other than you, Mel, Cindy and my mom. I don't have a need to talk to every woman that approaches me and that goes double for sleeping with them. I'm over all of that."

I stared at the phone in his extended hand. It would be easy to put my fears to rest by invading his privacy and making us both feel like shit. However, that wasn't the way I wanted things to be with us. If we were going to have anything beyond a friendship, we needed to trust each other implicitly. "I don't want your phone," I said quietly. "That would just make me feel like some kind of skeevy, asshole."

"So, what is it going to take for you to believe me?"

"I don't know," I muttered. "I wish I had an easy answer, but I don't."

"Jo, I thought we were already past this. I explained at work that I wasn't seeing Victoria anymore. It was a fucking one night fling and she went all bunny boiler on me. Hell, she calls up my mom and invites herself to lunch, but as soon as I find out she's coming, I cancel. I haven't hung out with her since that night. Not even as friends. I know she's obsessed with me, but there's nothing I can do about it. I certainly don't encourage it."

"That's not what she told me," I said, but even as I said it, I realized I believed Cooper more than I did Victoria. There was sincerity in his voice. Why would he offer me his phone if he had something to hide? Suddenly, I felt like a fool. Cooper had been nothing but good to me since I arrived and this is how I repaid him, by believing a known liar over him? I took a deep breath. I had to explain to Cooper why I brought this up, "She told me that you're still sleeping together. Apparently, you go over there whenever the bar closes, but I don't believe her. I believe you. I'm sorry I ever doubted you."

Cooper groaned. "The woman is a complete psycho and she's clearly jealous of the fact that I've been spending so much time around you." He shook his head. "How did you even talk to her that fast? Did she text you or something?"

I shook my head and nodded in her direction. "No, she's right there with a friend of hers."

Cooper turned and glanced at Victoria.

The woman wiggled her fingers and winked back at him.

My blood boiled and I wanted to slam her head into the table. I blinked. That was violent. *What was happening to me?*

I glanced up when Cooper shifted in his chair. He yanked out his wallet and flagged down our waitress before paying for the bill and telling her to keep the change. He took my arm and lifted me to my feet before he took my hand.

"We're just leaving?" I asked as I raised a brow. "This doesn't exactly make me feel confident you're telling the truth."

"Be quiet," Cooper said as he shook his head. "You'll see what's going on."

I pressed my lips together and let him drag me over to Victoria's table. As soon as we stood near it, my heart began to race.

Cooper squeezed my hand tight.

Victoria's eyes flickered down to our joined hands before she narrowed her eyes. "Cooper," she drawled. "How good to see you, darling. I didn't know you were here."

"Why are you lying?" Cooper snapped. "That's all you've been doing over the years and I'm fucking sick of it. You have no right to interfere in my love life and get the woman I love all upset over a bunch of lies and bullshit. We both know I dumped your ass a long time ago and I've never called you back, responded to a single text, message, or one of your ridiculous surprise pop ups at my work. I don't want anything to do with you, Victoria. Don't come around to the bar. Don't say hello if you see me somewhere. Don't try to make any kind of contact. Do you understand me?"

Victoria pursed her lips. "Y-you don't have to put on this front for her—"

"Stop it!" Cooper thundered and all eyes in the place flew to him. "If you don't stop right now, I'm going to go to the police and file a report. I told you ages ago that I'm not attracted to you like that and you still won't give up. Enough is enough. Don't come near me, or Ivy again. You got that?"

Victoria nodded slowly as tears filled her eyes. Finally, it seemed she had got the message.

Normally I'd feel horrible, but what she was doing was shitty not just to me, but to Cooper as well. He'd clearly made himself transparent to her ages ago and she still refused to see the truth. That was on her.

"Yes," she stated quietly.

Cooper sighed. "I really never wanted it to get to this point. We were friends once, and I hate to lose a friend, but you can't disrespect Ivy. Period. Maybe one day, we can all get over this and move on, but until then, just give us some space, okay?"

"Is there a problem over here?" a man asked.

I stiffened. Great, we're going to get kicked out and never be able to come back. I peered from around Cooper's back.

He dug into his wallet and passed the man some money discreetly. "Sorry to interrupt the other guests, that's not how my mama raised me. We just had to get something sorted out, and it's taken care of now. We loved the food by the way, especially my girlfriend."

I waved at the man, too dumbfounded to do anything else.

He looked me up and down and the snooty look was replaced with a soft smile. The man shook Cooper's hand. "Happy to have you and we'd love to have you both again, so long as the shouting stays outside."

"Of course." Cooper laughed. "We're usually better behaved."

When we could go, I breathed a deep sigh of relief. At least, we weren't going to be banned from the restaurant and Victoria had been put in her place. I thought about Cooper saying that I was the woman he loved and my heart fluttered.

We were quiet, until we reached the truck and Cooper pushed me up against it. "I don't feel anything for Victoria, do you believe me now?"

I nodded quickly. "Yeah, I do. I was pretty sure you didn't, but what she said got to me and I started to doubt you and then I just, I don't know, freaked out a little that everything was going to be the way it was before and—"

"I love you, Jo. I always have and I always will. If there's one thing you need to know about me it's that I don't want anyone but you. I don't care what we go through, what bull-shit crops up, none of that shit matters. The only thing that matters to me is you."

I nodded again, my eyes watery and my mouth pulled into a smile. I had been so upset about the situation, but seeing Cooper stand up for me changed that. Now, I knew for sure that he put me before anyone else and maybe, I needed that until I fully healed from what Brian had put me through. "Cooper," I breathed. "I'm really sorry I didn't believe you."

He cradled my cheeks in his warm hands. "You don't have to apologize to me. I have a lot of making up to do for the choices I made when I was younger and a whole lot dumber... Look at me."

I glanced up at him and tried to stop myself from crying. Why was I so emotional? Ever since I arrived back home, I'd been a train wreck of emotions. I'd learned to shut my emotions down while I was in New York, but something about Cooper brought them all back to life full force.

He wiped at my cheeks softly before he kissed each one gently as if I would break apart in his strong hands. "I want us to do this again, for real this time. You and I. And I don't want anything to get in the way. What do you say, do you think you want to go out with me again? Do you want to be my girlfriend?"

My head moved on its own volition as I nodded and happily accepted it before I could actually speak again. My voice caught in my throat and I fought through tears to give him a real answer, "Yes." I laughed softly. "Sorry, I'm really a mess, but I mean it. I want to be with you even if I'm all broken and damaged."

"I don't need you to be perfect, baby," he smiled as he kissed my hand. "All I need is you."

Cooper kissed me and I forgot the rest of the world existed. Every time his mouth pressed against mine he erased years of loneliness, damage and suffering. It was such an easy thing with him. And even though I had been livid just moments ago in that restaurant – thinking he was sleeping with someone else – it was just as easily forgotten.

Cooper had changed. It was apparent in everything he not only said, but the actions he took. He was the kind of man I could love and the one I had fallen for all those years ago.

I'm going to take a chance on him.

I couldn't do it if it were anyone else, but for Cooper? Yeah, I'd give him the opportunity to show me that this was real.

Chapter Thirty-Three

IVY

We barely made it through my door. The both of us were so desperate for each other. We were kissing, touching and fumbling with our clothes that we almost forgot to close and lock the damn door after us. Cooper reached back with his foot and slammed the door closed. I leaned against him, on my toes, as I kissed him wildly and he fought with the lock.

Click.

That was the sound of salvation. I was ready to rip off every shred of his clothing and feel those strong, calloused hands all over my body. I ached for it so hard it felt like I would die if I couldn't get to him right away.

"Bedroom?" Cooper breathed between pants and me tugging his bottom lip between my teeth.

"No time," I groaned as he yanked the dress off of me and threw it aside. "Couch. Go there. Sit."

Cooper plopped down on the couch and kicked off his shoes

and pants while I watched him get naked. I'd already taken off his shirt. When he was stark naked, I admired every line of his body. The man was built like a god with muscles and tanned skin that begged to be bitten, licked and caressed.

I ran my tongue over my lip as I stared at him in satisfaction. Cooper was a damn good looking man. When you matched that with his amazing personality, who wouldn't want to climb into his lap and ride him off into the sunset?

There was a light spattering of golden hair on his chest, neat but manly and I was glad for it because I loved having something to run my fingers over. His broad chest dipped into tight abs and there was a line of hair from his belly button down to his groin. I imagined licking his skin and following that trail to the thick prize that waited at the end.

Cooper grinned at me. "Are you going to stand there staring all day, or are you going to come over here and show me what a good little cowgirl you can be?"

"I could stare all day," I breathed. "You look like you should be on the cover of a magazine somewhere, not sitting on my couch."

"But I am sitting on your couch," he drawled.

"Lucky me," I purred as I reached up and released my bra. I flung it away as I walked up to him.

His enraptured eyes followed my every move.

I slid my panties down my thighs and kicked them away.

"Holy hell," Cooper muttered. "I'm never going to get tired of seeing you naked. I turn into an overly excited teenage boy every single time. You're fucking breathtaking." He reached out for me.

I pulled away. I held out a hand and shook my finger at him. "Uh...uh. You sit back and relax. I have something for you."

"Oh?" Cooper asked as he arched a thick brow. "And what is that?"

"You'll see," I said as I tossed a mischievous grin in his direction.

"I like the sound of that already."

I walked into my bedroom and gathered what I needed. When I came back, I dumped the condoms I had bought onto the couch. Cooper immediately went for one, but I smacked his hand.

"Those aren't for right now. I told you, I have something for you. Now, be patient, or I'm going to change my mind."

Cooper leaned back and licked his lips. He ran his hand up and down his impressively thick, hard shaft. "I like this side of you," he breathed deep and husky as he gazed into my eyes. "This dominant, take control thing is really hot on you."

I beamed at him. He had no idea how much it took to get me back to this point. I couldn't remember the last time I had been assertive, but it felt so damn liberating. He really had brought me back to life. Cooper had saved me. "I'm glad you like it," I said as I tossed a pillow onto the floor.

"Now what is the pillow about?" Cooper asked.

I ignored him. The man was amazing, but he was definitely still a man, impatient and eager to begin. Instead, I slowly sank down onto the pillow and my knees were protected from the carpet and the hard floor underneath. I wanted to be in that position for some time and I didn't want to kill my knees and have to interrupt the fun.

My hands started at his calves and I ran them up until I brushed over his knees and encountered his lean thighs. Even they were muscled, strong from the hard work he put in at the bar. I gave them a squeeze, feeling and exploring them as my eyes followed each twitch and flex of his body against my palms.

Slowly, my fingers traveled upward as I admired the satiny texture of his skin and the heat that radiated from his groin. I leaned forward and flicked my tongue against his pre-cum stained cock. I was rewarded with a shuddery gasp. My eyes flickered up and he regarded me with his heated gaze as if he was ready to throw me down and fuck me right then and there. I grinned up at him and lowered my eyes once more.

My hand wrapped around his cock and I squeezed it gently before I slipped my hand up to the crown and lathered him with his own pre-cum. I worked my hand up and down his throbbing shaft and he went from mostly hard to completely rock hard and ready to go, but I still wasn't quite ready.

I lapped at his flesh and Cooper muttered something incomprehensible as he jutted his hips out toward me for more. I traced the crevices of his inner thighs and watched shockwaves ripple along his skin as his length bounced against my mouth. Slowly, I opened my lips wider and accepted him. The head of his cock was warm and only slightly salty from his juices. I moaned at the delicious taste of him.

Cooper groaned and when I glanced up, he stared back at me

with his mouth slightly agape and his fingers looking for purchase. I grinned and took it as a good sign. With one hand, I encased his cock with my palm and with the other I fondled his balls, massaging and lavishing them with my tongue before I traced a path back up to his dick.

"Jo," he groaned and bucked his lips further into my mouth. "What the...Shit! What the hell are you doing?" He hissed.

"Enjoying you," I said shortly so I didn't break up the fun. "Really, *really* enjoying you." My tongue flattened as I licked the underside of him before I popped him back into my eager mouth. I twisted and bobbed my head as moans spilled from my lips and vibrated up his shaft.

Cooper leaned back, his head tilted as he panted and shivered under my tongue.

I took in more of him, inch after inch that stretched my mouth and left me nearly breathless.

"Oh fuck," Cooper spat as he lifted his hips from the couch and I breathed through my nose. "Fuck, Jo. I love this so fucking much. Your mouth is perfect. This is insane."

I grinned at each thing that fell from his mouth. It was like he couldn't stop himself and I loved each word that I heard. I slowly came off of his cock for air and he gasped. Apparently, I'd drooled a little and quickly wiped it away. When I glanced back up, Cooper had ripped open a condom and was furiously rolling one onto his length.

"What are you doing?" I laughed. "I wasn't done yet."

"I am," he countered.

Before I could protest, he scooped me up and wrangled me

onto his lap. I straddled him and felt his heat as I rubbed myself against his sheathed cock. Back and forth, I worked my hips making him even slicker with my wetness.

Cooper reached underneath me and rubbed my clit until I had to hold onto his shoulders to keep from falling off and onto the floor. "Cooper," I groaned as I squirmed against him. "No more. I can't—I can't take anymore or I'm going to—"

Cooper picked up speed and I threw my head back as I spasmed against him. My body rocked on its own, looking for more and more pleasure as he got me off with his hand. By the time the world made sense again, I was already grabbing him and I lifted myself a bit to slide him inside.

"Shit," he hissed. "You feel so good."

He was breathless and so was I. As he sank inside of me slowly, I felt myself open up for him bit by bit until I slid down his shaft and he was firmly inside me again. His cock twitched and I groaned as I shook my head and tried to remind myself to calm down a bit.

"You look amazing," Cooper mumbled as he leaned forward and kissed my chest. He lifted his head and pulled me down to him. "I can't believe I get to do this with you again and again."

I moaned and kissed him back just as hard and fast as he kissed me. Our lips fit so perfectly together. We pulled back, but only a little bit so we could still hold onto each other tightly. I raised my hips and lowered them a few times. Each movement made Cooper moan my name and I had to admit I could really get used to this.

Cooper sucked one of my breasts into his mouth and made my nipples get even harder. He sucked one after the other before his tongue flicked over them roughly. Just the nipple stimulation was almost enough to get me off alone, but I wanted a big one, one huge, ridiculous orgasm that would probably knock me unconscious.

I moved faster as I rode Cooper harder. He grabbed my ass and squeezed it while he lifted me up and down helping me so we could pick up the momentum. The wet sounds of our skin slapping together egged both of us on until we were whipped up into a wild frenzy.

Cooper lifted me up and turned me around until my back was pressed onto the couch.

I didn't even protest about having to give up being in control. Every muscle in my body ached and my legs refused to stop trembling.

"Look at you," he growled as he plunged himself deep and lifted his hips up to do it all over again. "You're amazing and you're all mine. I can't fucking believe it."

I caressed his cheek. "I can't believe it either," I breathed. "I never thought we'd end up together again, but I love it." I wrapped my arms around his neck and held on tightly. Cooper's hips lifted and fell over and over again until I knew it wouldn't be much longer before I couldn't take another minute of the intense pleasure and my eyes started to roll back.

Cooper kissed me from my lips, to my forehead and finally my throat. He licked there, tracing over a very sensitive spot before he nipped me roughly.

I cried out and held him tighter but my head began to shake back and forth. "I'm so close. I'm so close," I whispered. "Oh God I can't take it anymore, but I don't want this to stop."

"Then let go," Cooper whispered to me. "Let go and enjoy it."

So, I did.

My back arched and my breasts pushed against his chest. Every muscle in my body clenched and I tightened around Cooper.

He thrust a few more times before I felt his body stiffen then he groaned low, deep and primal before he completely collapsed on top of me. "Hold on," Cooper whispered.

"Hmm?" I was too out of it to focus on a word he said. When he slipped out of me, I cried out and instantly missed his big, throbbing cock deep inside me.

He carried me back to the bedroom and laid me on the bed.

I did feel grateful for how comfortable it was.

"I didn't want to move you, but that couch is kind of small to fit both of us," he explained, slightly out of breath. "Be right back."

I nodded and watched as he disappeared.

When he came back, he had water for the both of us and he climbed back into bed with me.

I immediately scooted closer to him and rested my palm on his chest.

Cooper sighed and kissed the top of my head. "That was

amazing," he breathed. "I can't believe how good it feels every time. You're something special, you know?"

I grinned up at him. "So are you. I loved watching you get all worked up."

"You mean you like to rile me up and see what happens for fun."

I chuckled. "Okay, okay you're right about that. I couldn't pass up the chance to get to you and, oh my God the way you moan and squirm while I was playing you? It was amazing and sooo hot."

Cooper shook his head. "Yeah, I don't see how anyone couldn't immediately see that we're meant to be together."

"Agreed," I hummed happily. "Would it be completely ridiculous of me to take a nap now?" I yawned and stretched myself. "And I could really use a massage too."

"I'll give you all the massages you want," Cooper said with a wolfish grin. "And no, I don't think it's such a bad idea. I mean, we have had a pretty eventful day, and I think I could use a little rest myself."

"Nap it is," I mumbled before snuggling against Cooper.

"And when we wake up, we can finally get everything together and be ready to go. I want to make sure we have you safe and secure at my place before it gets dark."

I smiled up at him. "You're so protective of me. Yeah, let's pack everything up and get it ready to move after we rest."

"Sounds like a plan." Cooper kissed me again.

I reveled in it. Every new hug and touch just made me feel

more loved by him. I could stay like this with him forever. I'd finally found someone that made me happy and I wasn't afraid to be myself around him. As I dozed off, I knew with absolute certainty that I had made the right decisions, especially when it came to Cooper. And I knew something else that couldn't be denied.

I was in love with Cooper.

Who was I kidding?

I had never stopped being in love with him

~

*P*acking up was made easier by the fact that Cooper hauled my things like they weighed nothing at all. I only packed the essentials I needed, but that still resulted in several bags to be taken with us over to his place.

"I can't believe I haven't seen your house yet," I mused as I handed him the last of my things tucked away into a bag while I shouldered a backpack.

"Well, I would have invited you over a lot sooner, but I wanted to give you some time to adjust to moving here and everything. I always planned on having you over sooner rather than later."

I bounced on my heels as he loaded the last of my things and we climbed into the truck. "What does it look like?"

"Why would I tell you when I can just show you? We'll be there soon enough."

"How long is soon?" I asked as I raised a brow.

"Trust me, we don't have very far to go at all. I specifically chose a place that was close to the park, a few restaurants and of course the bar, so just sit back and relax a little."

I groaned. "I hope all the suspense is worth it," I teased dramatically.

"Oh," Cooper grinned. "Trust me, it'll be worth it."

God, he's so adorable. The soft smile on his lips warmed my heart, so I calmed down and let him drive. No matter what his place looked like, it didn't matter to me. I just wanted to be with him.

Chapter Thirty-Four

IVY

"This is your place?"

Cooper burst out laughing. "How many times are you going to ask me that? Can you actually move instead of standing there staring? We need to get your things unpacked."

"There's no way this is your place," I muttered. "This is like one of those places you go on your phone to rent, so you can impress someone."

"Do you really think I have time for that?" Cooper asked as he arched an incredulous brow in my direction. "I barely have time to sleep or relax, working at the bar so much."

Cooper nudged me, but I was still in awe. His house was like something out of a dream of mine. It was one of those marvelous Texas houses, like something on the front cover a novel where you would see the heroine clinging to the hero dewy eyed and in love. Yeah, it was that insanely awesome.

The impressive building was two floors and huge and

painted a soft yellow. Large white columns supported the front of the structure with white balustrades. There was a balcony with the same stone balustrades on the first floor. Tall ceiling to floor windows covered the front and sides and I felt positive in the daylight the inside must glow with warm light.

"Jo," Cooper said as he stopped and pushed keys into my hand. "If you're going to stare, can you at least get the door for me. You have a lot of stuff here."

"I didn't know what to leave behind," I excused with a laugh.

"I can see that. Go ahead, I'll carry everything in."

I nodded and nearly jogged up the flagstone path to the front door. The key went in and my heart fluttered. *Click*. I pushed the door open and I was inside. The first thing I wanted to do was explore like an eager child, but then I remembered the fact that Cooper still had all of my things and I didn't want to leave him on his own. "Here, I'll help you with that," I said as I reached out for a bag.

Cooper shook his head. "No, no, I've got it. Why don't you check out the rest of the place?"

"Are you sure?"

"If you were any more excited you'd piddle on the rug like a puppy. Go on. By the time you're done, I should have everything put away upstairs. We can unpack everything after we eat dinner and have some beer."

I clutched my chest. "A man after my own heart," I purred. "Alright, just one little look around. If you need anything, just holler for me."

"I think I can manage," Cooper said as he winked and slapped my butt when I turned around.

I yelped and shook my head at him before I slowly made my way out of the entrance hallway. Right away, I fell in love with all of the real wood. No artificial crap or pressed wood bull-shit. It shone too, recently cleaned and polished and gorgeous.

"You clean this beast by yourself?" I asked Cooper.

"Are you kidding? I have someone who comes through three times a week for a deep cleaning." He walked up and wrapped an arm around my waist.

"Why did you get something so big when it's just you?"

Cooper smiled. "I thought one day I would want a family and if I had one, I would want them here. I fell in love with this view the moment I saw it and there was no going back. I know it's kinda ridiculous for a bachelor pad, but this place spoke to me and I couldn't ignore it."

"It is breathtaking," I whispered in awe.

"Go look at the rest of it." Cooper planted a kiss on my cheek before he walked ahead of me and up the stairs.

I didn't want to go up yet, instead I wandered the first floor. I'd expected warm light during the day, but even at night there was a softness that glowed. I dipped my head into the living room with its huge TV, comfy couches, and working fireplace. I found a sun room with amazing windows that would let in nothing but heat during the day. In summer, I couldn't imagine wanting to be out there, but with the cool nights and pleasant days it would be amazing.

The dining room was massive, and I could see entertaining guests around the long table and underneath that grand chandelier. The kitchen was even better. Creams and yellows were the dominating colors. It just seemed so homey and summery. I also found a large laundry room off of the kitchen and a breakfast nook tucked away in the corner.

I stared out of the back window in amazement. I could see a nice sized pool and what I could only assume was a hot tub built into the side of it. A barbecue grill and patio furniture were set up as well and I couldn't stop seeing myself standing there with Cooper in the summer while our friends enjoyed themselves.

Upstairs was even better. There were several smaller guest rooms and an office where Cooper kept track of everything that happened at the bar. After the study was the most magnificent room I'd ever laid eyes on. The master bedroom was huge, but even calling it that didn't really do it justice. It looked as if more than one room had been combined to make the master suite and the accompanying en-suite bathroom.

A large bed sat in the middle of the floor, a big screen TV on the wall and the colors were the same as downstairs, but with added tones of soft gray, making the whole space feel connected and down to earth. There were two walk-in closets, his and hers with a rotating shoe rack.

The bathroom boasted a large square tub that had jets and a glass shower stall that looked wide and spacious. I ran my hand over the white stones in the walls and stared, open mouthed as I walked back into Cooper's room in awe.

"What do you think?" Cooper asked as he set one of my bags on the bed. "You haven't said a word."

"I think my brain broke a long time ago," I muttered and shook my head. "I can't even believe this place is real."

"I'm really proud of it. I'm constantly improving it and expanding it bit by bit. I love it so far."

"I love it too," I breathed. "It's a lot like my dream house."

"You can always make suggestions," Cooper whispered against my ear.

I shuddered. "That sounds a lot like you want me to be around for the long haul."

"Of course I do." He grinned. "Who said I was ever going to let you go? Let's hold off on putting away everything and dinner," he whispered as his hand slipped into my clothes.

I clicked my tongue. "That sounds irresponsible."

"I'm okay with that as long as I get to have you."

I chuckled as he pulled me into a deep kiss. I could get *sooo* used to this.

Cooper's place was like paradise. The peace and quiet, the comfort of knowing he was around and the distance from all of the neighbors made it feel secluded and tucked away from the rest of the world. Going into work every day stopped being nerve-wracking and frightening and started to be enjoyable again.

Mel teased the hell out of us when she found out we were together before she beamed and secretly hugged me. "Don't tell Cooper I've stopped giving you shit. I'm going to torture him for a little while longer. I'm so happy for you, darlin'!"

I laughed so hard at her antics, but when Cooper asked me what was going on, I feigned ignorance and shrugged. Cooper glared at the two of us for the rest of the day, but I made it up to him as soon as our shift was over and I closed the door on the other two girls.

The more I was around him, the more I felt like I belonged with him. Cooper could read me in a way no one else could. As soon as I glanced over my shoulder one second too long, he was there with his arm around me and soothing words whispered in my ear.

I looked at his sleeping face and smiled. He really was everything I could ever ask for.

"If you keep staring at me when I'm asleep I'm really going to think there's something wrong with you," Cooper muttered with his eyes still closed.

I peered over the top of my pillow at him and smiled. "I was only looking a little. You look really cute when you're asleep."

"Weirdo," he grumbled before he pulled me into his arms and hugged me close. "You're supposed to be the normal one in this relationship."

I scrunched up my face. "Who told you that lie?"

Cooper chuckled and kissed my forehead before he opened his eyes.

My cheeks immediately flushed. I loved being so close to him. I could feel the warmth of his body and smell that unique aroma that could only be described as Cooper. Like cigars and fire and eternal comfort on a chilly fall night. My heart drummed in my chest and I gripped him a little tighter.

"Good morning," he whispered in that deep, husky voice that made my panties wet.

"Good morning to you too," I whispered back before I rubbed my nose against his and then laughed. "I'm really glad we don't have to work today. It's been non-stop."

"The only reason I'm not there is because you're here. Otherwise, I used to practically live at the bar."

"That's not healthy for you," I scolded. "Today, we're going to have some fun and not think about work. I was thinking we could visit the lake again. It's been a while and I'm dying for a swim."

"As usual your ideas are amazing." Cooper kissed me, then sat up and stretched. "Should we head out early then and stay all day?"

Cooper's words went in one ear and out of the other. My eyes ran down his body instead. As he stretched, every muscle rolled and dipped under his movements. I wanted to reach over and drag my tongue over his body. The man was an Adonis and I just couldn't get enough. I ran my hand down his back.

He leaned into my touch. "I keep telling you don't start things that you can't finish," he said.

I heard the smile on his lips without even seeing his face. "I don't mind finishing it at all," I purred. I shifted and crawled up to him as I littered his back with kisses.

"I thought we wanted to get to the lake early." He chuckled.

"Early-ish is good too," I muttered, concentrating on my lips as they connected with his skin over and over again.

"No," Cooper said as he stood up and grabbed my wrists. "Let's get ready to go or I'm going to have you in this bed all day and we'll never leave."

The desire on his face made my toes curl. "I'm starting to rethink this lake idea."

"Up you go!" Cooper pulled me up and with ease put me over his shoulder.

I wiggled and squirmed, but I couldn't get free.

Cooper chuckled, feeling really proud of himself apparently, as he carried me into the bathroom and finally sat me down.

"You're no fun," I pouted.

"You say that now, but you're going to love me when we're at the lake, soaking in the sun, drinking ice cold beers, swimming and fucking in the cabin until we're sore."

I contemplated his words. "That does sound amazing."

"Yes, it does. So please get in the shower before I have to drag you in there."

I laughed and stood up on my tiptoes to give him a kiss. "I'm going, I'm going."

Cooper smacked my ass as I walked by him and I yelped a little before I swiped at him. He chuckled and headed for the cabinet for towels while I adjusted the water in the shower. Once it was perfect, I slipped inside and grabbed the soap. I couldn't remember my life ever being so wonderful since I moved in with Cooper. All of the worry and fear I'd felt had been washed away like magic.

The glass door opened and Cooper walked inside in all of his naked glory.

As soon as he turned to close the door, I reached out and palmed his ass.

He jumped and turned on me with a glare. "What are you doing?"

"Grabbing your butt." I laughed.

"Don't do that." He laughed and reached for my ass instead. "That's my job."

I shook my head. "Hey, equal is equal. Besides, who could resist such a perfect ass? It's like the right amount of round and muscled, and hot as hell."

"I swear woman," he grumbled, but the smile never left his lips.

I finally gave him a break and stopped messing with him long enough to shower and get myself ready to go. I wiggled myself into a pair of jean shorts and a tank top to go with it before I slathered on some sunscreen.

Cooper walked out of his closet dressed in comfortable shorts in a red tank that matched my top.

I grinned and started rubbing sunscreen on his body.

He glanced down at me, a light smile on his lips as he let me work. "I still can't believe I got this lucky," he mused.

My cheeks reddened. "You say that all the time and my answer is still... I'm not that great."

"You're right," he said as he cupped my chin. "You're better than great. Seriously Jo, you're everything I want out of life."

I blinked up at him at a loss for words.

"Let's go swimming," Cooper said, placing a chaste kiss on my lips. "I'll grab the food, you grab whatever you need."

"Okay." I smiled and watched him turn, walking away.

Cooper deserved the world. I wanted to give it to him. He

deserved to be happy after how much he'd grown and how much he looked after me. I quickly gathered the rest of my things and we packed up the truck. Hitting the road, seeing our little town roll by, stirred excitement in my belly. I could definitely get used to this life.

Cooper's hand sneaked into mine and we squeezed each other. I loved having this comfort and knowing he was close. Just a squeeze of the hand and even if the smallest doubts cropped up, they were instantly swept away.

The lake came into view and I smiled as the sun sparkled off of it. Even from a distance, the water begged to be swam in. I bounced up and down in my seat unable to contain myself.

"I'm guessing swimming is the first thing we're going to do."

I beamed at Cooper. "You're right about that."

He chuckled. "I'll put away the food. Why don't you get changed and go for a dip?"

"Are you sure? I can help you."

We pulled to a stop in front of the cabin.

Cooper pulled me forward and kissed my lips deeply.

I melted into him.

"Go on and swim," he whispered as he rubbed his lips along mine. "I'll be there in just a few minutes."

"See you there." I gave him one last kiss then grabbed my bag and jogged toward the cabin. Within minutes, I was stripped out of my clothes and had slipped into the black and white polka dot bikini I'd bought a few days ago. I walked out of the bedroom.

Cooper whistled long and low. "You look sexy as hell," he muttered as he walked over and ran a finger underneath the fabric of my bikini. "I've changed my mind. Let's go swimming later."

My cheeks burned from his admiration as I slapped his hand away. "No way! You told me to behave earlier and now, I'm telling you to behave. Once I get done swimming, we can discuss it."

Cooper pouted like a little boy. "Fine, but I'm going to be hard as hell the whole time watching you in your itsy bitsy bikini." He kissed my forehead. "If I swim with this heavy thing," he grabbed his erection, "I might sink."

I burst out laughing. "I'm sure you'll be fine. See you at the water." I turned on my heels and walked away while feeling his eyes on me the entire time. It was powerful, this feeling of knowing he wanted me so much, but also knowing he would wait.

If it were with Brian, he would have torn me down, ripped me apart until I felt small and somehow pushed me into the thing even if I didn't really want to do it. Cooper was nothing like that. He let me be me and I thrived because of it.

The lake was cool when I dove into it. I treaded water and smiled. It was so wholesome, being back at the lake in my hometown. I didn't realize just how much I had missed it. I swam until my arms were sore and my legs burned.

When I stepped out, Cooper made his way over and wrapped me up in a towel. He rubbed it against my skin and led me over to a thick blanket he'd laid out on the ground. "Beer?" he asked.

"Yes, please." I smiled. "I could really go for one after that."

"Yeah, you swam hard," he agreed, as he pushed hair out of my face. "Are you okay?"

I nodded. "I just felt like pushing it today."

"Since you're all warmed up, do you want to go over some of the moves that I taught you?"

Slowly, I nodded. I didn't want to think about the past or Brian, but he crept in at every chance. My pleasant swim had turned dark and dangerous and it was why my body felt like a noodle. Cooper had decided to teach me how to defend myself in case I was ever face to face with that bastard again. So when I was all wound up and worried, he would push me to practice. It sucked some off the energy out of me and made me calm down, so I wasn't drowning in panic.

"Arms up," he said and nodded at me as he pulled off the towel and tossed it onto the blanket behind us.

I shivered for only a moment before the sun started to warm my skin. I put my hands up, ready for him to tell me what to do next. Every muscle in my body was tense, ready to strike as I imagined taking down someone.

"Hammer strike," Cooper called grabbing my attention.

I balled up my fist and aimed for his face. Cooper caught my hand, of course, but the fact that I had been so close to striking him made me proud. I moved back and tried it a few more times before he changed instructions. Hell palm strike, getting out of a headlock, escaping if my hands were trapped. We ran through the gambit of self-defense moves until I was panting and sweat was dripping down my body.

"You're getting a lot better at this," Cooper said as he ran a hand down my arm. "I think you're almost ready to take care of yourself without me now. It's really important that you can protect yourself if I'm not around."

"Thanks for teaching me," I said as I drank down some water first, then happily took the beer he offered me. Exhausted, but feeling good about myself, I settled onto the blanket. It was so quiet and I loved the stillness. I cracked open the beer and Cooper got down beside me.

"Man," I whispered. "I really missed coming here."

Cooper smiled as he watched the surface of the lake glinting in the sun. "I didn't come here very often when you weren't here," Cooper said finally. "I missed when it was just the two of us coming here and messing around."

I grinned. "We did that a lot. If my parents knew all of the bullshit I got into when you and I hung out, they never would have let me go with you. You were kinda their worst nightmare."

Cooper beamed. "I take that as a compliment! Hey, your dad eventually liked me. I mean, he didn't glare at me as hard as he did when I first started coming around and he even said a few words to me from time to time. I think I was growing on him."

"You were." I sighed. "And mom loved you. At first, she was worried I'd end up getting pregnant, but then she saw how I came out of my shell. I was so timid and reserved before we started hanging out. And then I lost my virginity to you right over there," I said as I pointed out a spot not far down from us.

"That was the best night," Cooper said as he grinned and conjured up images of that night. "We couldn't even go back home because my parents were looking for me so desperately. I probably should have expected it, but I didn't think they'd realize so fast that I'd stolen all of the fireworks."

"Oh, they were so fucking pissed," I said with a laugh.

Cooper reached over and took my hand.

I glanced at him and saw the way his eyebrows were

furrowed. Slowly, I reached over and trailed my fingers down his cheek to his jaw. "What's wrong?"

"That night was an amazing one." He sighed. "I never thought you would actually sleep with me, but you were so eager. It was an amazing time and I took it for granted back then. I thought I was hot shit and I thought sex was always going to be like that. It wasn't. It was never like that with anyone else."

My heart swelled. "I know," I said softly. "It was the same for me."

Cooper shook his head. "I'm still really sorry. I shouldn't have ever treated you like that."

I smiled at Cooper. How could I not forgive him? He was so sincere and honest now. I was convinced he really felt bad about the way things happened between us in the past. It made me want to wrap my arms around him and comfort him and I did just that. "It's okay," I said quietly. "I forgive you. We were young and dumb and that's so far in the past. What I care about is how you treat me now and you haven't let me down once since I got here. No matter how many glasses I break you never fire me."

He smiled lopsidedly. "Don't think I haven't thought about it."

I reached up and cupped his cheek. "Don't be so hard on yourself. Let's just go forward and not look back anymore, okay?"

Cooper smiled down at me. "Okay," he said before he leaned forward and his lips pressed against mine.

The kiss deepened and deepened. My body heated up. I

reached out, grabbed the string on his swim shorts and loosened them.

Cooper got the hint immediately. His fingers slid up my back and my top came undone. He released my breasts from it and I wiggled out of the swim bottoms as well. Completely naked, I deliberately opened my legs so the warm sun's rays would fall on my open pussy.

Cooper followed suit, but before he could get to me, I was on him. I pushed him down onto the blanket and he went willingly. My lips ran down his body, inch by slow inch as I kissed every bit of him. His skin was so warm and inviting, I could kiss him forever and be perfectly content.

Cooper's hand ran down my back and through my still wet hair as his stomach rose and fell and a soft moan escaped from his lips. "Jo," he groaned as his hips rolled up toward my mouth. "Fuck, that feels so good."

I smiled at him and kissed down along his abdomen. A kiss was placed on top of his groin before I slowly moved down and traced my tongue along his inner thighs. There was something about the way Cooper tasted that made me drip with desire. A heady, intoxicating aroma that screamed man and made me want to feel him inside of me.

My fingers traversed his tanned flesh and he sucked in a breath as soon as I touched his cock. It was already rock hard, ready and waiting for me.

I did that.

I turned him on so much that he was already hard for me. Just from being kissed. As always, it helped to boost my confidence to know that someone as gorgeous as Cooper wanted me so badly.

I glanced up at him as my tongue slid over his length from bottom to top. He shuddered when I reached the head and my tongue lavished his crown with warmth. I opened my mouth and swallowed him slowly as he reached out and grabbed ahold of me while his breath became mere ragged pants.

I wanted to tease him and drive him to the brink before anything happened. When I pushed him a bit further than I thought I dared, he turned into a beast of a man and I adored him then. Unlike Brian, Cooper didn't scare me when he was filled with lust. No, he made me feel that desire and made me long for him to take me. Sometimes roughly.

My mouth popped free and he groaned as he rolled his hips and reached down for his cock. I slapped his hand, and he growled with frustration. Every inch of my body shuddered in response. That primal part of him, unfettered and hot made me want to climb on top of him and ride him until he lost it. "You taste so good," I breathed as I licked him slowly. "I can never get enough of this. Did you hear that? I. Can. Never. Get. Enough. Of. You."

Cooper groaned. "If you keep talking like that I'm going to come faster then you're already trying to make me."

"I mean it," I said, cupping his balls and rolled them gently between my long fingers. "You taste like heaven on my tongue."

"Fuck," Cooper growled. "That's it."

Before I could stop him, Cooper rolled over and he was on

me. His mouth attacked my throat even as his hand fluttered between my thighs. He shoved them apart further, and rubbed at my clit with his eager fingers.

A gasp left my lips and my back arched forcing my breasts against his body. "Cooper," I groaned.

"Shhh..." He grinned as one thick finger dipped inside me. "You're not the only one that can tease, you know. Maybe you shouldn't poke the bear if you don't know how to climb trees."

I started to say something, but the words were ripped from my lips when his finger slid in further as he hooked it and brushed that sensitive spot inside me right away. I shuddered in response. Pleasure built up fast and hard until I rolled and jerked my hips, trying to get more as he milked an orgasm out of me with a single finger in the right place.

My body tingled from his weight on top of me. I wrapped a leg around his waist and ground myself against him. Cooper growled, low and deep. The sound vibrated through my body when he sucked one of my nipples into his mouth. His tongue flicked over it nice and slow before he picked up speed then sucked it hard and deep into his mouth.

"Fuck," I screamed. "I can't take it anymore!"

"Yes, you can," he said sternly as he nipped my breast. "Come for me. I'm going to make sure I give you every orgasm that I couldn't over the years, so you're going to be here a while."

I shook my head. "You're kind of evil, you know."

"And you kind of love it."

I did. I loved that Cooper was my sweet, protective angel, but that in the bedroom he turned into an insatiable beast that wanted to eat me up day and night. He moved down from my breasts and buried himself between my thighs. His tongue attacked my clit as soon as he was in range and my hips jutted upward for more.

My legs shook as my orgasm slammed into me.

Wave after wave crashed down and my eyes rolled back in my head. I forgot to breathe, I forgot how to think. All I could do was sink into the pleasure that surrounded me until I was flying with ecstasy.

"There we go," Cooper crooned as he lapped at the juices that had flowed out of me. "Look how fucking wet you are," he said as he devoured my pussy.

"It's your fault," I muttered as I slowly regained the power of speech and my body craved more.

"You taste amazing. I could do this all day."

"No more teasing," I begged. "I want you inside me. I need your cock to fill me up again."

Apparently, that was all Cooper needed to hear. He removed his finger and positioned himself between my thighs.

I sucked in a breath, ready and waiting to feel him stretch me and fill me up.

He froze and stared down at me with a slight frown on his lips. "Wait, I need to go get the condoms. I didn't think we'd get into this out here."

I shook my head as he started to pull away. "No, fuck it. I don't want to wait," I breathed.

He rubbed himself against my opening, his brows still knitted in thought.

"I'm not saying I want a kid right now, but would that be the worst thing in the world?"

Cooper's eyes widened. "Are you serious? I want that more than anything in the world. You, a house full of kids. That's my dream."

I chuckled. "I'm not saying right now! I'm just saying that..." I paused and bit my lip. "It wouldn't be the worst thing in the world. That being said, pull out?" I laughed. "I want you and I want to feel all of you. And one day, we'll talk about babies and all that entails. Okay?"

Cooper grinned. "Okay, baby. Whatever you want."

I beamed up at him and then gasped as he slid inside of me firmly. Right away, I groaned as he filled me up and stretched me out in the most delightfully fulfilling way. I ran my hand down his chest and my head tilted back against the soft blanket.

"Jo," he moaned as he laid on top of me and rolled his hips inside of me. "Fuck, you feel so good. I love feeling you rub against me."

I nodded my head hard. We had sex without a condom before, but there was emotions now. Far more. And that made it hotter. More special. "I know what you mean. This is —God, this is crazy. It feels so damn good. Too good—I love it." Feeling the unrestrained heat from his cock and the soft-ness of his skin made me gasp and moan as he picked up speed and really started to rock into me.

I held onto him and clenched around his rigid cock. My

wetness slicked his strokes and he rutted deeper and harder inside of me until the sound of our flesh slapping against each other echoed around us and the lake. I wrapped my arms around his neck and shook my head. "It's *too* good," I panted. "I know I'm gonna come. Cooper, come with me."

My man groaned and I swooned. That deep, guttural sound that left his lips let me know that he was as close as I was. I didn't care about drawing it out forever, I wanted to come. I wanted to feel good and I wanted Cooper to join me.

"Jo" he groaned as he kissed me so hard my toes curled. "I love you so fucking much."

My heart raced. Every time he said he loved me, I desperately wanted to say it back, but I just wanted to wait a bit more before I gave in to that final commitment. I couldn't take it if it all crashed and burned and I was left clutching the broken pieces of my heart in my hands, alone, damaged and shattered.

I yearned to say it to Cooper. If I could just say it once, I knew he would be over the moon, but I wasn't ready. Not yet. I pushed my fingers into his hair, but my mouth stayed closed. Not yet. I can't do it yet.

Cooper held me close as he lifted and dropped his hips without ever missing a beat, but I felt it. Sadness. He wanted me to say it too, I know he did, but I couldn't bring myself to do it and he didn't pressure me to do it. That's why I cared for him and why I would walk through fire for Cooper.

Our words ceased, but our bodies spoke volumes. We pulsed, rolled and grinded against each other until the pleasure built and we were both right on the edge. We balanced there, precarious and dangerous until we both fell off together. My

legs wrapped around him tightly and squeezed as I rode out
my orgasm. I pushed and jerked my hips, enamored with the
feeling until it slowly subsided.

Cooper pulled out and jerked his cock as he panted.

I was astonished by the way his eyes and skin sparkled. His
strokes increased until he shuddered and came hard all over
my belly and thighs... this turned me on all over again. I
swiped a finger through it and tasted it. The taste of Cooper
was as intoxicating as his personality.

"God," he groaned as he finally released his cock and laid
beside me, one leg thrown over my body. "We have to go
wash off now, don't we?"

I laughed. "Give me that towel and fuck washing. I want to
drain this beer and eat whatever you have tucked into that
cooler."

"Strawberries." He grinned. "Strawberries, grapes, melon, and
even a bottle of champagne."

I clicked my tongue. "You've been holding out on me."

"Of course." He chuckled. "And don't fill up on it, okay? I'm
taking us out to dinner."

"Good luck with that," I murmured. "I can't feel my legs and
I am perfectly content in lying here forever."

My stomach growled and Cooper burst out laughing.

"Okay, I lied. Sue me," I said with an embarrassed laugh.

Cooper leaned up and kissed my lips. He crawled over to the
cooler then came back with a fruit and cheese plate.

Yeah, he'd definitely been listening to me when I told him

about the things I liked. I popped a grape into my mouth. Sweet cold juice squirted onto my tongue. "That's perfect right now," I sighed. "I didn't realize how much I needed this."

Cooper bit into a strawberry and I groaned as juices ran down his lip. "If you keep that up, we're never going to make it to dinner."

"I don't mind," He winked, then grinned. "I could eat you for the rest of my life."

My cheeks burned. Yeah, Cooper was definitely perfect for me.

"O h, my God," Jo groaned as she finally tasted her linguine and clams. She bounced a little in her seat. "This is amazing."

I grinned. Whenever she was excited, I couldn't take my eyes off of her. She was like a child, eager, happy, and totally mind-blowingly amazing. I stared at her, my own food forgotten. I wanted to marry her. Everything about Jo screamed for me to slip a ring onto her finger. When the time was right, I would.

Even if she hadn't said she loved me yet.

I knew there was a reason for it. One of the first things I did when she told me about her ex was research. Trauma made it hard to move forward, to embrace someone when everyone else had betrayed you. I understood this and I wasn't going to push her into anything she wasn't ready for. I knew she loved me, she just couldn't say it aloud yet.

"Sorry!" She laughed. "Am I being a complete pig?"

I chuckled. "Don't worry. I think pigs are really cute."

"Did you just call me a pig?" she demanded, her eyes twinkling.

"Since pigs are one of my favorite animals, consider it a big compliment."

She beamed at me. "I don't want to be greedy, but the food here is just so delicious. Plus, I worked up an appetite." She gave me a flirtatious wink. "I'm definitely not complaining though."

At her beaming, my heart stopped. Her smile and playfulness just did things to me. "Good, because I would hate to have to take it away," I teased.

Jo rolled her eyes, her smile still on her gorgeous lips.

I was constantly reminded of how much I couldn't let her go. Even if she decided to up and pack her bags again and head out for New York, I would be right there with her, ready to give up everything to make her mine.

"What are we going to do after dinner?" Jo asked as she sipped at her glass of wine.

"I was thinking we'd go home, watch some old movies, then fall asleep after we work off some of this food." I smiled.

"You're so damn lusty," Jo crooned. "I don't know how I ever got so lucky, but I love having you around." She took another bite of her food and hummed. "I can't wait for tonight."

"Me too," I watched her over the rim of my glass. I put it down and cut into the chicken on my plate.

Suddenly, Jo reached over and touched my hand. "Thank you." She smiled. "For everything. You didn't have to take me in and you didn't have to do so much for me. I know we're together now, but you always go above and beyond and I'm so fortunate to have you."

I cleared my throat and gave her hand a warm squeeze. "I'm the fortunate one. I can honestly say I feel like I'm exactly where I belong for the first time in my life."

Her smile was enough to light up my entire world. I felt that pang again, the need to hear her say that she loved me too, but I was determined to be patient.

We enjoyed our meals until our plates were cleared, then we indulged in one portion of delicious dessert called tiramisu. She definitely had some of that New York sophistication in her, as I was learning things about food I'd never known before.

I dug into my pocket and pulled out the box that I'd kept tucked away for a few days now. Slowly, I laid it on the table and slid it across.

Jo glanced up from her dessert and smiled. "What's this?"

"Open it." I grinned. "I think you're going to like it."

She raised a brow at the rectangular box before she opened it and gasped. Inside was a gorgeous bracelet of silver and diamonds.

It was perfect for her and I watched as she carefully lifted the bracelet out in awe.

"Cooper," she breathed. "You didn't have to do this for me."

"I wanted to." I reached across and took the bracelet from her. She laid her wrist into it and I fastened it, my fingers brushing against her soft skin.

Jo turned her hand back and forth, as she admired her new bracelet. "This is beautiful, Cooper. Thank you so much." Her eyes watered up, so she quickly yanked her napkin and dabbed at her eyes. "Sorry. I didn't mean to be so emotional."

"I told you." I smiled. "I would do anything for you. I'm so glad you like it." I reached over and rubbed my thumb over her cheek. "You don't ever have to apologize to me. Not for feeling things. I love that I can be the one that you're vulnerable in front of."

"You're going to be the death of me," she said, smiling softly at me. "I love it." She cooed and stroked her fingers over it. "Thank you."

"You're welcome. Shall we get going?" I asked when our plates were cleared.

"Yes," Jo chimed. "I'm nice and full and ready to get home and relax." She reached across the table and held my hand. "Might as well relax as much as we can before work starts tomorrow."

"Sounds like a plan." I wrapped an arm around her waist as we walked out of the restaurant. My eyes wouldn't stop taking in how cute she looked in the black dress that clung to her gorgeously full curves. I'd noticed the stares that she got in the restaurant and it made me smile. They could look all they wanted, they would never have her.

She was mine. And only mine.

The sun had already started to set when we made our way out of the restaurant. It was a perfect evening. The air was still warm, but it had cooled off a bit. Fall was right around the corner and thankfully, it seemed like the heat would subside and leave us with a pleasant season. I wanted to enjoy it with her. "Let me go and get the car," I told her as we stopped at the sidewalk. "I'll pull it around."

Jo smiled. "You don't have to do that. I can walk it."

I shook my head. "We parked down more than a little bit far and you're wearing those damn heels." I pointed to her ridiculous shoes. "Let me get it for you and I'll be right back."

She chuckled. "I won't lie, my feet are killing me a bit," she said as she winced and then smiled up at me. "Hurry back?"

"Of course, beautiful."

I kissed her deeply and she leaned against me. Every time her lips touched mine I was floored. No woman had ever done that to me before, but she did it without even trying. Just by being who she was, Jo drew me in and I never wanted to be away from her.

"I'll be right back," I whispered against her soft lips.

"I'll be right here."

We finally pulled apart and I grinned at her. She gave a little wave and my heart fluttered. She's the one for sure. One day we're going to have a wedding, a family, the works. I was going to give Jo the world.

I finally turned and headed for the car. The street was clear, so I started across.

As soon as he was in the middle of the road a car revved its engine. I turned to the right and saw a sleek, black car with tinted windows. I couldn't see who was behind the glass, but that didn't matter when they slammed their foot on the gas, and the car leapt toward Cooper at top speed.

Cooper was a sitting duck. Whoever was in that car wanted him hurt or dead. Unless he could avoid that vehicle, he was going to die before I ever got to have the life that I wanted with him.

"Cooper!" I screamed.

I didn't think as he stared at the charging car. I moved. My heels clacked hard against the ground, but I couldn't hear or see anything besides the man I loved. I ran for him, my heart pounding in my chest. Even as I ran I saw Cooper jerk back, but that didn't stop my momentum. I flew forward and would have landed on my face on the tarmac if Cooper hadn't thrown himself down to catch my fall.

The car sped off at full speed and never slowed as Cooper laid on top of me.

"Are you okay?" Cooper asked, his forehead creased in a frown.

"Are you?" I asked, slightly out of breath.

"I'm all right," he said and touched himself all over as he spoke, "I'm in one piece." He quickly scrambled off of me as people poured out of the restaurant. "You sure you're fine?"

I nodded. "Wind knocked out of me a little," I strained to say as I tried to catch my breath.

"Shit," Cooper cursed and checked me closely. "We should get you to a hospital."

"Me? You're the one that almost got mowed down!'

"Are you two all right?"

I turned to the manager who'd walked over concern all over on his face.

Cooper took his hand and let himself be pulled to his feet. He limped a little, but quickly thanked the man and then reached out for me. "Can you stand?"

I nodded. "I'm fine, really." I let him help me to my feet and dusted off my dress. My gaze scanned the area around us, but I didn't see the car that had tried to flatten Cooper. A touch to my shoulder startled me and I nearly leapt out of my skin. I turned around and looked up at Cooper with concerned eyes. "I'm fine, but you're limping."

"Just a little," he said as he ran a hand down my arm. "Might have sprained my ankle a little, but it's fine. Don't worry about me." He kissed my forehead. "Let's get home, okay?"

I nodded. "I'll drive."

Cooper happily handed over his keys and I saw the effort to keep the pain off of his face. We climbed into the car and I stared up and down the street.

Cooper reached over and squeezed my leg. "What are we waiting for?" he asked.

"I was wondering if there were any cameras, but there aren't any on this street," I huffed, angry that nothing had been there to capture what happened. "We should go to the police."

"What good would it do?" Cooper asked. "It was just some moron that doesn't know how to drive. Those are a dime a dozen. Besides, like you said there are no cameras here and we were the only two people that saw anything. Might as well let it drop." He grunted and adjusted himself in his seat. "Let's just go, okay? My ankle is starting to kill me."

I nodded and didn't push the subject anymore. It was clear that he was sore and starting to get cranky. I didn't want to tell him I was worried. Not just because he almost got hit, but because I was pretty sure it was on purpose. My stomach churned at the thought, but I didn't want to upset him.

I can't believe I didn't get a damn license plate number. I had stood there scared and frozen for too long, but at least Cooper was safe. What if this someone tried again?

What if it was Brian?

I couldn't stop looking in the rearview mirror the entire trip home. I kept expecting to see a car come out of nowhere and follow us back to his place. My eyes shot to the mirror multiple times, but there was no car behind us. At least not the same one.

We finally reached his place. I quickly hopped out and moved to his side.

Cooper limped a little and held onto me a bit for support as we made our way into the house.

"Why don't you sit on the couch, and I'll get some ice for your ankle and painkillers?"

"That would be great." He grunted as I helped him sit down and he let out a breath. "Thank you," he said as he held onto my hand and kissed it. "I'm sure it'll be fine by tomorrow."

I smiled at him. "I hope so."

As soon as I was hidden away in the kitchen, I slapped a hand over my mouth. My body shuddered as I tried to keep the sound to a minimum and I thanked God, that Cooper had turned on the television when he sat down. I didn't want him to hear or see me when I was completely breaking down.

"Hey."

My head shot up and I sucked in a sharp breath.

Cooper stood in the doorway. The frown on his face was so deep and even with a hurt ankle he crossed the space between us to pull me into his arms.

I buried my face in his chest and the sobs wouldn't stop as I clung to him.

"Shhh...it's okay," he cooed. "You're okay."

I shook my head. "It's not about me," I sniffled as I pulled back and wiped at my face. "It's about you. What if I lost you? I love you so much and I couldn't handle it if anything bad happening to you, Cooper. You mean everything to me and if you weren't here I-I... I would—I don't know what I would do. I love you so much!"

Cooper caressed my cheek and smiled softly. "I know I shouldn't be happy right now, not while you're panicked and hurting, but do you realize what you've just said?"

I blinked up at him. The words had spilled out of my mouth and heart so quickly that I really had no idea what I'd said to him. I shook my head softly and tried to think before I froze. *Did I just say that I loved him?*

"Is it true?" he asked as he rubbed at my cheeks gently and pushed my hair behind my ear. "Do you love me?"

I nodded hard. Why would I ever deny it? Thinking about how difficult it had been to say earlier, it just felt stupid now. What if Cooper had died and I was never able to tell him how I truly felt about him? I never wanted anything like that to happen. I needed to be more in the moment, more honest about everything going on in my head. I quickly glanced up at him and saw the way he beamed down at me.

"I love you, Jo Johanson," he smiled. "More than you'll ever know."

Cooper kissed me and my knees wanted to buckle. This man, this amazing, hot, caring, big hearted man loved me and I loved him too. I would shout it to the world if I could because I wanted everyone to know. Cooper was mine and I was most definitely his. "Let me get you those pills," I said quickly as I remembered that he was in pain.

Cooper nodded. "Once you do, come back into the living room, and sit with me."

"I'll be right there." I watched as he disappeared back into the other room. I splashed water on my face and swiftly dried my face with a paper towel, before grabbing the pain pills and a bottle of water. When I walked into the living room, I dropped the bottle of water and the pills and they clattered to the floor. "What are you doing?" I gaped as I stared at him sitting on the couch completely naked.

Cooper ran a hand down his muscled chest and over his hard abs. He traced his tongue over his soft lips.

With a will of their own, my eyes followed each and every movement. When he sucked his bottom lip between his teeth, I damn near fainted.

"I'm celebrating the fact that you said you love me. I always said the minute you said it I was going to mark the occasion and now it's here."

I shook my head. "You're hurt!"

"I told you, it's just a little sprain," he said as he gestured toward it. "Besides, I don't need it anyway. As long as you can climb into my lap, I'll be just fine."

Even while I was still freaked out and it had been weird, seeing Cooper completely naked and turned on made my heart throb in my chest. I wanted to celebrate too. Before the car, I'd been thinking about getting him home, stripping off his clothes and giving him a wild night until both of us were too exhausted to keep going. "Are you sure?" I pushed. "I don't want to injure you more and we have to end up at the hospital because I couldn't stop being a thirsty bitch."

Cooper burst out laughing. "It's not like you asked me to do this for you," he reassured me. "I'm offering because I want to feel you and I want to make love to you after hearing you say that you really love me." He extended a hand toward me. "So come and show me just how much you need me and let me hear you say you love me a few more times. I've been waiting to hear it for so long."

I took no more convincing. The same way I recognized that I should have said I loved him sooner was the same way I recognized I didn't want to miss a minute of being with him. If we were sitting together not saying a word or if we were mixed up and tangled in the sheets, it didn't matter. What did matter was the fact I craved him so hard it hurt and I never wanted to miss an opportunity to celebrate us.

 He didn't need to convince me. I kicked off my heels and stripped off the dress. The bracelet I left on my wrist. I would never take that off. I sailed over to him and climbed onto his lap. Cooper's hand pressed against my back as I leaned down and kissed him passionately. Heat swept the entire length of my body as I ground myself against him eager to feel his touch and to have him fill me up.

My nipples became rock hard as they rubbed against his chest. Cooper did that deep, toe curling groan that made me want to come right then and there, but I kept going. I wasn't done with him yet.

My lips kissed his throat and my teeth nipped at his shoulder. Cooper's breaths turned to pants and I loved how I could reduce him to an eager, desperate thing that craved me. Cooper gripped my ass and squeezed as his other hand slipped between my thighs. He opened me up. Then I felt a finger slide into me and coax more wetness from my aching pussy. It didn't take long at all before his fingers were slick with my juices and he rubbed my clit with them.

I threw my head back and gripped his shoulders for dear life. "Oh my God," I moaned. "That's so good."

"I know, baby," he whispered. "I know it is. Sit on my cock. I need to feel you so fucking bad, I can't even think straight."

It was different from all the other times. We were always the types to love long, slow bouts of foreplay. Those times dragged on and on and usually, we were so worked up by the time we were done that the sex was just the fireworks after the show. Still amazing, but part of the experience, not all of it.

This time, I felt it between us. Both of us were ready to fuck the other's brains out now. The emotions, the closeness of losing him and me saying I loved him for the very first time all culminated into a wild storm that wouldn't be tamed until we were spent, clutching each other and moaning as we tried to keep our brains functioning.

That's what we needed at that moment. Unfettered pleasure and closeness and I never wanted to let him go in fact. After seeing how close he had come to being snatched away from me—so very, very close...

I shook the thought from my head so violently it throbbed in protest. All I wanted to focus on were those fingers that rubbed me into a euphoric oblivion. I lifted myself above his thick, raging cock and rubbed it along my slit.

Ripples of anticipation ripped through me as I impaled myself on him. I cried out his name at the top of my lungs as I took him into my body. We were secluded enough that I could be free, but I knew that even if we weren't, I still would have shouted his name out. Cooper was mine and I didn't give a damn who knew it.

"Right there," Cooper moaned as I lifted and dropped my hips. "Fuck, you feel so good," he breathed.

He sucked one of my breasts into his mouth and I rolled my head at the tight tug of his lips and the gentle scraping of his teeth. My skin would end up slightly bruised, marked by his mouth, but I didn't care. I wanted that bite, that claim that showed the world I was his completely. "Cooper," I whispered as I felt the quick burning orgasm building in my belly. "I love you so much. I love you so fucking much."

"I love you too," he breathed and held me tightly. "I'm always going to love you. I always have."

There was awe and admiration in his eyes and I knew without a doubt that he was telling the truth. I picked up speed and clenched my pussy around his shaft until I felt his cock pulse and throb inside of me. Each stroke of my tightness hurled him closer to the edge and dragged me along with him.

I cried out as I came so hard my body convulsed against his. My nails dug into his shoulders, but all Cooper did was growl as he pumped upward into my body. It only took a few rough, deep thrusts before he shook his head. "Get up," he moaned. "I need to come."

I did him one better. Still dizzy and high on the orgasm that had just ripped through me, I slipped between his thighs to my knees. I wrapped my mouth around his cock and bobbed my head up and down on his shaft. Cooper's muscles strained and tightened before he bounced his hips up sharply and I swallowed inches of his cock in one go. I breathed through my nose and watched him with wet eyes before he gasped and hot cum splashed into the back of my throat.

I leaned back and showed him his cum inside. I swirled it before I swallowed while my hand traced down my throat. Cooper shuddered in response and it brought a smile to my lips. Yeah, when I loved someone and they showed how much they loved me, I had absolutely no problem going above and beyond. If anyone deserved this, it was Cooper.

"Good God," he muttered as he ran a hand down his thigh. "That was... Good God."

I chuckled. "I'll take that as a compliment."

"Oh, you should," he muttered. "That was amazing."

I stood up and placed my hand on his chest. He tilted his head up toward me and I kissed him softly. I clutched him hard never wanting to lose him. The thought of him being gone, taken away from me—well it had wiped away any fear or doubt in my heart. I loved Cooper and I wanted to spend the rest of my life with him.

"Time for bed?" he asked as he gazed up at me with hazy eyes after our kiss.

"Oh, definitely. I'm dying to pass out," I admitted as I stretched and yawned. "Do you want those pills now?"

"Probably a good idea." Cooper nodded. "I don't want to wake up in even more pain."

I narrowed my eyes. "You said it didn't hurt that much."

He grinned. "I wanted to have sex with you."

I slapped his shoulder. "Really! You're just as bad as you were when we were teenagers."

"Worse, because now I know how to use this thing," he said, pointing to his dick that already seemed to be growing hard again.

A groan spilled from my lips. "You are literally the fucking worst. Why do I love you?"

"I'm charming, sexy, funny, and I worship you."

I grinned. "Never mind, I remember now."

"That's what I thought." Cooper kissed me.

I hummed against his lips. When I stood up, I gathered some more pills and water for him and he happily took them. I started picking up the clothes that we'd scattered around the room.

He carefully stood and tested his ankle. He started reaching for things, but I slapped his hand away. "Go ahead and go to the bedroom. I'll be up in a minute."

"You don't have to clean up. I feel bad having you do that alone."

I smiled. "That's exactly why I don't mind. Go ahead, I'll be up soon."

"Alright." He smiled and slapped my ass making me yelp. "I'll be up until you're in bed with me."

"You're the sweetest," I purred.

Cooper climbed the stairs and I went back to cleaning up our things. When I grabbed my phone, I noticed a new text message. It was probably Mel. I hoped everything was okay at the bar. I opened it and dropped the phone as if it had bitten me.

*D*o you want him to die? Break up with him or next time, I won't miss.

I reached down with a shaky hand and picked up my phone. The number it had been sent from was blocked, but I knew who it was from. Brian. Who else could have sent it? No one else would threaten to kill the man I was dating.

Why wouldn't he leave me alone?

Brian didn't want me when I was right there next to him, but suddenly he was desperate for me. It suddenly felt eerie as if he was right behind me. I even glanced over my shoulder and expected him to be there, but of course, it was empty. My heart fluttered in my chest and I quickly ran up the stairs as if something was on my heels.

I had to escape him. I had to do something before he hurt Cooper. If he got hurt, I would never forgive myself.

"Jo?" Cooper asked when he glanced up at me from the bed as I stood in the doorway, frozen. "What's the matter?"

I couldn't speak. Wordlessly, I crossed the room and handed my phone to Cooper. He glanced up at me, but I just shook my head and gestured toward it. If I spoke, I was afraid I would sob because the nightmare was never ending. I couldn't get away from Brian, no matter how fucking far I went.

Cooper opened the phone and read the text message. His face darkened. He turned it off and set the phone on the nightstand. "Come here," he said and crooked a finger at me.

I dropped the clothes I'd been holding and ran over to the bed. When I hopped in, he grabbed me and held me close against his body. Whenever he touched me like this, all of the worries and fear I held evaporated. How could one man calm me so much?

"It's going to be okay," he whispered as he stroked my hair. "If that asshole thinks I'm going to let you go because of some vapid threat he's a dumbass. I'm not going anywhere and neither are you."

I sat up and wiped my eyes. Despite trying my hardest, tears had rolled down my cheeks and dripped on my arm. I shook my head and toyed with my fingers nervously. "You don't know him like I do, Cooper. If he says he's going to do something, he always does it. The man is a psychopath and he'd do anything to make sure that I suffer." My throat squeezed and I sucked in a breath. "I shouldn't have come back here. I popped up and brought all of my baggage and bullshit with me. It's not fair," I said as I broke down again.

"Hey, hey," Cooper said, lifting my head and cradling my face between his palms. "You are not the one at fault here. He is. You deserve to be happy, safe and loved and he can go fuck off with his bullshit. I'm going to be right here and protect you no matter what happens."

For some reason, this statement made me cry harder. Cooper would get himself killed because he wanted to keep me safe. I couldn't let him do that!

"You don't get it," I said as I pulled away from him. "Brian is like a shark that has scented blood. He won't give up that easily. I need to get away. I have to quit the bar and move somewhere else. I'm not going to be selfish and put you at risk when you didn't ask for any of this."

"Jo," he said and grabbed me to keep me from getting out of the bed. "I didn't ask for any of it, but I signed up for supporting you and protecting you when I asked you to give me another chance. I love you and there is no way I'm going to let that bastard take you away from me."

"Cooper I—"

"No," he said firmly. "You are not going to quit working at the bar, and you sure as hell ain't moving anywhere else, especially when that psycho is still out there ready and waiting for you. Do you understand me?"

I stared at Cooper. So much love and care radiated from him that I didn't know what to do with it. I buried my face in his chest and let him hold me close to him. I didn't hold back this time and I sobbed as my shoulders rose and fell.

Cooper stroked my back and hair the whole time. When I was done, I rubbed at my eyes and he handed me a tissue. "Better now?" he asked softly.

I nodded and blew my nose. "I don't know what has happened to me. I've become such a crybaby lately."

Cooper smiled softly at me before he squeezed my naked thigh.

"What are we going to do?" I whispered. "If I keep working there, you know he's going to do something like what he did today. What if he doesn't miss next time? Cooper, I would lose it if anything ever happened to you."

"Then nothing is going to happen to me," he said confidently. "If it's a choice between hurting you and making sure I stay safe, guess what's going to happen?"

I sniffled. "You'll stay safe."

"Exactly. I know how to handle myself and you've learned to defend yourself too. We can't live in fear because of him, okay? That's exactly what he wants and we're not going to give it to him." Cooper lifted the blanket and pulled me underneath it. "Now, we're not going to think about him for one more second. We're going to go to bed, have an amazing rest, and then in the morning we'll go for round two."

I grinned at his words. "Is that the only thing on your brain? Sex?"

"Have you seen how you look? Of course, that's all I think about," he scoffed.

"I love you," I said.

"I love you too," he said before he leaned down and planted a kiss on my lips, my neck and my cheek. "Now get some sleep. We'll figure this out together. That's what couples do. They stay together come what may."

"Okay." I yawned and nestled into my pillow.

Cooper shut out the lights.

I was engulfed in darkness, the scent of his clean sheets and his body. Before I knew it, my eyes grew heavy. I snuggled against him and forgot the world, even if it was just for a little while.

Chapter Forty

I woke up with my body pressed against Cooper's. His warmth soothed me as well as the way his breath tickled across the back of my neck. I smiled and pushed back against him, wanting to be as close as humanly possible to him. It felt right being so close, so comfortable and safe in his arms.

As I shifted, I felt something else press against me. I laughed under my breath. Seriously, it really was like we were two teenagers. I grinned and rocked my hips back and forth against his body grinding against his dick until he groaned and tugged me against his body sharply.

"If you start shit, just know that I will end it, woman," he muttered.

"You talk a big game, but I don't believe you. I guess you're just going to have to prove it to me."

"Really now?" he asked.

Now I heard the way his voice suddenly sounded alert.

"I'm going to the bathroom then we're going to have a very deep discussion," he growled against my ear. "About teasing me and the consequences of teasing me."

I shivered. "When you use that voice it really drives me crazy."

"I know. That's why I do it." Cooper kissed my shoulder and climbed out of bed.

I watched his deliciously bare ass as he made his way to the bathroom and disappeared inside. The man was ridiculously gorgeous and he knew it. Not that I was complaining.

I reached over to the nightstand and picked up my phone. When I turned it on, I thought about the message that I'd received from Brian the night before. The threat hung over my head like a cloud, but I wanted to believe Cooper. I didn't want to be afraid of Brian. That was giving him more power than he deserved and I wouldn't let him get to me like that anymore.

There were no new messages, so I sat my phone back on the table. No one was going to take me away from Cooper.

"You're a million miles away," he said as he padded back toward the bed. "What are you thinking about?"

I glanced up at him. "Nothing important," I said as I held my hand out toward him. "I'd much rather you climb back into bed with me and we don't talk at all."

"I can make that happen," he said as he leaned down and kissed me.

"Good."

We stayed in bed for so long that my stomach growled in the

end and broke up our happy morning. I'd completely forgotten about Brian's text message and I wanted it to stay that way. I rolled over and stretched out on the bed as I yawned. "I'm starving. We should get breakfast."

Cooper was sprawled out beside me, still catching his breath. "I think you're on your own. I can't move. I don't even know why I thought I could keep up with you that many times in a row."

I grinned. "That's the power of a woman," I teased. "I could go a few more times."

Cooper nipped my arm.

I chuckled.

"Do we even have food?" he asked. "We've been on a restaurant kick and I can't remember the last time I went grocery shopping."

"I can get some food. I've been meaning to go to the supermarket anyway."

Cooper grabbed my wrist as I tried to roll out of the bed. "Hold on, I'll go with you. Just give me another minute."

I shook my head. "I think you need to let that ankle rest today. Besides, it won't take me long to get a few things and come back."

He frowned. "I don't really want you leaving on your own."

"If I was going somewhere deserted then I would agree, but it's the grocery store. There's plenty of people around and it's broad daylight. I promise, I'll be fine."

"Alright," he finally relented and pulled me down for a long, slow kiss. "Be careful and call me if you need me."

"I'll be fine. Like you said, I can't live like I'm afraid and I'm not going to. If you weren't here, I would still have to live and navigate the world on my own and this is no different."

"Do you have to be so smart?"

"Yes," I said cheekily.

"As logical as that thought is, I still worry about you."

"I know you do and I adore you for it." My hand trailed over his cheek. Then I left him to lie in bed and relax. I found a pair of comfortable shorts and a tank top then twisted my hair up into a ponytail. I placed one more kiss on him before I wiggled my fingers at him and left.

The drive to the supermarket was uneventful and it reinforced the thought that I would be okay. I headed into the store and slowly walked down the aisles with a smile on my face. It felt nice to be doing something so normal and mundane, and to know that when I arrived back home, Cooper would be waiting for me eagerly.

Home. I'd thought of Cooper's place as home, hadn't I?

The thought made my smile spread. It was home when I was at Cooper's. The soothing, relaxing atmosphere, the warmth he displayed toward me, the way I was completely comfortable when it was just the two of us. It was amazing.

I decided I was going to make us a big breakfast; eggs, steak, home fries, fruit, bacon. It would be delicious and I couldn't wait to see Cooper devour it all. He'd done so much for me that I wanted to pay him back and just making him breakfast didn't feel like nearly enough.

"I'll think of something," I muttered to myself. "Something he'll love."

I didn't want to leave him waiting for too long so I finished up grabbing food and paid for it. He'd slipped me his credit card when I wasn't paying attention, but I still had some cash and I used it. Still, I smiled at his attempt to make sure I really was taken care of. I happily took the bags and carried them to the car when I was nearly yanked off of my feet.

Before I could scream, a hand slapped over my mouth and cut off any sound that might have escaped as I was dragged into an alley. I struggled against the hands that held me and tried to kick, but he was stronger. Finally, I was able to bite into him and he howled before he shoved me against the brick of a building. I was slightly dazed and looked up to see Brian sneering at me.

"What are you doing?" I shouted as I touched my head to make sure there was no blood. "What do you want?"

"You know damn well what I want," he snapped. "And if you even think about screaming, I'll make sure you never scream again."

I swallowed thickly. My eyes shot up and down the alley, but there was no one in sight. The busy street was close enough, but there was no guarantee that I would reach it before he got to me. "Brian, we are over. There's nothing else to talk about. I left because I didn't want to do this anymore and you're still following me. I don't want to fight with you. I just want to be done with this and move on with my life. I'm happy. If you ever gave a shit about me just let me be happy," I cried.

"You are mine," he snapped. "The only way you'll ever be free of me..." He wrapped his hand around my throat and I pried at it. "... is if I let you free and I'll only do that if you're dead. You can either leave with me now or I'll go and hurt that boyfriend of yours too. Don't think I won't do it. I don't need an excuse at this point, but you're really giving me one. Let's go."

Brian yanked me off of the wall and I stumbled forward. I could feel him behind me huge and intimidating. I had to get away from him. If he got me alone, I would be in more danger than I was in now.

I spun on my heels and grabbed his wrist when it shot out toward me. The heel of my hand crashed into his nose in a palm strike at the same time that I brought up my knee and shoved it deep into his groin.

Brian howled and fell to the ground.

I didn't stick around to make sure he was really down, I jumped over him and got the hell out of there.

The groceries stayed on the ground, but I wasn't going to stop for anything. Instead, I ran for the truck and jumped inside before I slammed and locked the door. I peeled out of my parking space with my heart in my throat and blood rushing in my ears.

I thought about going back to Cooper's place, but then I remembered Brian's words. He was going to hurt Cooper if I went back there. Someway, somehow, he would do it and then I wouldn't have anyone anymore. Cooper meant so much to me, too much to simply let him get hurt because of me and my stupid life choices.

I turned from the direction of Cooper's place and went in the opposite direction. If I wanted to do anything for Cooper, it should be keeping him safe from harm the same way that he would do for me. I knew what I had to do. My heart broke at the thought, but there was no other answer left.

I hopped out of the truck and dashed up the stairs to my apartment. My hand shook as I inserted the key into its lock. I struggled with it for a moment then... Finally, thankfully, the key shoved into the lock. I turned it and let myself in then shut the door after me. It felt weird being back in my place. Cooper's house really had felt like home and being back at my place felt... odd.

I had no time to wander around thinking about old times though. I needed to pack and get the hell out of town. I ran to my bedroom and rooted around in the closet. There was a duffle bag in the back, one I'd made in case I ever had to leave in a hurry and now it would come in handy.

I yanked open my dresser drawers then dumped clothes and shoes into the bag. Everything else I could leave behind. Maybe Cooper would send it to me and I would be okay.

Cooper.

I froze when I thought about him. There was no way I could

just take off without letting him know. He deserved at least that much.

My heart sank into my stomach—I knew that he wouldn't love the fact that I was getting up and disappearing on him, but it was all I could do. If I didn't, he wouldn't be safe and I couldn't risk it. As if he could sense something was wrong, my phone started to ring and it was Cooper's name on the display. I nervously hovered my thumb above my screen before I slid it over and swallowed hard.

"Jo? Where are you? I thought you'd be back with breakfast by now."

I bit my lip. "I have to leave."

"The store? You're still there?"

"I'm leaving, Coop. For good. I need to get out of town before you get hurt because of me."

"What are you talking about?" he demanded. "You can't just take off! Where are you going to go? What are you going to do?"

"I don't know," I breathed. "I'll leave your truck at the bar and grab a cab from there. Trust me, it's better this way. I love you so much. I won't let anything horrible happen to you."

"Horrible?" he asked. "Why would something horrible happen to me? What's going on?"

"I ran into Brian," I said as I found my backup stash of money buried inside of an old DVD player. "He's going to hurt you if I stick around. I really can't stay."

"I love you," Cooper growled. "I'm not going to lose you again. Where are you?"

"It doesn't matter. I have to go, okay? I love you."

"Jo, don't hang up this phone!"

I didn't want to. I wanted to talk to him for the rest of the day, go home to him, sleep with him, but I knew that wasn't a possibility. I was doing what was best for him. Anything else would be horribly selfish and I couldn't be selfish when it came to Cooper.

Before I could say another word, pain shot up my back. The phone spun out of my hand as Cooper called me over and over. I turned around in time to see Brian glaring at me.

"I told you that you wouldn't get away from me."

"Brian..." My voice quivered. "Please, don't do this."

He circled around me, but he kept his eyes fixed on me at the same time. As I watched, he raised his heel and slammed it into my phone. It crunched under his boot. No way out. My breathing quickened. He walked closer and terror shot through my body.

Brian's face pulled into a grin and a shiver passed through me. He pulled his hand back and the world began to spin.

I was going to die.

He had come back to finish the job he'd started in New York.

Chapter Forty-Two

COOPER

I stared at the dead phone for one instant longer. I'd heard the coward's voice. I never knew how he sounded before but it was clear that it was him. I hated the terror I heard in her voice and it angered the fuck out of me.

I didn't think. I jumped out of bed and tugged on my clothes ignoring the howling pain in my ankle. Nothing mattered when Jo's life was on the line.

If he hurt her...

I wasn't going to finish that thought. I would end up in prison for murdering him and I didn't want to think about her being gone. I searched for my phone and quickly pulled up the app on it. There was a blinking red dot moving on the map and I frowned.

"Where the hell are you taking her?" I muttered to myself.

The dot continued to travel and I hoped that as long as they were moving, she was safe. The minute they stopped, things might get really bad for her and I wasn't going to think about that either. All I knew was that I had to stop him.

My truck was gone and the only way to get to Jo was to find a car. I quickly thought about Mel and called her.

Five minutes later, she screeched to a stop in front of my place and hopped out. "What the hell is going on?"

"Her ex-boyfriend got her," I said as I tugged on my shoes and winced. "I need to go get her."

"What the fuck?" She breathed. "Let me go with you."

"No. There's already one person in danger and I'm not going to involve you too."

Mel tightened her fists. "Son of a bitch. How dare he touch her!"

I smiled softly at Mel. "You're a good friend, to both of us. I promise we'll be back soon enough and everything will be fine."

Mel nodded. "You better be. I'm not about to look for another boss that I can stand and a friend that I adore. Both of you better get your asses back here safe and sound."

"We will. I gotta go."

"Go get her!" She tossed me the keys. "I'll lock up and see you guys later."

"Thanks, Mel!" I was glad Mel didn't live far from me. If she had, I have no idea how things would have gone, but now I could go get her and bring her home. I sped off down the road and glanced at my phone. The dot blinked and kept moving. I wasn't too far behind, but it would still take a while to catch up.

Please be okay, Jo. You have to be okay.

My head buzzed as I tried to move my limbs.

It felt like they were filled with sand and so was my dry mouth. I licked my lips, but it didn't help in the least. Where the hell was I? My head went from buzzing to throbbing as the darkness slowly cleared. For a moment, I couldn't remember a thing until memories of Brian came rushing back.

I jerked back to being fully awake and glanced around the room I was in. The dingy bedspread and carpeting was a dead giveaway that I was in a motel. I tried to move, but my wrists wouldn't come around from the chair that I'd been placed in. I knew I was tied up to it. "Shit," I cursed under my breath as I tugged and yanked at the rope that rubbed against my skin and burned. "Shit, shit, shit!"

Brian had gotten me. I'd been so sure that I had gotten away from him and then he had to come back to cause trouble all over again. What the hell could he possibly want from me? When I was trying my hardest in our relationship, he'd wanted nothing to do with me and now he wouldn't let me go. Why wasn't I allowed to move on from him?

"Good, you're awake."

I jumped at the sound of his voice. Brian walked out of the bathroom and his grin chilled me. I yanked at my ropes harder before I growled at him. "You can't do this to me! Do you have any idea what you're doing? I've already let the police know about you and what you've done. Let me go, Brian!"

"You talk too much as usual," he muttered as he walked over to the bed and yanked up a roll of tape.

"Don't!" I yelled.

Brian's hand connected with my throat and I sucked in half a breath before my air was cut off. His hand squeezed and I whimpered under his tight grip. When he pulled his hand away, I panted and sucked in a desperate breath.

"If you scream like that again, I'm going to slap the shit out of you, do you understand me?"

When I didn't respond, he raised a hand, so I quickly nodded.

"Good," he said approvingly.

Tape was slapped over my mouth and my heart raced. I was trapped. Tied up, gagged, and no one had a clue where I was. I was really going to be trapped alone with Brian so he could finish what he started, or he could rape me. He always had a fantasy of tying me up and playing pretend rape, but I wasn't into it. This could be his fantasy come real.

Both options chilled me to the bone.

"It took me way too long to find you," he said as he opened the bag he'd sat on the bed. "Thankfully, I'd noticed you were slowly taking stuff to the office. I knew the only person at work that you spoke well of was that cleaner Maria, so I hit her up. Told her a pack of lies and the stupid broad let me into the broom cupboard. It wasn't hard to find the address and track you down." He chuckled. "If you wanted me not to find you, this place wasn't really wasn't a smart choice, was it?"

I glared at him.

It had been the only place I could go and he'd made sure of that. No money on me, nowhere to live. No job. I couldn't go anywhere else but home and even if I had gone somewhere else, I knew it wouldn't have mattered. Brian would have tracked me down anyway, and we still would have been where we were now. I wasn't going to let him get into my head.

"Do you know what I'm going to do with you?" he asked conversationally as he turned around with more rope in his hands. "I'm going to make up for lost time. I have all kinds of marvelous plans for you little Ivy."

I made a noise through the gag.

"Did you really fucking think I wasn't going to get what was mine again?"

Brain gripped my chin and I couldn't turn away.

"We're going to be just the way we were. You're going to go home with me and do what you're told and this time. I'm going to keep you in the apartment and you're going to be my doll. I always wanted my own sex doll. I'm going to dress you up and I'm going to do what I want with your body. You will never say no to me again. Then I'm going to put my baby in your belly. Maybe I'll break your legs, so you really won't ever be able to get away from me."

My eyes shot open wide. I struggled against him as that grin I had seen when he was strangling me, widened on his face. It made me ice cold inside.

Brian's hand ran over my cheek and my skin crawled. He leaned forward and pressed his lips against my forehead, my cheeks, even the tape on my mouth as I started to struggle and try to scream behind it.

"If you keep moving away from me, you're going to piss me off," he snapped. "Don't make me have to hurt you too."

Too? Was there some other woman before me that he had hurt?

I closed my eyes tight and shuddered in revulsion. Brian was talking like a mad man, or a serial killer. I did not know this man at all. Somewhere along the line, he had snapped. He was now criminally insane.

At least, Cooper was safe. He would never have to be exposed to this bastard. It was the one good thing I'd done and I felt glad that I had at least protected him the way he'd protected me.

My eyes flew open as someone banged on the door. It flew open and Cooper charged into the room, his face full of rage. Before Brian could react, Cooper punched him in the face and Brian went down like a sack of potatoes.

As much as I wanted to keep him away, my eyes lit up. Cooper was here to get me away from Brian's psychotic ass. I pulled at the rope, but it was tight and it wouldn't give no matter how hard I tried.

Brian managed to get back on his feet, but Cooper was ready for him. He bawled up his fist and slammed it into Brian's face. When he was down Cooper, climbed on top of him and kept pummeling.

I tried to call him, tell him to stop before he ended up killing Brian and going to prison, but the tape still held fast over my mouth.

As Cooper raised his fist to deliver another blow the doorway was filled with bodies, and cops poured into the room. They drew their guns and pointed them down.

One cop hauled Cooper off of Brian. "We've got him, son. It's all right," the gruff man said as he patted Cooper's shoulder. "Somebody get her untied."

I recognized the man. Officer Jones had been at the police station, he'd taken my statement and promised to look into it. For some reason, I hadn't thought he'd actually do it but he had come through. I was so grateful he did.

The ropes were removed from my wrists and ankles then the tape was carefully peeled off of my lips. My wrists burned and my head still throbbed, but I didn't care. I shot out of the chair and threw my arms around Cooper's neck. He held me tightly and the heat of his body soothed me more than anything else could have done.

"Are you okay?" he asked urgently, when we finally pulled apart. He touched my face and hair, checking me over for injuries.

"I'm fine now," I said in a shaky voice. "I'm so glad you're here. How did you find me?"

"I got a GPS tracker in my truck and the tracer is on your bracelet. It led us straight to his motel." Cooper pulled me into another tight hug.

I hugged him back. I didn't want to be apart from him, not for another minute. I'd been so close to losing it all and now, I had another chance. "I thought I wouldn't see you again," I whispered.

"I'll always come for you," Cooper said as he kissed my forehead. "I told you before, I'll do anything to protect you, and I meant that."

"You're still not going to be free," Brian's voice cut in,

I clung to Cooper as I gazed at him.

"Do you really think I'll give you up that easily?" He grinned even as the cuffs were put on him and he was yanked to his feet. "You're mine Ivy. I'll be back."

"Get him out of here," Officer Jones snapped. Once they'd hauled him off, he walked over to us. "You don't have to worry about him. He won't be getting out anytime soon."

"How do I know that?" I asked. "I need to be sure that he won't be able to hurt us."

"Well, we have him on breaking a restraining order, abduction, assault and that's just with you," Officer Jones explained. "I looked into it and Brian has a rap sheet. You're not the first. You're one of the lucky ones in this situation. His two other exes were held much longer and sustained injuries. He will go up on charges from those cases too. I'm just glad we got to you in time."

I shook my head. "I can't believe any of this is actually happening."

"We're going to make sure he can't hurt anyone else, Ivy," Officer Jones stated softly. "I know you need a bit of time, but if you could go downstairs and get checked out that would be great. We also need to get your statement, but it can wait for now."

"Thank you," I said softly. "At least he won't be able to do this to anyone else."

"That's the only upside to this situation. I'm sorry we couldn't get him earlier."

"It's all right. You did everything you could."

Officer Jones smiled and walked away leaving me alone with Cooper.

He wrapped an arm around my shoulders and led me from the room. I couldn't be in there anymore anyway. Every time I thought about it, I knew how close I'd been to something I could never recover from. I shuddered.

"We're going to get you checked out and then we'll make it through this together. Okay?" Cooper spoke softly.

I nodded and gripped his hand hard. "I know we will. All I need is you to comfort me right now."

"I'm not going to leave your side."

I knew he wouldn't leave me, but hearing him say the words out loud gave me comfort. He led me over to the ambulance and I let them examine me. For the most part, I was okay. A slight concussion from where I'd hit the floor, a few bruises and rope burns on my wrists. I had a feeling his other victims hadn't been so lucky, so I felt thankful that help had arrived when it did.

"Would you like us to take you to the hospital?" Officer Jones asked.

I shook my head. "No, I just want to go home and have a shower. I can give a statement tomorrow, right?"

Officer Jones nodded. "Just come down in the morning. I'm sure you need to rest for now."

"I do. I'll be there first thing."

"I'll be there," he said and nodded.

Cooper shook his hand and thanked him. His fists had been bandaged up too from where he'd cut them punching Brian, but he didn't seem bothered in the least. All of his attention was focused on me and making sure I was all right.

"Can we go home now?" I asked when he was done talking to the officer. "I feel like I need to scrub my skin raw first, then lie down, and just disconnect from the world for a long while."

"Okay. Let's go home," he said, rubbing my arm.

Home. It hit me then. I could be there with him forever now. I didn't have to disappear. This gave me untold comfort and I couldn't believe it was actually coming true after everything we had been through. "I love you so much," I breathed.

"I love you more," he replied looking deep into my eyes.

I leaned up on my tiptoes and kissed him.

Cooper held me close, his lips claiming mine sweetly before the kiss deepened and I felt all of his fear and anxiety pour into it. He'd been just as scared as I had been and that only made me love him more. I followed him to a waiting car, too tired to ask about it or anything else. All I wanted to do was get home and pretend the rest of the world didn't exist, especially a world with freaks like Brian in it.

month later...

"How are you doing?" Mel asked as she sat on our front porch and sipped at her iced tea.

"Better." I nodded. "Much better."

"Good. I miss you at work." She smiled. "It'll be nice to see you back on your feet and dropping things soon."

I flipped her off. "How dare you? I haven't dropped anything in ages."

"Will you leave my fiancée alone?" Cooper said as he walked out and handed me another beer. "You're supposed to be celebrating with us, not aggravating her."

"Jo-Jo knows I love her." Mel grinned. "Besides, I'm just as happy as you two. That asshole was finally sentenced and locked up where he belongs. Good riddance!"

I tapped my beer against her glass. "Yeah, good fucking riddance."

We watched the sun as it dipped behind the clouds. I'd never felt so much relief in my life and I couldn't wipe the smile off of my face. Cooper had proposed as soon as we heard the good news that Brian was no longer a threat as he'd gotten thirty years with no possibility of parole. Now, we could live our lives in peace.

"I better get out of here," Mel said as she checked the time. "If I leave the bar alone for too long, I'll be the one having to do a lot of cleaning up." She sighed. "Hurry up and come back to work, please?" She laced her fingers and begged.

"We'll be back soon." I laughed. "This is the last week of our vacation."

"Then you can get sick of me again." Cooper grinned. "I've saved up a lot of things for you to get annoyed at."

Mel rolled her eyes. "Why am I friends with you two?"

"You love us," I purred. "Thank you for coming over and celebrating with us."

"I wouldn't miss it for the world."

I stood up and Mel hugged me tightly. Cooper hugged her as well and she waved before she headed for her car. When she reached it, she winked at me. "Have fun!"

I raised a brow. "What is she talking about?"

"I have no idea," Cooper muttered.

As I watched her speed down the street, Cooper pulled me close to his side and smiled down at me. That radiant smile made my body heat up.

He reached down and brushed the hair off of my cheek. "I have a surprise for you."

I tilted my head. "You do? What is it?"

Cooper picked up my hand and kissed it. "You'll see when we go inside," he said as he took my hand into his. "Close your eyes."

I smiled. "Okay, but don't let me fall into anything. One concussion in a lifetime is more than enough for me."

Cooper chuckled. "Don't worry. I'm not going to let you get hurt. Close em, so I can show you."

"All right," I said and closed my eyes.

I let out a little yelp as I was scooped into his arms. I leaned my head onto his shoulder and sighed as he carried me up the stairs. Whenever he held me like this, I felt so safe and complete in his arms.

We reached the top of the stairs and he gently put me down before he guided me by my shoulders. "Ok," he said as his breath tickled my ear. "You can open your eyes now."

I opened my eyes and sucked in a breath. Our bedroom had been completely transformed. Candles flickered on every surface, soft music played in the background, while the bed and floor were decorated with rose petals. "You did all of this?" I breathed as I stared around the room. "Is this why you snuck off when Mel was here?"

"She was in on it." He grinned. "I told her to keep you distracted while I took care of everything and she was more than happy to do it."

I laughed. "Of course she was. God, I love that woman." I ran a hand over the bedspread. "I can't believe you did all of this for me."

"We're not done yet," he said as he opened the closet and set a black box on the covers. "Go into the bathroom and put that on when you come out, I'll have a glass of champagne and a very naked me waiting."

I bit my lip. "You really know how to treat a woman right."

"I try my best," he purred against my ear before he nipped it. "Go and get changed."

I picked up the box and smiled as I walked into the bathroom. When the door was closed, I stripped off my clothes and opened it up. Inside there was a set of lacy black lingerie. I pulled it out and slipped into the top that was comfortable and easy to slip my breasts out of I noticed. There were garters and stockings too and I put those on before I looked at myself in the mirror.

I turned back and forth and smiled at my reflection. The material hugged my body lightly and showed off my ample curves. I teased my hair in the mirror and threw my shoulders back. I looked hot as hell. I couldn't wait for Cooper to see me in it and watch his jaw drop.

Slowly, I stepped out of the bathroom and Cooper turned and stared. I watched the surprise turn to shock and he licked his lips in anticipation.

He reached out a hand and offered me a glass of champagne. "I knew you would look amazing in that, but I had no idea you would look that fucking good," he whispered in awe. "Come here."

I walked over to him and placed my hand on his naked chest.

The champagne glass touched my lips and I sipped before I slid my hand down. My fingers traced over his inner thighs and down over his semi-hard shaft and sensitive balls.

Cooper sucked in a breath. "God, you're so fucking beautiful," he groaned as he tilted my head up by my chin. "I can't wait to marry you."

My heart throbbed in my chest. "I can't wait to marry you either."

Cooper's mouth claimed mine and I moaned and leaned against him. His fingers ran over my body before he gripped my ass and gave it a firm squeeze.

I sat the glass of champagne down and wrapped my arms around him. "I think I'm going to need to finish this drink later." I gazed up at him with hooded eyes. "Right now, I need only you."

Cooper didn't say a word. He led me over to the bed and pushed me onto my back gently.

I waited for him to climb on top of me.

Instead, he went into the nightstand and fished something else out.

The toys he laid out made me raise a brow and I swallowed thickly. "You're really prepared," I gushed. "What do you have in mind?"

"You'll see." He chuckled. "Let's just say when you talk, I listen. To everything," he added with a wink. "Get comfortable for me."

I did what he said and wiggled myself back against the pillows.

Cooper parted my thighs and ran a finger over the panties that separated him from my already wet pussy. He leaned forward, pushed them aside, and lapped at me as he groaned.

It felt so good. I closed my eyes and gave into the amazing sensations rolling through my body.

He stopped just long enough to toss my panties on the floor and went right back to it.

My fingers wandered down to his hair and slipped against his scalp. The vibrations from his humming moans racked through me and I shivered against his tongue. Every single time it flicked over my clit my back arched and my legs pushed further apart.

The minute I relaxed into the sensations my eyes flew open and I jolted.

Cooper grinned up at me as he pressed the vibrator to my clit and rolled it in little circles.

The buzzing sent me over the edge and I held on tightly. "Oh god," I panted. "Too much. It's too—oh, fuck!" My back arched up and my legs trembled as an orgasm shot through me so powerfully that I cried out at the top of my lungs. I felt my cum as it ran down my thighs and groaned.

Cooper pulled the vibrator away and lapped at my wetness eagerly. "Now we just need to have a few more of those from you." He chuckled. "Keep your legs apart. I want to use this next."

I stared at the toy in his hand. "Is that a butt plug?"

Cooper nodded. "I know you've been wanting to try it. Are you up for it, sweetheart?"

I nodded, my head still spinning from the orgasm that had just washed over me.

Cooper lubed up the toy and slowly pushed it inside of me.

I gasped as I was stretched more than I'd ever been before. The slight burn gave way to a feeling of being full and I moaned as it rubbed against my insides.

"How's that?" he asked, his voice husky and deep.

"It's so different," I moaned. "I'm not used to it, but I like it."

"You'll like it better in a second."

I opened my mouth to ask him why when the toy started to vibrate. A gasp slipped from my lips and I tensed up as my hole clenched around it.

Cooper climbed on top of me and settled between my thighs. He rubbed himself over my wetness.

I felt the head of his cock as it slowly pushed inside. "That feels so good," I moaned as I reached up for him. "Kiss me."

Cooper kissed me deeply before his kiss turned passionate and wild. His tongue slipped between my lips and nipped my bottom lip as he slowly pulled away. When he came back down, he pushed his cock inside of me harder.

I moaned as he filled me up completely.

"You're so hot," Cooper mumbled against my mouth. "I'm never going to get enough of you."

"Good." I smiled up at him. "I know I'm never going to want anyone but you."

Cooper slipped out and then thrust back inside. As he buried himself deep, my walls closed around him and he pumped in and out. He maneuvered my breasts out of my top and ran his tongue over my pert nipples. When he sucked one into his mouth, I threw my head back and bit my lip.

"I can feel the vibrations," he grunted as he picked up speed. "You feel fucking awesome."

I could listen to Cooper's groans and compliments about me all day. The more he rocked and shifted his hips, the wetter I became.

He leaned down and nipped my earlobe as he started to whisper dirty little compliments into my ear about how tight and wet I was just for him.

His dirty whispers almost undid me as he made them in that low sexy voice of his. I wrapped my legs around his waist and tightened them as my body rocked up and down. His fingers slipped around my nipples and he pinched and rolled them. My mouth went slack and moans poured out until I couldn't take another minute of his thick cock without losing it. "Cooper, I'm gonna—" I cried out as the orgasm took over and my world went white and full of mindless pleasure. I felt Cooper rock inside me harder, his mouth on my throat as he called my name against my ear. I clung to him and heard his gasp when he shuddered and came deep inside of me. Heat filled me up and I sighed, as Cooper stayed buried inside me.

"Wow," I muttered. "I'm still trembling."

Cooper groaned. "I'm just going to lay right here for a while," he muttered back. "I don't think I've ever felt you climax that hard before." He kissed my shoulder. "Give me a bit and we'll do it again."

I laughed. "Can we drink a few glasses of champagne first?"

"Of course, that's what it's there for," he said as he raised himself up and grinned. "I love you so much."

"I love you to the moon and back," I said, reaching up and stroking his hair.

EPILOGUE

One Year Later
Ivy

"That was the last customer," I announced as I traipsed into the back of the bar. "It's just the two of us now."

"Finally." He sighed as he pushed back and patted his lap. "Come here. I've been dying to hold you all day."

I smiled and sat in his lap. I rested my head on his shoulder.

He sighed again, this time he sounded content.

My fingers traced over his chest and I smiled at the ring on my left hand. We still hadn't had our wedding just yet, but we were already planning it and I knew it was going to be beautiful. "Want me to count up the till?" I asked.

He shook his head. "I can handle it, sweetheart. I keep telling you that you don't have to work as a waitress anymore. You could stay home, or work on your career, or even take over and help me manage."

I smiled. "I like where I am though. All of the pressure on my shoulders is gone and I like the people here. Besides, I'd be bored out of my skull if I had to sit around the house all day." I leaned up and kissed his chin. "And I don't want to take what's yours."

Cooper's eyebrows knitted together. "What have I told you a thousand times already? Everything I have is yours too, that's the way it works when you agreed to marry me."

I grinned up at him. "Then one day, I may want to do it, but right now I like what I'm doing. It's nice to just be able to talk to people and see how much fun they're having."

"You've turned into such a people person," he said.

"You don't like it?" I asked as I poked his cheek playfully.

"I love seeing you come out of your shell, but you should see the way some of these guys look at you."

"Awww, are you jealous?"

"Irrationally," he admitted right away. "But I know it can't be helped." He sighed elaborately. "You're just way too beautiful."

I burst out laughing. "Have you seen the way women look at you?"

Cooper grinned and reached to the mini-fridge. He picked up a bottle of scotch. "Grab those glasses."

I stood up and grabbed a couple off the shelf.

Cooper filled it up a bit before he waited for the other glass.

I handed him the one with the scotch, then I filled mine with water from the bottle on his table and sat on his lap again.

He gave me a puzzled look. "You don't want a drink?"

"It's not that," I said with a smile. "It's more like I can't drink right now. Or for the next seven months."

"Seven months," he mumbled before the truth dawned on him and his eyes widened. "You're pregnant!"

I nodded. "I found out a little while ago. I wanted to make sure everything was fine before I told you," I said rubbing my belly. "And I wasn't sure how you would react."

"How I'd react?" He repeated before he lit up and squeezed me in his arms. "Are you kidding me? This is the best fucking news I've ever heard in my life! I can't believe you're pregnant with my baby."

"I can't believe it either. I never thought I would want kids when I was living in the city, but here? This is home and I'm here with you. Of course, I want to settle down and have kids with you."

Cooper blinked. "Kids? Multiple?"

I realized what I'd said and my face flushed. I hadn't meant to say that out loud, but now it was out there. I fiddled with my fingers and smiled softly. "Well, yeah I want to have at least three. That's what I was thinking anyway. I know you might not want that many—"

"We can have as many as you want! Actually, I was thinking of six," Cooper said grinning so hard I was sure his face would break.

"Six?" I screamed.

"I don't care as long as you're happy, I'm happy."

I wrapped my arms around his neck. "I'm so glad I came back home. That asshole was awful, but I'm thankful to him. He gave me the reason and the impetus to come back to you. Otherwise, I would have missed all this."

"I'm not grateful to that piece of shit, because I believe you would have come home on your own steam anyway," Cooper said.

"You know there will be changes with the baby coming, right?"

"We're going to need a nursery and a car seat, clothes, toys," he ticked everything off on his fingers as he grinned widely. "There's so much to get ready for. I feel like I'm already behind."

"You're going to be one good dad, aren't you," I said with a happy smile.

"Do you know if it's a boy or a girl?"

I patted his cheek. "Not yet, hon. I'm hoping to find out in a few weeks." I rubbed my belly. "I really want a boy first and then a girl."

"Me too." He grinned. "Especially to keep away boys like me."

I laughed. "You didn't turn out to be so bad you know." I

squeezed his hand. "In fact, you turned out to be exactly what I need in my life."

"If you keep talking like that, we're never going to get home," he muttered. "I'm already way too happy and energized after that news."

I chuckled. "Who says we need to make it home?"

"Really?" he asked as he wiggled his eyebrows at me. "I'll take that permission to go ahead."

"You may," I said standing and tugging my shirt over my head.

Cooper's eyes never left my body as I shimmied out of the black skirt that I wore and the flat shoes on my feet. I reached up and released my bra, before I let it drop to the ground. Finally, I pulled down my panties and dramatically tossed them at him.

Cooper's mouth closed and he grinned at me.

"You know I always want you," I purred. "Every single minute of every day. That's something you never even have to doubt or worry about." I walked over and trailed a finger down his thigh. "I will always want you."

Cooper sucked in a breath. "And I'll always want you," he said, staring up at me until his eyes were distracted by my stomach. Leaning forward, he kissed my belly. "I'm so fucking happy I can't stand it."

My fingers combed through his hair and I knew exactly how he felt. I'd never felt my heart feel so full of love and joy as it did in this moment. All I wanted to do was stay by his side, grow our family, and live the life we were meant to live. I tilted his head up with my fingers. "I love you so damn much it hurts, Cooper."

"Words can never describe what I feel for you, my darling heart."

His smile made my heart skip a beat. I knew how much he meant it and how true those words were when they came from his lips. Cooper was my first love, my protector, and soon he would be the father of our child. I knew for a fact that I was insanely lucky and I would never take anything for granted with him.

Once he'd said, '*Let's start over.*'

And we did.

And it worked.

The End

ABOUT THE AUTHOR

Thank you so much for reading!

Do come visit me here:

ALSO BY RIVER LAURENT

Made in the USA
Monee, IL
14 June 2021

71281588R00187